Stolen
COURSE

Aly Martinez

Stolen Course
Copyright © 2014 Aly Martinez

Stolen Course is a work of fiction. All names, characters, places, and occurrences are the product of the author's imagination. Any resemblance to any persons, living or dead, events, or locations is purely coincidental.

Cover Design by Ashley Baumann at Ashbee Designs https://www.facebook.com/AshbeeBookCovers

Edited by Mickey Reed at I'm a Book Shark
http://www.imabookshark.com
Formatting by Self Publishing Editing Service

ISBN-13: 978-1499540444
ISBN-10: 1499540442

For Mandy

It's been way too long since we lost you. I still remember the smile on your face when you walked away from me that last time. I have no idea what we were talking about, but I can almost still hear your laugh. I miss it.

"She isn't weighted down here on earth the way I am. She's soaring, I'm sure. Manda never knew how to do anything else."

Prologue

"IT'S NOT fucking them!" I punch the dashboard and scream at my partner, Brett, as he weaves through traffic.

Just moments ago, we received a page that will destroy one of us forever. It said a bunch of words, but the only four I can remember are "one fatality, one injury." I reject the very possibility that this has anything to do with my Manda, but the vise currently holding my heart still twists even tighter. I drop my head to my hands as I wage war with reality. If that message is accurate, I have a fifty-fifty chance that my life is over. Done. Finished. I'll never survive losing Manda. Never.

It can't be her. We haven't even gotten married yet. We are supposed to get married and have a life together. We have a plan. A knife lands hard in my stomach as I try to reason my way out of this mess. *It can't be her.* Manda is strong and healthy. No accident in the world could steal her from me. Yeah, she's tough. She's got to be the one who's injured. Something simple, maybe a broken arm. We can fix that. I just need her to be alive—anything else, we can deal with *together.*

The car barely slows before I'm out and sprinting toward the twisted metal on the side of the highway. Every hope I have of this being a big misunderstanding vanishes into the night when I recognize Sarah's car. Reality slices me open, but the promise of only an injury keeps my legs moving forward.

"Detective Jones!" I hear shouted, but I continue to run. I slow only when I get to a group of officers.

"Where is she?" I demand, but deep down, I'm terrified to hear the answer.

"Caleb, take a second and catch your breath."

"Where the fuck is she!" My eyes scan the faces lining the road, desperately searching for Manda's fiery red hair and green eyes.

But instead, they land on a white sheet covering what I know is a body. My heart begins to race as I once again try to fight all rational thinking that tells me that it's her.

"That's not her," I say, desperately trying to catch my breath, but the panic that has lodged itself in my system prevents it. "Oh God, someone please tell me that's not her." Tears well in my eyes as I glance up to see my good friends, Stephens and Perez, step up beside me. From the look on Stephens's face, I know I don't want to hear whatever he has to say.

"She didn't make it, Jones." With one sentence, the little breath I have left is stolen. My legs buckle, forcing me helplessly to my knees.

"No." I refuse to accept that my Manda no longer exists.

The earth starts to tremble as my world begins to crumble around me. It only takes a minute to realize that my body is violently shaking as the physical pain of reality courses through my veins. This is *not* happening.

"That's not her," I begin to repeat.

She can't be gone. My eyes never leave the body that used to house my soul mate. This isn't real, and any minute I'm going to wake from this horrible nightmare. I'll roll over in bed and pull Manda hard against my chest. I close my eyes, willing myself to wake up, but it never comes.

I rise to my feet and take a step towards her. "Manda!" I yell. I need to see her. To touch her. It's fucking cold tonight and she's just lying there under a sheet. Oh, fuck. That's not her.

Perez grabs my arm, effectively halting me. "Don't do this to yourself. You don't need to see her like that."

"Get your fucking hands off me. If that's Manda, I need to see her."

"Not now you don't. Let them get her to the hospital and clean her up a bit."

The pain in my chest is quickly being replaced with anger.

"Get off me, Perez," I say calmly while leveling him with a menacing glare.

"Not happening. I won't let you do this to yourself." He pulls me back a step, and that is all it takes for me to lose it. My rage needs somewhere to go, and it just so happens that it chooses Perez's face. My hands fly, landing directly on his jaw.

"I need to see her!" I scream, landing punch after punch. Stephens jumps in, tackling me from behind. He uses his weight to pin me to the ground.

"Goddamn it, Jones. Stop fighting. We're trying to help you."

"She's not fucking gone!"

"She *is*, and you *don't* need to see her."

An image of her laughing at dinner flashes behind my eyes as once again reality takes hold. *This is not happening.* The temporary shield of anger fades away as devastation settles in. As I'm lying facedown on the side of a highway, gut-wrenching sobs spring from my chest.

"Oh, God. Please, not Manda."

Chapter ~~ONE~~

Emma

"PERFECT. OH that's great. A little to the left. Little more. Tiny bit more. Yes, yes! Now hold it!" I yell at the dumbass blonde I'm photographing.

I know I probably shouldn't think like that about my clients. After all, they are paying me. But this woman really is frustrating. She is paying me to take pictures of her stupid historic house for a dumb, ridiculously popular home magazine. I have no idea why she needs to be in every shot. They are just going to crop her out to focus on the house, but regardless how many times I tell her that, she still squeezes into every shot. I just took a picture of her ugly King Charles spaniel sitting in a rocking chair on her front porch. *Fuck my life*.

My phone rings with a Chicago area code. I don't recognize the number, and my heart begins to race at the very idea of what this phone call could be about. Just another update from Brett? Or maybe it's the call I've been dreading since the night that changed everything.

My sister, Sarah, was involved in a car accident five years ago. It completely fucked her up, and then it fucked me up. About six weeks after Sarah's accident, our father died. He wasn't exactly young, but that didn't make his stroke any less unexpected. It was the worst day of my life. When it came time for his funeral, on a day when I needed her more than ever, Sarah wasn't there. I would have been a heartless bitch if I'd said that I didn't understand her reasons. She had just lost her best friend and was suffering from a pretty serious head injury herself. But I can't say that it didn't hurt like hell when she told me that she couldn't make Daddy's funeral.

A few weeks after the wreck, Sarah tried to kill herself. I've never been able to wrap my mind around why she would cross that line, even with as many times as I have tried to put myself in her shoes. When I got the phone call about her first suicide attempt, I was pissed. I knew she had been dealing with guilt, but she and I were always close. And after the accident, I really tried to be there for her. If she had emotional stuff going on, she could have reached out to me. Hell, she *should* have reached out to me. One phone call—that's all it would have taken. I would have been on a plane the same night. I could have helped. But she never once picked up the phone. It was bad enough that she'd moved almost a thousand miles away, but she could have fucking called.

So on the day we buried my father, I stood with my mom and said goodbye, praying that I didn't have to say goodbye to my sister soon too.

After Sarah's accident, she didn't just change, she lost it completely. Her husband, Brett is a total sweetheart. He has been taking care of her for the last few years, but for reasons known only to Sarah, she hates him—has ever since the accident. He's a really good guy, and he doesn't deserve the shit she gives him. He's done nothing but stand by her side, waiting for her to reemerge. But Sarah is hidden so deep inside this new woman that I'm not sure anyone can reach her—at least that is what I tell myself.

As the phone rings in my hand, I suck in a quick breath and prepare for the worst.

"Hello."

"Hey, Emma. It's Brett."

I listen closely to his voice for clues on how bad this call is going to be.

"Is everything okay?" I chew on my lip, waiting for his response.

"She's fine," he says, reassuring me right off the bat. "A lot of stuff happened today. She tried...again." I know exactly what he means by *tried*.

Brett is the big brother I never knew I wanted. I love him, and he's super protective of me. He and Sarah started dating when I was only six-teen years old. I've grown up with him watching over me from afar.

"How bad?" I immediately jump to the heart of this phone call.

"She's okay. But this one isn't going to be brushed under the rug. She did some really shitty stuff yesterday, babe. Stuff that will have legal consequences for her."

"What?" I shriek across the line.

He lets out an audible sigh, and if I know Brett at all, he's pinching the bridge of his nose. "Emma, she tried to shoot me last night. She locked herself up in an apartment, and when I went in after her, she actually pulled the trigger."

"No," I whisper in disbelief. "Shit, are you okay?"

"Yeah, I'm fine. Her aim is shit." He tries to reassure me with a joke. That's what Brett does, he makes jokes. But the absence of his laugh makes me worry more than anything else he just said. "When can you get up here?"

"Are you asking me that, Brett? Because if you want me there, it must be pretty fucking bad."

"You'll call me when you land?" he asks, both answering and ignoring my question.

"Yeah. Where is she right now?"

"The hospital," he answers shortly, offering no more information.

"The one by your house?" I digging a little deeper.

"Please just let me pick you up. We need to talk anyway."

"The one by your fucking house?" My voice rises from the frustration. I know he is trying to protect me, but Sarah is my sister. If he won't give me the story over the phone, I'll get it from somewhere else.

"Emma, we need to talk, and not over the phone."

"I'll call you when I get there," I say, knowing that I have no intention of calling him. I'll see him at the hospital when I get there.

If this is as bad as he says, I don't want him to leave just to come pick me up. She may pretend to hate him, but I know Sarah, and a part of her still needs Brett.

I hang up the phone and stare into the annoyed eyes of my client.

"Are you done chatting?"

I let out a laugh, turning off my camera and twisting off the lens to pack up. "Yeah, I'm done."

She rolls her eyes at my non-apologetic answer. "Well good. I'd like to get some more out in the garden."

"No, I think I've gotten everything the magazine will want." And probably a week's worth of editing her ugly ass out of pictures.

"But I wanted some in the garden. Our time isn't up yet," she whines

6

in the most ridiculous way.

"Something came up, but I have more than enough pictures for the magazine. I took every picture they asked for, and because I'm leaving early, I'll even send you a few of the stupid ones with the dog in the rocker."

"What!" she yells, but I just continue to pack up. I can't be bothered with this forty-year-old spoiled brat of a woman. I need to get home, book a flight, and get my ass to Chicago.

"Sorry. I've got to go." Without another word—and especially not the attitude I want to give her—I head out the door.

I make the short drive back to my house. My mind is racing with plans the entire way.

"Hunter!" I yell when I walk through the front door.

"In here, sugar," he calls from his office/our living room.

I roll my eyes at his stupid use of the word sugar. You have to be either an eighty-year-old man or a pimp to use that one successfully, and Hunter Coy is neither of those.

"Hey, can you take me to the airport in about an hour?"

"Yeah. What's up? You planning a little vacation and not inviting me?" he laughs with a sexy grin.

"My sister tried to kill herself last night," I blurt out.

"Fuck, Em." He immediately stands and pulls me into a hard hug.

Hunter gives good hugs. He's a really good guy and hot as hell—a combination so rare that, when I met him two years ago, I snatched him up. Unfortunately, three months later, he admitted that he was still in love with some girl back home. We stayed up all night talking about her and how she ended up with his best friend. Poor guy was really struggling and I'd had no idea. After that, we decided to just be friends, but Hunter has become so much more than that. He's my *best* friend. I don't know what I would do without him.

"She's okay, I think," I say to his chest.

"You want me to go with you?"

"No. I don't know how long this is going to take. You stay here."

"You sure? I've got some vacation days saved up. I've never been to Chicago." He pulls away to look me in the eye.

As tempting as the idea of having Hunter with me is, I know this is something I need to do alone. "I'm sure." I offer him a fake smile and back away. "Okay, be ready to go in one hour." I head to my bedroom to pack.

An hour later, I'm Chicago bound to try to help my broken sister, who I haven't seen in over two years.

Chapter TWO

Caleb

"CALEB," I hear from behind me as Jesse hugs me around the waist.

I can't help but smile. No matter how tough things get, Jesse Addison always makes me smile. She is so tiny and innocent. If she weren't my best friend's girl, I would keep her for myself. Don't get me wrong. I don't have feelings for Jesse or anything, but she's low drama and low maintenance. I need a woman like that. Manda was nothing like that, yet I loved her harder than any person should be allowed. If I'm really being honest with myself, I still love her like that. It's been almost five years and Manda Baker still owns my heart.

But that's before I was robbed.

Manda was stolen from me. Stolen from herself. Stolen from a world that is clueless as to what they are missing but will be nonetheless be worse off without her. She lost her life, and it's all Sarah Erickson's fault.

Oh, Sarah didn't intentionally kill the love of my life. What she did was far worse. She was drinking and decided to get behind the wheel, essentially playing Russian roulette with every man, woman, and child on the road that night. It was just my luck though. Sarah didn't kill herself that night. No, Manda was the one who paid the price for Sarah's stupidity. And I was the one who had my life ripped out from under my feet. Not fucking Sarah. Me. Yet here I am, in a poorly lit hospital waiting room, trying to find out what the hell is going to happen to that bitch.

This isn't the first time I've ever been here for Sarah, but it is the first time I actually feel okay with it. Sarah has tried to kill herself four times since the accident. Last night was her most recent attempt. Before today, it was always her husband—and my best friend—Brett who came to pick up her broken pieces, but today, I sit in this waiting room alone. No one else is here for her. She has long since forced everyone who loved her away.

Last night, with a gun in her hand, she ran off the only person who would never give up on her—Brett. It was a long time coming. He should have walked away from her years ago. But Brett has a bleeding heart. According to him, Sarah suffered some bullshit traumatic brain injury as a result of the accident. While that really sucks, I have trouble feeling bad for her when my entire life is buried six feet under. Brett was insistent that something was wrong with her. Her personality changed, and she didn't want anything to do with him anymore. I just call it guilt for killing her best friend, by making the ridiculous decision to drive drunk.

Unfortunately for me, Sarah was never prosecuted for her drunken activities for a couple of different reasons. The first is that she wasn't drunk when her blood alcohol level was taken. No one seems to care that her blood wasn't taken until hours after the accident. Sarah was a cop's wife. No one in that entire hospital was excited about pointing the finger at her. Oh, and there is always the fucking debate about who was driving the car that night. That conversation always makes me heated. Technically no one can prove who was driving that night. Witnesses on the scene said that it was a redhead, like Manda, driving the car. I've always wondered how the hell they saw that in the dark though. Other witnesses at the restaurant said that it was a tall blonde who pulled out of the parking lot. I tend to trust those people a lot more.

Tonight, as Brett tried to talk Sarah out of killing herself, he uttered the only words that could ever make me help her. "What would Manda say about this?"

It wasn't a new idea. I've thought about it a million times. But after spending the day at her grave with Jesse at my side, those words finally hit home. Manda would kill me if I let anything happen to Sarah. She would never forgive me if I didn't do everything in my power to help her get better. She wouldn't even be mad at Sarah for killing her. Manda was amazing like that. She loved Sarah. So when Brett said those words, I broke every promise I'd made to myself after the accident and saved Sarah from herself. I walked through the door, dropped to my knees in front of her, and told her the truth.

"Manda told me I need to help you. I still hate you, but she never would. I'm going to help you, Sarah. Not for you, but for her." Then I picked her up and carried her out.

Thankfully she didn't fight me. She wrapped her arms around my neck and repeated over and over again how sorry she was. I didn't tell her that it was okay. I will never tell her that. I did, however, tell her how much Manda loved her and how she wouldn't have blamed her for any of this. Manda always was a better person than I am.

So here I am, wrapped in the tiny arms of my very own guardian angel, Jesse Addison. Brett stands behind her, angry and frustrated. It's obvious she made him come here today. I don't blame him. Last night, Brett thought Sarah had a gun to Jesse's head. He heard the gun shots, and I know they lodged directly in his heart. The fact that he's here at all speaks wonders about how much he loves Jesse. And I know because a ghost dragged me here today.

"Hey, baby girl." I give her a tight squeeze.

A few months ago, Brett would have blown up at me for touching Jesse, but he knows I'd never try to come between them now. Jesse is a little sister to me, and after everything Brett and I have been through, he's more than a brother to me...whatever that may be. I'm happy for them yet still so jealous it hurts.

"How is she?" Jesse asks, looking up at me with tender brown eyes.

"She's fine, I guess. They sedated her. You know she's going to go into police custody after all that shit, right?"

She looks away and sadly nods. I have no idea how Brett got so lucky. Here is a woman who is genuinely worried about her boyfriend's soon-to-be ex-wife—even after Sarah broke into her house with a gun. I have no doubts that Sarah would have harmed Jesse if she had been there. Suddenly, it hits me. Fuck, Manda would have loved Jesse for dragging Brett here. And just for that, I squeeze her just a little tighter.

"What are you doing here still? Have you been home at all?" Jesse asks.

"Nah, I just figured someone should be here for her. Even if it is just me."

My words cause Brett to let out a string of cuss words then roughly drag his hands through his hair. He's a good guy, and he loved Sarah. But after she pushed him away for years, he finally moved on with Jesse. I know Brett, and I'm sure he feels guilty as hell. He may not love her anymore, but he loved Sarah once.

"Hey, man. I'm not trying to make you feel guilty. You're a better man than I am to be standing here right now at all. I just meant…someone should be here, but it definitely should not be you. You did the right thing this time. You two needed some alone time after yesterday."

"Thanks, Caleb." Jesse finally releases me and returns to her position at Brett's side, tucked securely under his arm.

Without even thinking, Brett leans down and kisses the top of her head. I have to look away to keep the burning jealousy from seeping out.

"Brett!" I hear a woman yell.

I turn to see a tall blonde running full speed down the hall. She so eerily looks like Sarah that I unconsciously take a protective step towards Jesse. Brett, however, doesn't move, and as she gets closer, the resemblance fades.

Sarah was always beautiful, but this woman, who barely slows when she reaches us, is easily the sexiest woman I have ever seen. Her long, straight hair is so blonde it's almost white. It's natural—I can tell that much. No color from a bottle could ever produce this shade. Her eyes are so bright that they must contain flecks of every color blue imaginable. It's unbelievable. She's dressed in jeans that hug her long and lean figure and a tight T-shirt that is barely able to stretch over her large breasts. She completes the ensemble with an unlikely pair of flip-flops. It's February in Chicago, and we still have four inches of snow on the ground. It's obvious that this woman isn't from here. *Interesting.* I could use a temporary long-distance distraction, and I have a feeling that body would more than do the job.

"Brett, oh my God. I'm so glad you called."

He steps forward, pulling her into an awkward one-arm hug, never releasing Jesse. Her sweet Southern accent causes my cock to quickly stiffen. My mind instantly drifts to all the fun things I'm going to make her say with that accent while I'm fucking her mouth tonight. Although that wouldn't give her much time to talk.

"Hey, Emma. I shouldn't have called. You didn't have to come right now," he says gently.

The vision of her round tits bouncing while she rides me immediately shatters into a million pieces. Damn it, I recognize that name. Fuck, this is Sarah's little sister.

Chapter
THREE

Emma

"YES I did have to come! Sarah tried to shoot you. God, I'm so sorry," I say, feeling guilty as hell that things have gotten this bad with her. "Is she going to be okay? Have you seen her?" My words have barely come out of my mouth when I notice that his arm is draped around a pretty brunette. "Um…" I stutter, looking back and forth between Brett and the short woman.

It's obvious that they are together. Her arms are lovingly looped around his waist. Brett is hesitant to answer and stares at me with awkward discomfort, but she boldly looks up at me with a soft, warm smile. I have to give it to her—she's really fucking cute.

"Em, this is my girlfriend, Jesse Addison. Gorgeous, this is Sarah's sister, Emma Jane."

I am stunned into silence. I probably look like the human version of Wile E. Coyote with my jaw unhinged and on the floor right now. I can't believe he did it. He finally left her. Sarah's attack on Brett yesterday now makes a lot more sense.

"Oh my God, is this what yesterday was all about? Is she pissed you started dating?"

"Pretty much. She stole one of my guns then broke into Jesse's apartment. Led everyone to believe she had Jesse, but thank fucking Christ, she wasn't home."

"Jesus, Brett. That sounds horrible."

"Sarah's fine, but this is going to be a long legal road for her. The

police were involved this time, and she didn't just try to hurt herself..."
He trails off, and I can tell that he is uncomfortable with what he is about
to say. "Listen, Em, we need to talk. I'm not just dating again. I'm in love
with Jesse. I filed for divorce, and I'm done with Sarah."

"Brett..." Jesse tries to softly interrupt.

My eyes slide down to her, but she's staring up at him, silently pleading. Although I can't for the life of me figure out why the hell she would
be pleading for Sarah.

"No, babe. Don't. I'll never forgive her. You told me how you feel,
but I'm not you and I can't just get over it. I'm sorry, but this is something
I have to do."

I honestly can't believe what I'm witnessing. Since the accident, Brett
has never had balls when it comes to Sarah. For the last five years, he has
been at her mercy. Babying her and letting her run all over him. Now, this
Jesse chick is arguing with him about protecting Sarah. I know I must look
confused when he looks back at me.

"I can't take care of her anymore. I know you two aren't speaking,
but she's going to need you more than ever. I washed my hands of her last
night."

I can't help it. I all but plow over that little girl and launch myself into
his arms.

"Finally!" I scream. Brett deserves so much more than Sarah. Not old
Sarah—they were perfect together. However, he doesn't deserve the person she has become.

"Jesus, be careful," I hear a man hiss.

I turn to give him an annoyed look when I hear Jesse giggling and
wiping off her pants where I knocked her to the ground.

"Oh shit, I'm so sorry." I try to help her the rest of the way up, but
the angry man pushes my hands away.

"I've got her. Just be more careful. Maybe even act like an adult."

My eyes lock with his and I sway back a step as the heat of a sexual
fire emanates from his skin. Jesus, he's hot. That messy sandy-blonde hair
and steely blue eyes. Crap, if he weren't being such a dick right now, I
might pause to check him out. Oh, who am I kidding? I'm totally checking
him out. He's wearing a fitted grey sweater that clings to his perfectly
sculpted pecks and tattered jeans that I'm sure cling to a tight ass. He's at
least six foot two, and for a girl who is five foot ten, that's golden.

"So nice to meet you, Mr. Pleasant. Do you have a name to match your warm and fuzzy personality?" I launch full-on sarcasm.

Brett introduces me. "Emma Jane, this is Caleb Jones."

And with those words, I become the ass. I know exactly who he is, and I have a very good idea of why he's being rude.

"I'm sorry. Hey, Caleb," I say awkwardly. He silently glares at me, so I continue to nervously spew words. "I'm really sorry for your loss. I met Manda once when she and Sarah came down to Savannah. She was hilarious, and I'm sorry you lost her."

"I've got to make a few calls," he mumbles before walking away.

"Okay, then. That was awkward," I say, turning my attention back to Brett.

"Don't worry about him. He didn't get any sleep last night. He stayed up here with Sarah all night."

"Um, why? Doesn't he hate her?" I ask, once again confused.

"No clue. Caleb isn't exactly acting like himself. He was also the one who carried her out last night. I'm not really sure what he's doing here."

"Shit. I should thank him for staying with her. Although I might just send him a fruit basket, because the idea of talking to him again isn't really all that appealing."

Jesse quietly speaks up. "Just ignore him. He's had a rough twenty-four hours. I bet Caleb doesn't even know why he's still here."

I let out a sigh and get back to the matter at hand. "Okay, back to Sarah. What happens next? Can I see her?"

"Probably not. Usually in situations like this, once she is stable, they will release her into police custody."

"What? They are going to send her to jail? She doesn't need jail! She needs help!" I scream, drawing every eye in my direction.

"Yes, she does need help. Unfortunately, after what she did yesterday, it's up to the courts to make those decisions for her now," Brett says with a bitter mixture of anger and sadness in his voice.

"They won't let me see her at all?"

"I'll ask, Em. But I'm really doubting it."

I lower my head. I'm virtually helpless when it comes to Sarah—yet again. "So what *can* I do?"

"You can head back to Sarah's place, maybe get some rest. I know you're exhausted from traveling. There's nothing you can do tonight." He digs in his pocket and pulls out his keys. He slides a gold key off the ring and looks at it for a second before shaking his head and handing it to me. "Here. This is the key to her place. We can give you a ride over there."

"I think I'm going to hang around here for a bit." My eyes flash over to Caleb in the corner talking on the phone. Jesse's eyes immediately follow mine, and my interest causes her to let out an adorable giggle. I drag my attention away from Caleb and look down at her. She's still attached to Brett's hip. "You're cute," I say with a smile.

"Jesus, don't call her cute! I made that mistake on more than one occasion. Trust me. It won't win you any points."

"Oh, shush." She gives Brett a gentle tap on the stomach. "She's a girl. She can call me cute," she says with the tiniest of attitudes. It's almost comical, and I watch as Brett's lips twitch when she looks back at me. "Thank you. You're really pretty." She offers me the warmest of smiles like we have been friends forever.

"I like you." I look back at Brett and repeat, "I'm liking her."

"Okay, before you two start exchanging recipes and painting each other's nails, I'm getting out of here. Emma, it was good to see you. I'll see if I can pull any strings to get you in to see her in the morning." He pulls Jesse into his side and walks away. I'm so wickedly happy for him. Brett deserves a good woman, and it looks like he just might have found one.

I stand for a minute, immediately regretting my decision to stay. I hate hospitals. Everything is so freaking sterile, but they still make me feel gross. I sit down on a worn-out chair in the waiting room and glance around when my eyes settle on the muscular back of Caleb Jones. I'm a real ass for checking out this man. My sister basically killed his fiancée. I wasn't lying before—from what I knew about Manda, I really liked her. And I know Sarah loved her. I just can't sit here without saying something to him. Apologizing? I already did that, and he didn't exactly seem receptive. Maybe I should take a different approach.

"CALEB, CAN we talk?" I hear Emma ask from in front of me.

"Nope," I reply, never looking up from my phone.

"I love Sarah, but I'm not my sister," she rushes out. I slowly lift my eyes to hers, trying not to rake them over her tits but failing. "I understand why you don't like me, but I just wanted to say thank you for being here last night. I'm glad she wasn't alone. I haven't been there for her, but that's about to change."

"I didn't exactly sit at her bedside, holding her hand or anything. I just sat in the waiting room," I reply, disinterested in her gratitude but very interested in her panty preferences. *Fuck!*

"That's more than I did. I haven't spoken to her in years. I get the occasional update from Brett, but I never came up here. I couldn't stand watching her fall apart. So I'm sorry. I know Brett thinks the world of you, and the last thing I wanted to do is piss you off." Tears well in her eyes. Jesus Christ, is she going to cry? *Fan-fucking-tastic.*

"Look, I don't hate you. I don't even know you. You didn't piss me off, it's just—"

"Oh good. You want to grab a drink?" She smiles, perking right up and bouncing on the balls of her feet.

"What? No! I mean yes, I want a drink, but not with you. Did you just fake cry?"

"No, they were real tears. I've been under a lot of stress. The only fake part was when they threatened to escape my eyes. I'm not a crier." She shrugs. Holy shit, crazy must run in the Erickson family.

"Okay, well, sorry if I was a prick earlier. I just didn't realize who you were, and by the time I did… Anyway. Sorry. We're good."

"Wow, you're easy," she says with a smile so sexy it leaves me unable to drag my eyes away from her mouth. I've got to get out of here and get laid.

"Okay, well I should probably go. It was good meeting you, Emma Jane," I lie.

It was horrible meeting her. I'll have to fuck everything in a fifty-mile radius to keep from thinking about her. God damn. Just my luck—Sarah's fucking sister.

"Hey, wait, Caleb. Can you do me a big favor?"

Sure, as long as the favor is stripping you naked and spending the rest of the night between your legs.

Instead, I answer, "Maybe. What do you need?"

"I have to go home tomorrow and pack up all my stuff. I've decided to move up here and do what I should have been doing all along—taking care of Sarah. Do you think you could call and give me updates about her until I can get back? It might be a few weeks. I just don't know who else to ask. I don't want to involve Brett anymore. He and Jesse seem so happy. He deserves to move on."

"Yeah, sure. I can do that. Just so you know, I won't actually see her, but I can definitely keep you in the loop."

"That would be great." She breathes a sigh of relief. "Here." She reaches into her back pocket and pulls out a card. "That's my cell number. It's also my work number, so I never leave home without it."

I look down at the small rectangle business card in my hand that reads:

Magnolia Photography — Owner Emma Erickson

"You're a photographer?" I ask surprised.

"Yep. For five years. Why the shocked face?"

"Oh, no reason. I dabble in a little photography myself. Nothing *professional* though." I lift her card teasingly.

"Do you think she's going to be okay?" She suddenly shifts to serious.

"If there is one thing Sarah is, it's a survivor." I try to fake a smile, but that's all it is—fake.

"Thanks," she returns with a sad smile. "You sure you don't want a drink?"

"I shouldn't. I've got to work in the morning."

"You still a cop?"

"Yep."

"You think you can sweet talk the nurses and get me back to see Sarah?" she asks without even a glimmer of humor in her eyes. Despite how hard I try, I can't stop the smile from crossing my lips.

"Probably, but the uniforms outside her door don't respond nearly as well to my charm," I respond dryly, and her smile immediately grows to match mine.

"Well, it's obvious you don't try hard enough then." She smirks, and I let out a small chuckle.

"Emma Jane, it was really nice to meet you."

"You'll keep me informed, right?"

19

"Of course." And before I have a chance to flirt any more, I force myself to walk away.

Chapter
FOUR

Caleb

"MARRY ME." I thrust inside her so hard it pushes her up the bed and slams her into the headboard.

She answers the same way she always does. "No."

Her rejection never gets easier. She loves me. I know she'll spend the rest of her life with me, but I want more. I want to share a last name and make beautiful redheaded babies with her. I just want her to be mine. I don't know why I need a marriage certificate to do that. She's never been anything but mine since the day I first laid eyes on her.

"Manda, fucking marry me. You're wearing the ring, so stop playing games and set a date."

"I'm not playing games." she whispers while moving to flip me.

I roll over and settle on my back as she begins to slowly ride me. She's beautiful. The very idea of her tight, slender runner's body moving over me is enough to finish me off, but it's more than that. She owns me.

Reading my mind, she leans over, whispering into my ear, "I'll love you for the rest of my life." Her voice is distant and sad. It immediately causes worry to flood my veins.

I try to open my eyes to get a read on her, but they won't budge. I struggle motionlessly underneath her, desperate to see those emerald greens. But no matter how hard I try, I can't force my body to cooperate. Oblivious to my struggle, she never stops moving—harder and faster as the minutes pass.

Suddenly her scream pierces through the darkness. "Caleb!" It's not pain or pleasure. It's pure unadulterated terror.

I'm paralyzed against the bed, but I can't grab her or save her from whatever demon that has taken hold. All the while, her relentless rhythm on my cock never falters. I fight under her, trying to see her, touch her. But I can't move. It's too dark, and my arms must weigh a thousand pounds.

"Manda!" I try to yell as fear rushes through my body, but no sound escapes my throat.

I strain, immobile under her touch. Her voice suddenly changes, and words I don't immediately recognize hit me hard.

"I'm not my sister."

I freeze as my mind tries to process who said it. Suddenly, a tall blonde with blue eyes flashes into my mind.

"I'm not my sister," she repeats.

"Emma?" I silently whisper. She continues to move, and images of her dance through my blindness.

"Oh God, Caleb, yes!" she sighs as her body pulses around my cock.

My eyes suddenly open, and the shit storm known as my life rushes back into focus. Sitting on top of me is a raven-haired beauty. By any man's standard, she is insanely sexy, yet the very sight of her makes my stomach turn.

"Get off me." I roll to the side, causing her to fall to the bed.

"What the hell?" she shouts as I stand, snatching off the condom and gathering my clothes from the floor.

"What the fuck was that, Lisa?"

"That was me getting off, you dick."

"No. I wake up from a sound sleep to you riding my dick?"

"Fuck you, Caleb. You started that shit. Don't act like I was raping you or something. I woke up to you sliding into me. You should be thanking me. I might have been half asleep but I at least had the good sense to use a fucking condom."

"Shit!" I run a rough hand through my hair. "I've got to get out of here."

"Manda again?" she asks quietly, rising to her knees.

"Don't you say her name. Ever," I say to the wall, not wanting to make eye contact with her. I don't even bother to offer her a second glance. I barely tug my jeans over my ass before I'm out the door and pulling on my shirt as I walk to my truck.

This isn't the first dream I've ever had about Manda, but it is most definitely the first time she has ever morphed into a different woman. And of all women for her to become, it had to be Emma fucking Erickson. I shouldn't be thinking about her, and she sure as shit should not be invading my dreams. But as I drive home, I can't stop thinking of those two seconds she was riding me. The way it felt with her long blond hair sweeping over my face and her blue eyes piercing into mine. Worst of all, I can't help but remember the way it felt when she came, even if it was Lisa I was inside. *Fuck.*

WHEN I get home from Lisa's, I'm desperate to escape these thoughts of Emma Erickson. I know just the way to do it, too. I walk into my dark and empty house, flipping on the lamp, and head straight to my hall closet. I open the door to retrieve the cardboard file box I keep hidden away on the top shelf. I'm the only one who knows it's there, but that doesn't mean I don't pull it out almost daily. Living alone has its perks sometimes.

I carry the box to my kitchen table and follow the same sick routine I always do. After pulling off the lid, I begin my nightly investigation. Laying each picture of the wreck out in front of me, I scan every single image. I've looked at them so many times over the last few years that I could probably draw them from memory. I can't even begin to tell you how many hours I've spent reading and rereading witness statements from that night. I have them memorized at this point, but that doesn't stop me from poring over them, wishing and praying the answers will somehow jump from the page.

Even though the wreck that stole Manda from me was almost five years ago, my need to know what happened that night is still as strong as it was the night I vowed to never stop searching.

Five Years Earlier...

"CALEB!" I hear wailed from outside my door. "Caleb, please open up." I immediately recognize the voice as Sarah's. Her tone softens as she

begins to beg and, if I'm not mistaken, cry. "Please." I hear a loud thunk that I can only imagine is her head dropping against the door.

I pause for a second, trying to make sure I'm fully awake before opening the door. I don't need to face this situation with a groggy head. I scrub my face and glance round the room. My eyes land on the small potted violet on my end table in the corner. I stare at it for a minute, remembering why it's there and losing my breath in the process. The guys at the station all chipped in and sent me that ridiculous flower the day of the funeral. I'm sure Dana, the receptionist, ordered it. None of them had any clue how much Manda hated the color purple. Oh yeah, I need to go back to bed. This is all too fucking real. My Manda is still gone.

I can't help that I immediately flash to Manda's face as I kissed her goodbye that horrific night. She had a bright smile and shining green eyes. She was clinging to my leg under the table when Brett announced that we had to leave. When I look back, it's as if she were subconsciously trying to keep me with her. The permanent knife in my gut twists just a little deeper at that thought. Not a minute has passed in those three months since the accident where I haven't imagined the 'what if I had stayed' scenario. But I didn't, and that one decision cost Manda her entire life.

There are a lot of things I would change about that night, and all of them would leave my fiancée laughing beside me. Manda and I fought a lot, including on the way to Westies that night. Looking back, I realize that it was a stupid argument, but I would live it on loop for the rest of my life if it meant I just got to keep her.

"Caleb, I..." Sarah sobs against the door, reminding me all over again that this is my reality. Anger courses through my veins as I stomp toward the door, desperate to release my grief on someone else.

"Are you fucking kidding me?" I snatch open the door.

Sarah stumbles inside like a drunk on heels. I watch her crash to the ground. I almost reach out to catch her, but at the last second, I pull my hands away.

"Shit," she says, standing back up on shaky legs. I don't even offer a helpful hand. I just stand there and watch her struggle.

"What the hell do you want?" I slam the door, narrowly missing her body.

"Do you have Manda's necklace?" she asks, rocking me back on my heels.

She didn't come here to talk or to apologize for stealing my entire life. No, she came here for a fucking cheap-ass necklace that they got on vacation. It's one of those cheesy heart "best friends" necklaces. She and Manda both had half, and neither one of them ever took it off. My already boiling blood makes my cruel words come even quicker than I would have thought.

"You fucking bitch! You have some serious balls to show up at my door asking for anything!"

"I don't feel her anymore," she whimpers, dropping back to her knees. "I just... Please, I need to feel her."

"Guess what, Sarah? I don't feel her either. That's because she isn't fucking here anymore. She's gone, and you want to know why?"

She expects my answer and quickly looks up at me with sad eyes. "I wasn't driving," she whispers.

"Yes, you fucking were! Own it!" I scream at the top of my lungs.

"Caleb, please. I love her. I would never knowingly hurt Manda."

"No, Sarah. You loved her. It's past tense now. She is fucking dead, remember?" I spit out the words as I watch her flinch with each syllable.

I need someone to pay for what happened to Manda, and I don't give two shits if it is her best friend. I need something to make me feel again. I've been so numb over the last few months, and I don't care if doing this will make me feel like an asshole. At least I'll feel something. I was already pissed at Sarah, but when she showed up here tonight, asking for something of Manda's? Well, she may as well have thrown herself into the lion's den. I'm not usually a cruel man, but I can definitely make an exception for the woman who killed the love of my life.

"You are one selfish bitch, Sarah. Not three months ago, you killed the only woman I have ever loved. She was my fucking life and you murdered her!" I roar so loud my voice actually breaks. "Then you show up on my doorstep, asking for her most prized possession? And you're delusional enough to think that begging will actually make me to give it to you? If it were up to me, you would be rotting in a jail cell right now, but as it stands, you are prancing around town, while Manda is buried six feet under." That admission hits me hard as my mind flashes to an image of Manda in a casket. I stumble over my words, trying to erase the image that can't be unseen. "You need to really listen to me right now. I will spend the rest of my life trying to prove that you were drunk and driving the car

that night. And when I do, I am going to take everything from you—the same way you did me."

"I don't have anything left for you to take." Her chin begins to quiver as tears openly flow from her blue eyes.

"Oh, I think you do. Now get the fuck out of my house," I say, staring down at the floor with my hands securely on my hips. I can't look at her without my rage bubbling over.

"Please, Caleb. I need something, I'm dying here without her." She all but crawls across the floor to my feet.

It catches me off guard to see this devastated side of Sarah. I almost feel sorry for her for a split second, but just as quickly as that feeling passed over me, it disappears.

"Get out!"

"Please," she whispers, still holding my leg.

I look down and lose whatever calm I thought I had. "You want her necklace?" I ask, and she immediately perks up. The tears still run down her face, but for the first time since she arrived, she appears to have some glimmer of hope.

I walk to my bedroom and pull Manda's necklace off her nightstand. It's been there since they handed me her belongings at the hospital. I stomp back into the den, where Sarah is standing, trying to collect herself. She is rubbing her fingers under her eyes where her eye makeup is running down her cheeks. My mind jumps to the million times I've watched Sarah and Manda swipe the makeup away after hours of drinking and dancing.

"Are you drunk right now?" I pause, edging toward the door.

"What? No!" she screams.

"You sure?" I ask again, pulling open the front door.

"I'll never drink again," she solemnly swears, but it does nothing to quell the flame burning inside me.

"Sarah, I'm going to destroy you the same way you did me, even if it's the last thing I do in this life. Now get out," I repeat as I extend my hand, showing her Manda's half of the necklace.

Her eyes light before her whole face crumbles in despair. She rushes toward me, ready to claim her reward. But as far as I'm concerned, there will never be a reward for her. I turn just as quickly and sling my arm as hard as I can toward my front yard. Her eyes go wide while trying to track the necklace's trajectory, but the darkness cloaks everything.

Stolen Course

"No!" she screams, rushing outside.

I slam the door behind her and move toward the window to watch her scramble. She frantically starts searching the grass, collapsing to the ground for a better view. I watch with a sick sense of triumph as she pulls her cell phone out of her pocket for extra light. I smile to myself before walking back to the door, casually flipping off the outside lights and heading for bed.

I stay awake for hours, constantly looking out my window. Sarah must have combed every inch of that yard, and I took great pleasure in watching her look. By the time she finally relents, her knees are covered in mud and her face is streaked with tears.

Five hours after she pulled into my driveway, Sarah pulls out of it.

Thirty seconds after she leaves, I reach into my pocket, pull out Manda's necklace, and gently place it back on her nightstand. Right where it should be.

Chapter
FIVE

Caleb

FOR FORTY-EIGHT hours, I've done nothing but think about Emma Jane Erickson. I've tried everything to stop, but the brief memories from my dream won't let me go. I can't figure out what it is about her that consumes my every thought. You know, if I don't count her Victoria's Secret runway model good looks. Fuck, I couldn't jerk off enough to forget how she looked running down that hospital hallway. Trust me. I tried.

My visit to Lisa made things even worse. She usually helps me forget everything. She's great in bed, even if she is crazy as a circus sideshow out of it. This time, even she couldn't dull the ache in my body for Emma. I've almost broken my phone twelve times calling for updates about Sarah. I needed a reason to dial Emma's number, but I had nothing new about her sister to share.

Finally I caught a break this morning. It seems Sarah's neurologist got involved in her criminal investigation. I have no doubt that the pixie finger that dialed that doctor's number was any other than Jesse Addison. She is hell-bent on saving Sarah, even if it is from afar. She has this silly notion that Brett needs Sarah to be okay. Truth be told, Brett just needs Jesse. Sarah isn't even a blip on his radar anymore.

I've been sitting on my couch for forty-five minutes staring at my phone. Debating on what to tell Emma. Of course, I'll tell her the truth, but how do I sugarcoat it? Fuck it, I'm just going to do it. She doesn't strike me as a woman who needs to be coddled.

"Hello." Her smooth Southern drawl slides through the phone.

"Emma?"

"Hey, Caleb. I'm so glad you called. I've been worried sick. What's going on?" She jumps right to the point of the call.

"Sarah's fine. She's still in the hospital. Sorry I didn't call you sooner."

"She's still at the hospital? Why? I thought they were taking her into police custody?" she shrieks across the line.

"It seems her doctor got involved, and he's keeping her there, claiming she's incompetent. He's basically cock-blocking the police from touching her."

"Oh my God, Caleb. That's fantastic news!" she says so excitedly that I almost want to be happy with her. I can't though. Sarah belongs in jail, if for no other reason than what she did to Manda.

"Yeah, so we are just waiting to see what happens with her doctor and attorney tomorrow."

"Caleb! I wish I could kiss you right now!" she screams through the phone.

"Oh yeah? I should call more often then." I laugh at her enthusiasm.

"I've been sick all day about the idea of Sarah sitting in a cell. This is the best news in days. I'm getting drunk to celebrate."

"You calling up all your girlfriends and going out or staying in for your little celebration?"

"I don't have many girlfriends. My two best friends are guys. They are always up for getting drunk."

My blood boils. She's going out with two fucking dudes. Of course they are always up for getting drunk. They probably spend the whole night staring at her tits and imagining putting their dicks in her ass.

"Fuck!" It just comes out. I know I sound like a douche right now. I've met this woman exactly once and I was a bastard. I was inside another woman less than twenty-four hours ago, yet here I am getting pissed off at the idea of her with another man.

"What? Something wrong?" she asks sweetly.

"No, just be careful. Make sure you catch a cab." I try to get off the phone, but she stops me.

"Caleb, the guys I'm going out with tonight are my best friends and roommates. We share a small townhouse in downtown Savannah. No one will be driving tonight. The bar we go to is just down the street. Actually, all the bars are within walking distance. Okay?"

"Emma, you don't owe me any explanations. I just didn't want anyone drinking then driving."

"That's funny. You didn't get pissed off until I mentioned Alex and Hunter."

Christ, I've got to end this call. She is entirely too perceptive of my moods.

"Listen, I need to go. I'll let you know when they move Sarah."

"Thanks, Caleb," she breathes into the phone, and I have to suck in breath of my own. I can feel her words, and not just in my pants. Yeah, definitely time to say goodnight.

"Bye, Emma." I hang up the phone before she has a chance to say anything else.

My ass stays glued to the couch for the next twenty minutes while I try to figure out what the hell to do about Emma. I don't know her. She's probably a total bitch just like her sister. Damn it, why the fuck does she have to be Sarah's sister? That one relationship complicates everything. It's not like I can fuck her out of my system like I do with other women. Then again, I've never had a woman *in my system* since Manda. I can't touch Emma. No matter how much I want to. It would be seven million shades of fucked up when things got messy. And there is no doubt things would get messy. Sarah would flip her crazy shit if she found out I was sleeping with her sister. Hell, that little thought alone makes me want to do it all the more.

IT'S WELL after midnight, but I'm still awake and sanding down the new coffee table I just finished. After trying to run off the Erickson trance, I retreated out to my workshop. I always feel better after a few hours of decompressing with a belt sander. The sound of Sarah McLachlan's *Blackbird* is blaring through the speakers. It might be an odd choice to some, but it stays on repeat when I'm out here.

My phone lights up from across the room. It's late but it's not unheard of for me to get calls this time of night. But when I see Emma's name on the screen, I'm immediately worried. She was out drinking tonight with two dickheads. I swear if those asspucks let anything happen to her, I'll kill them myself.

I immediately snatch up my phone. "Emma?"

"Caleb," she says, crying through the phone.

I start scanning the shop for my car keys but pause when I realize there is nothing I can do. I'm helpless. What the fuck am I going to do? Jump in the car and drive sixteen hours down to Savannah?

"What's wrong, sweetheart? Are you all right?" I ask as she continues to sob over the phone.

"I'm sorry. I shouldn't have called so late. It's just... I had way too much to drink, and I feel like shit about not being there for Sarah over the last few years. I'm such an asshole for abandoning her like I did. She needed me, but I just walked away because I was so afraid of losing her." My pulse begins to slow and I begin to relax as she continues blubbering over the line.

Fuck. Why do I always overreact to shit when it comes to woman I care about? I was never this way before Manda died, but now I always assume the absolute worst. I have a need to save people and do what I couldn't do for Manda. Shit, did I just admit that I care about Emma Erickson? This little obsession I have with her just went from bad to fucking ludicrous. I've had two conversations with her. I really should go back to being a dick. At least then she will hate me.

"Caleb, are you still there?"

"Yeah, I'm here. Did you need something or were you just calling to bitch and cry?" I ask, pulling some old-fashioned asshole out of my back pocket.

"Don't be a dick just to keep me at a distance," she says, shocking the shit out of me. I pull the phone away and look at it as if Siri is going to explain to me how the fuck she just read my mind.

"I thought you weren't a crier?" I decide to keep it up even though she's onto me.

"I'm not usually, but I just had a threesome with my roommates and it made me all emotional."

"What the fuck, Emma?" I scream over the phone.

At the exact same time, she screams, "I knew it!" Damn, if she didn't just trick me into blowing my own asshole cover, and it only serves to piss me off for real this time.

"What do you want, Emma? A pep talk about what a great sister you

31

are? Because I am fresh out of those tonight. I'm glad to hear you got tag-teamed. Every woman deserves a good dick in the ass every now and again. But if that's all you called for, I'm headed to bed."

"Tell me why you got upset earlier when I told you I was going out with Hunter and Alex?"

"Oh Jesus Christ, Emma. What the fuck do I need to say to get off the phone right now?"

"The truth would work," she says, annoyed. And guess what? It pisses me off even more that she has the balls to be annoyed with me. I didn't call her at midnight. I barely even know this woman. Still, somehow I'm so attracted to her that I find myself trying to protect myself from her and what is sure to be a train wreck.

"Okay. The truth. Fine. You're sexy as fuck, and I can't stop thinking about drilling into that smartass mouth of yours. And after hearing about your little double-play action tonight, you can add your ass to that list too."

"Wow. That really was honest," she says, taken aback by my outburst.

"Great, I'm glad you approve. Now, I'm going to bed."

"Caleb, wait."

"Goodnight." I hang up before I can say anything else I'll fucking regret.

I stand in the center of the room for a few minutes just trying to catch my breath. I can't believe I just said all of that to her. So much for not complicating things.

I lock up my workshop and barely make it back into the house before the phone chirps in my hand.

I just called tonight because I needed to talk to someone who understood the whole Sarah situation. I'm sorry if I bothered you. - Em

Great, now she's texting. This woman is obviously not used to men ignoring her. I can definitely see why. She's beautiful and I'm treating her like shit for no reason other than self-preservation. Why the hell do I feel guilty now? I let out a loud sigh before picking up my phone to text her back. I type out about twenty different replies but delete them all without sending.

What exactly do you say to a woman after you blow up and tell her you want to fuck her in the ass? I'm pretty sure that is the moment you just cut your losses and move on. But this isn't just any woman. This is Emma, the person I promised to keep updated about Sarah until she can finally move up to Chicago. Before I have another chance to reply, my phone chirps again.

FYI: Now, would be a good time for you to apologize. If you don't respond, I will just have to assume your silence is the Jones version of a profuse apology. :) -Em

As frustrated as I may feel, I can't help but burst out laughing. It is almost one in the morning, but I'm off tomorrow, so I head to the fridge and crack open a beer. I toss the phone around in my hands for a few minutes, debating how to respond. But I knew what I was going to do as soon as I read her last text. I shake my head at myself and dial Emma's number.

"Jesus, Caleb, do you always call people so late?" she says sarcastically when she answers.

"Not all people. Just the lucky ones."

"Well I'll consider myself very lucky tonight then."

"Yeah, it sounds like you were really lucky tonight. Two guys, huh?" I try to lighten things a bit. I know she was just fucking with me, and I played right into her hand with my reaction.

"You know I didn't really have a threesome tonight." I can hear the smile in her voice.

"I know you didn't." I let out a guilty sigh. "I'm sorry."

"Do you always act like a kindergartener when you like a girl?"

"Who said I like you?" I mock surprise.

Yeah, I gave myself away. She knows that I think she's hot, but wanting to have sex with someone is very different than actually liking them. At least it is in my world. I've had sex with numerous women since Manda. Never once have I even thought twice about them though. That is until Emma ran into my life.

"You called back, didn't you?"

Damn it, busted again! She's right. I like her even though I know absolutely nothing about her. I need to remedy this without acting like a broody, sullen teenager. Who knows. Maybe I will be able to shake her once I get to know her a little better.

"What's your favorite color, Emma Jane Erickson?"

"What is this, the get-to-know-each-other portion of the night? I never thought you would be so cliché, Detective Jones." She laughs for a second before answering, "Orange."

"Oh, come on. No one likes orange."

"I do."

"Why?"

"Why not? It's different and bold. It stands out amongst a blank world of black, white, and gray. Orange is the early morning sun stretching across the sky and the color of a burning ember standing tall in the middle of a beach bonfire. It's leaves in the fall, carrots in Nana's vegetable soup on a cold winter day, tulips in the spring, and the ladybugs in the middle of the grassy park on a hot summer afternoon. Orange is life. It's unexpected but beautiful." She stops talking, and her depth silences me too.

I consider myself a very artistic person. I draw, paint, and build. Creation is my escape. And to listen to this woman wax poetic about a single simple color steals my breath. It embeds itself somewhere deep inside. A place where no woman, especially an Erickson, has any business being.

"Oh, and it's my favorite flavor of candy too."

And with those simple words, I know I'm in trouble. So fucking much trouble. I begin to laugh, and I mean really laugh. The kind that sticks with you even after the joke is long since forgotten, and I do it for the first time in almost five years. *Fuck.*

"What about you, Caleb? What's your favorite color?" The curious tone in her voice piques my interest. Is she as attracted to me as I am to her? If she feels anywhere close to what I feel, that could be seriously dangerous.

"Brown," I answer simply.

"You gave me shit about orange when your favorite color is brown?" she yells, making me laugh harder.

God, I miss this. For the last few years, I've met nothing but she-bots. You know the kind—robots who always say what they think you want to hear. They say all the right things, are always aware of their surroundings, and read the people they interact with but never show you their true colors. I fucking loathe she-bots.

"What did you do tonight?" I ask when my curiosity gets the best of me. I may know she wasn't having a threesome, but that doesn't mean I'm not dying to know what she was doing.

"We went dancing at the gay club. It was so much fun. Hunter and Alex had this ridiculous bet going."

"Shit. Your roommates are gay, aren't they?" I ask, and she starts laughing so loud I have to pull the phone away from my ear.

"Oh my God, no, they aren't. But I can't wait to tell them you assumed that. It was actually ladies' night at the gay club."

"Are *you* gay?" I shout, which only causes her to laugh even louder.

At this point, I have no doubt that she is rolling around on her bed in a fit of laughter. I can even picture it. She's probably half naked, wearing only a tight little see-through tank top and thong. Her nipples are peaked from a chill in the air. No, wait. Strike that. Her nipples are peaked from how turned on she is from being on the phone with me. She's probably even stroking her clit through her panties…

She interrupts my daydreaming with an equally stimulating answer. "No, I prefer my lovers with a dick."

We are both in luck, because I just so happen have one of those growing in my pants as we speak. I'll keep that large tidbit to myself though. Honestly I'm not even sure why we are having this conversation right now. But I know I don't want to get off the phone yet.

"So what were you doing at a ladies' night at the gay club?" I try to change back to a subject that won't have me picturing her naked.

"The guys had a very interesting drunken conversation last night. It basically consisted of them debating if lesbians really only like women because they can't get guys. So they decided to make a bet about who could get one into bed first."

"Wow. They sound like idiots," I say little too roughly, but douchebags like that make my skin crawl.

"Yeah, they are. They are also really good guys, but total meatheads sometimes."

"They don't sound like meatheads. They sound like assholes," I say very matter-of-factly. I have zero tolerance for ignorant tools like them.

"Hey, stop judging people you don't even know. That makes you an asshole. They were just joking!" she yells, and I can tell that her hackles have risen. She must be pretty tight with these guys to get all mama bear over this. If she only knew what I really wanted to call them.

"My sister, Lindsey, has been happily married for over three years to a woman she has been with for over twelve years. Sorry, but I don't find trolling for homosexual woman in an attempt to *change* them even the slightest bit humorous."

"Shit," she whispers to herself.

"Yeah, 'shit' about sums it up."

"I'm so sorry, Caleb. I wasn't trying to be insensitive. They were just being stupid."

"It's okay, Emma. I know you didn't mean anything by it. However, I stand by my earlier description that they are assholes."

"No, it's not. I should have stopped them, but honestly it was hilarious watching women shoot them down over and over again. Both of them left with their tails firmly curled between their legs."

"Well, at least they got put in their place." I just wish it were me who had put them there.

"I got hit on a few times though."

"Oh yeah? How'd you handle that?" I ask, sipping off my beer.

"I very kindly told them that I was straight then offered a compliment on their shoes, shirts, or hair. By the end of the night, I had quite a few friends."

"I bet you had more than just a few friends," I tease.

"Well I had more than the guys, that's for sure." She laughs before the phone goes quiet with uncomfortable silence. "So. You've been thinking about my ass?" she questions, referring to my outburst earlier.

"Ah, that. Yeah, that was the truth, but I'll be happy to tell you it was a lie if it would make you more comfortable."

"I can't stop thinking about you," she boldly admits, surprising me once again. I can't believe she is being this forward or…well, honest. But based on our earlier conversation, it's not exactly like I've been good at hiding my attraction either.

"Shit, Em. That makes two of us."

"This is going to be really bad, isn't it?" she says quietly.

"Probably," I answer shortly. It's not exactly the truth. This is going to be far worse than bad. This is going to be epic proportions of horrible, but I still ask, "When are you coming back?"

"Hopefully late next week. Just depends how quickly I can get packed and finish the photos for my clients here before I leave."

There is no doubt that this is going to end in disaster, but once again, I add fuel to the fire. "You want to meet for dinner or something when you get back?" I have no idea what I'm doing, but if she is going to be this open, then I am too.

"Yeah, I think I'd like that." Once again, she sounds happy, and the seriousness fades from my voice too.

"I need to go before I have a chance to ask you something stupid, like the color of your bra," I say, equally praying to God that she will and won't answer.

"Nude," she announces without hesitation.

"And now I *have* to go!" I stand up off the couch. I don't know where I think I'm going to escape when the phone is still securely anchored to my ear, but I know I need to stop this conversation.

"Okay. Go to bed," she says with a small laugh that proves that she knows exactly how much she's affecting me. "Oh, and Caleb?" She catches me before I can say goodbye. "I didn't mean nude the color."

I have to bite my lip to keep a groan from escaping. What the fuck happened here tonight? I went from being an absolute dick to having a date and all-too-vivid image of Emma's lack of undergarments. Fuck. Me.

"Goodnight, sweetheart." I quickly pull the phone away, ending the call.

I fall back on the couch, shaking my head at myself. I just opened a door, and Emma all too willingly walked right through it. Let the shit show begin.

Chapter SIX

Emma

AFTER CALEB and I got off the phone last night, I struggled to fall back asleep. I went to the living room and had a long talk with Hunter and Alex. I love those guys. They were half drunk, but that only made the conversation more interesting.

Hunter has been moping around since I told him I was moving out. He was pissed at first, but after a little chat, he understood why I needed to go. He just didn't understand why I was making it a permanent move instead of just an extended stay. I love that boy, but damn he is so hardheaded when he wants to be. I know he's going to miss me. Hell, I'm going to miss the shit out of him too. He and I have been through a lot together. He leaned on me about his girl and his best friend. And over the last few years, I've really leaned on him about Sarah. He swears he is going to come visit once a month, and I don't doubt that for one second.

Alex is much more laid back about my up and leaving. I know he loves me. It's nothing personal. He's just a big tough guy, and even if my leaving devastated him, he'd never tell me. He and I just have a very different relationship than Hunter and I do. While Hunter is my overprotective best friend, Alex is my overprotective big brother. I've known him since elementary school. He lived next door for most of our lives. Truth be told, he actually made out with Sarah on more than one drunken occasion growing up. He's always been a part of my life.

When Alex graduated, he went off to the University of Georgia on a football scholarship. The following year, when I graduated, I followed him up there. He took me under his wing, and when I say that, I mean he ran off any guy who tried to look at me. I was off-limits to the entire football team, yet I still managed to date two of them behind his back. He's a big teddy bear. I know he means well, but we still butt heads a good bit.

I've spent most of the day editing photos for clients, trying to wrap up my jobs before I take off. Most of this can be done remotely, but when I first get to Chicago, the last thing I want is deadlines looming over my head. I've watched the clock all day, waiting for a time I could call Caleb. I barely make it to eight p.m. my time—seven p.m. his—before I give in and dial his number. However, the call goes unanswered. I open my laptop back up and settle in with a glass of wine. It's probably for the best that he didn't answer. I have a lot of work to be done if I'm ever going to be able to move to Chicago.

Two glasses of wine later, my phone starts ringing. I glance at my phone and bite my lip when I see Caleb's name light the screen.

"Hey, you." I try to hide my giddiness.

"Hey, sweetheart. What's going on?" Caleb purrs over the line.

"Not much. Just hanging out in bed, trying to finish up some work. What are you up to?"

"I'm on my way home from the gym. Sorry I didn't answer earlier. I was in the ring when you called."

"The ring?" I teasingly let out breathy sigh. It causes him to laugh too.

"Yeah, I box three nights a week. I hate running, so it helps with my cardio."

"You hate to run?"

"The only time I run is when I have something serious on my mind. I can usually forget whatever it is with loathing when I run."

I laugh at his logic. "I guess that's one way to do it." He doesn't immediately respond, so an awkward silence falls over the phone. "So have you heard anything about Sarah?" I ask. I know he would have called me if he had, but it seems like an acceptable question to ask.

"She's still at the hospital," he answers shortly.

"You okay?"

"Yeah, I'm a little tired. Listen, can I call you when I get home?"

"Oh, yeah. Sure," I answer, suddenly feeling awkward to have called him. "You can just call me tomorrow. I'm probably heading to bed pretty soon."

"Yeah, okay."

"I'll talk to you later."

"Bye, sweetheart."

I hang up the phone, baffled by how distant he sounded.

Last night, he was funny and sweet. Caleb might have been a dick at first, but I knew it was only because he liked me. I've met him exactly once, but I could tell that Caleb is all man. The minute I mentioned Hunter and Alex, he became a dick—typical alpha-male syndrome. He probably got off the phone, put on a leopard-skin loin cloth, and pounded on his chest like a caveman for a few minutes too. I mean, hell, just the way he reacted when I knocked Jesse down at the hospital gave him away.

I figured he'd be stoked to hear from me, but whatever. I can't sit here trying to analyze Caleb Jones. I've got pictures to edit, wine to drink, and a pillow calling my name. He can figure out his shit on his own, but I can say that that will be the last time I call him just to shoot the shit.

I finally fall asleep with images of ugly King Charles spaniels floating through my head. I couldn't have been asleep long when my phone starts ringing beside me. Caleb's name flashes on the display, sending fear through my veins. No way would he call this late without it being horrible news about Sarah. I snatch it off the nightstand and immediately click the green button.

"Is she okay?" I don't even bother with a hello.

"What?" he asks.

"Sarah? Is she okay?" I repeat.

"Oh, yeah. I mean, I guess she is. I haven't heard anything today."

"Shit, Caleb! You scared me to death. I thought if you were calling this late it had to be shitty news!" I yell as I try to calm myself down.

"Jesus, I'm sorry. I didn't even think about that."

"Yeah, we definitely need to develop a system for Sarah updates. Maybe one ring for bad news, two rings for good."

"Um, you picked up on the first ring this time. I didn't have a chance for it to get to the second ring." He starts laughing.

I amend my brilliant idea. "Okay, one ring for good, two for bad."

"What exactly am I supposed to do after these one or two rings? Hang up? What if you don't hear the phone ring and just see a missed call from me? Is that good news or bad?" he asks, continuing to laugh at me.

"Damn it! I don't know! I didn't exactly have time to think this plan through." I sit for a minute, trying to catch my breath, then burst into laughter right along with him.

"How about if I have *any* news about Sarah, I'll text first and ask you to call me? Would that keep you from worrying every time I call?"

"Yeah, that works. Although I'm kind of hating on you right now. Your plan is good, and mine sucked."

"It really was a bad plan," he answers.

I'd give anything to see the grin that I know he's wearing right now. I only saw him smile once at the hospital, but it's etched into my memory.

"Okay, so what's up? I didn't expect to hear from you again tonight."

"Why not? I told you I'd call when I got home."

"But then I said I was going to bed and to just call me tomorrow."

"Yeah, but I said I'd call you when I got home, so I'm calling you now that I'm home," he says firmly. "Don't worry. I'll still call tomorrow too," he tries to tease.

"Wow, you're just getting home? Did you hit the strip club on the way? Get a little Friday night eye candy before heading home?" I laugh at the silly joke, but Caleb is silent. "You still there?" I say, pulling the phone away from my ear to make sure the call didn't get dropped.

"Yeah, I'm here," he says before letting out a loud sigh. "I stopped at Manda's grave. It's on my way home from gym, and I can't pass by without stopping."

"Shit." I bite my lip, feeling like a total asshole. "I'm sorry. I was just being funny. My jokes obviously need a lot of work these days."

"It's okay," he says dryly.

"Fuck. I just… I'll let you go."

"Does it bother you?" he asks, catching me just before I hang up.

"What? You going to Manda's grave?"

"Yeah," he says sadly, and it makes my heart ache for him.

"No, it doesn't bother me at all. You lost someone you loved. I'd be a bitch if it bothered me. I just didn't know, and I made a stupid joke. I'm sorry."

"I go about three times a week," he oddly announces.

"Okay…" I trail off, not sure how to respond.

"I just thought you should know. I wasn't sure if it would bother you or not. You know, now that we are kind of talking, I guess. I don't know.

I just wanted you to know."

"Caleb, does it bother *you* that I know? Because you don't have to share stuff like that with me if you don't want to. But just so you know, I will never in a million years have a problem with any part of Manda or your past together. She's gone, but I don't expect you to forget about her just because we have started…talking." I repeat his term from earlier.

It's true. Caleb and I really aren't doing anything but talking, and we have only done that once. Yet, it still seems like this is more, and we both know it.

"Emma, I have no idea what the hell I'm doing." He lets out a loud sigh. "I haven't dated anyone since Manda."

"What?" I yell across the line. "Never?"

"Nope. Never."

"Damn, it's been five years! You must jerk off like twelve times a day!"

What the fuck is wrong with me? Why I would say that to him in the middle of a serious conversation? However, acting like a raving lunatic, for once, works in my favor. Caleb actually starts chuckling.

"I said I haven't dated anyone, not that I haven't had sex. But thank you for worrying about how many times I jerk off. It makes me feel a lot less pervy about where my mind has been when thinking about you."

"Oh, okay. That makes more sense! Wait, what exactly have you been thinking about me?"

"Nothing you haven't been thinking about me, obviously."

"Well, I don't masturbate twelve times a day."

"Stop ruining my daydreams, woman!" He laughs into the phone.

I play along. "Actually, I do it thirteen times."

"That's my girl," he rumbles over the line, ensuring that today's real count will be at least one. "Go back to sleep, Em. I'll call you tomorrow."

"Hey, Caleb? Before you go… I'm serious about Manda. I don't have any issues with you having a past. I'm not an insecure girl who is trying to compete with her memory. So if you ever want to talk about her or anything…I'm here, okay?

"You really are an amazing woman, Emmy," he says in a joking tone, but I know he means it.

"Yeah. I know. And I get a new nickname? What, Emma wasn't short enough for you? What happened to sweetheart?" I try to keep the end of this conversation lighter than the beginning.

"I was just trying something a little different."

"Oh good. I like sweetheart. It makes me feel all warm inside."

"I like the idea of you feeling warm. Wet is preferred, but warm is good too."

Okay, make that two times tonight.

"Oh yeah? I took a shower earlier. I was wet then. Is that the kind you're talking about?"

"Not exactly, but I'm going to assume you were naked in the shower, so I guess that will work."

"Definitely naked...and wet." I take a deep breath, hoping this crosses into full-fledged phone sex, but Caleb cuts it off.

"When are you coming back?"

"Hopefully soon."

"Well hurry up. I want to see you again."

"I probably won't be naked or wet when I get off the plane," I say, attempting to take it back to sexy.

"Probably not, but I'll make sure you are both very shortly after." His words cause me to let out a quiet moan. "Goodnight, Emmy."

"That was mean, Caleb," I whisper into the phone.

"Go make it fourteen, and we'll talk tomorrow."

I let out a frustrated groan as he begins to laugh. "Night, Caleb."

"Night, sweetheart."

Chapter
SEVEN

Emma

JUST STEPPING out of the shower, I hear my phone ringing across the room. I don't recognize the number, but I immediately recognize it to be yet another Chicago area code.

"Hello."

"Emma Jane?"

"Yes?"

"Hey, it's Jesse, Brett's girlfriend."

I release the breath I didn't even realize I was holding. "Shit! I mean… Hey, Jesse."

"Bad time?"

"No, not at all. I was just getting out of the shower. What's up?"

"Well, I just got off the phone with my new friend Eli Tanner, and he said he is going to have Sarah call you in about an hour."

"What?!" I scream.

"She's still at the hospital, but as a favor to Brett—"

I can hear Brett bitching behind her. "No, I had nothing to do with this shit. Damn it, Jess." I can almost picture him pinching his nose and pacing.

"Jeez. Okay, fine," she says, answering his complaining. "As a favor to *me*, Eli volunteered to head up there at lunch and pass her his cell phone."

"Seriously? Oh my God! That is fantastic news!" I shout as she begins to giggle on the other end of the line. "Jesse! I love you!"

"No you don't, but you are still very welcome." She continues to laugh.

"So one-ish my time?"

"Yep. Just keep an eye on your phone."

"Thank you so much. I… Damn. Jesse, I really appreciate this."

"It's no problem, Emma. She needs you right now."

"Thank you." I hang up with a renewed hope.

A FEW hours of staring at my phone later, it finally rings.

"Sarah?" I quickly answer.

"Hey," her broken voice comes across the line. It's so dull and flat I barely even recognize it.

"Are you okay?"

"Well, that depends on your definition of okay. I'm handcuffed to a hospital bed, waiting to be sent to the psych ward, while talking on the phone of a man who hates me to a sister I haven't spoken to in years. Does that sound okay to you?" She goes from sad to bitchy with just one sentence.

"Jesus, Sarah. Don't be like that. Can we just have a conversation, please?"

"I'm sorry, I…" She trails off and starts to cry—something else I'm not used to with Sarah. Before the accident, she was always so strong, but now she just sounds lost. "Did Brett tell you he moved on? He found a little brunette and basically tossed me in the trash."

"Sarah, that's not what happened and you know it. You've been trying to get rid of him for years. Don't you think it's about time Brett moved on with his life? Hell, don't you think it's time *you* moved on with yours?"

"Probably," she answers but gives no further explanation.

"Hey, guess what? I'm moving to Chicago!" I try to move the conversation to a happier note, but Sarah brings it right back down again.

"Why?" she asks rudely.

"Because I like the pizza?" I answer sarcastically. "Why do you think?"

"Oh God, you're going to try to fix me, aren't you?" she says with an annoyed groan.

"No, there's nothing to fix. You need a lot of help, but as far as I can tell, there is nothing broken about you."

She barks out a laugh. "Did Brett tell you I tried to shoot him the other day? I'm probably going to jail."

"Maybe," I answer nonchalantly even though the very idea scares the shit out of me.

"Maybe? That's all you have to say about me trying to kill my husband then rotting in jail?"

"What do you want me to say? You want me to yell and scream? Tell you what a horrible person you are? Tell you you're a crazy-ass bitch?"

"Yes!" she screams into the phone so loud it hurts my ear.

"Well screw you, sis. It's not happening. I think you have serious issues that you have never taken care of, and while I'm not going to fix you, I sure as hell am going to make sure you fix yourself."

"I've done some really fucked-up shit, Emma. I think I'm damaged beyond repair," she whispers between choking sobs.

"When the hell did you become a quitter?" I ask in all seriousness.

"The night I killed my best friend." And with that, I hear the call end.

"Damn it!" I scream, throwing my phone onto my bed.

I flop down next to it, getting more and more pissed off at this entire situation. Damn it, when did *I* become a quitter? I snatch up my phone and call back the number.

A man's voice answers. "Tanner."

"Take her back the phone," I demand.

"Look, she's pretty upset. I shouldn't even have given her the phone to begin with. As soon as she gets—"

"Eli! Take her the God damn phone!" I shriek into his ear.

"Christ, you really are related."

"Yep, now take her back the phone." I return to my casually sweet tone.

He doesn't say another word, but I can tell he's walking.

"Sarah, it's for you."

"I'm done talking," she says, once again sounding defeated.

Eli picks the phone back up. "She doesn't want to talk."

"Put me on speaker."

"Jesus fucking Christ," he growls, but I hear the abstract sounds of the room fill the silence. So I start talking.

"Sarah, you need to listen up. I'm done with this. I let you push me away years ago, but it's not happening again. You can hang up, run away, cuss me out—whatever. But I'm not going anywhere. You don't want a savior, and I get that. But you fucking need some family right now. I'm sorry to say it, but I'm all that's left. So while you are wrapped up in your head, trying to figure out your next move, you need to remember one thing. No matter how dark you get, I will trudge through the quicksand of your guilt and drag you out—every single time. Get fucking used to it. I may not have been there before, but I'm here now.

"No matter what you might believe, you didn't kill Manda. There's a reason they called it an accident. You need to let it go and lean on me to deal with your bigger issues. Get ready, because you're about to get your life back. I refuse to accept it any other way. I love you and I'll see you soon." Before she can even utter a word, I hang up the phone.

Tears stream down my face and over my wide smile. I'm heartbroken and elated all at the same time. I've messed up over a million different ways with Sarah. And every single one of them was because I was terrified of losing her. Well guess what? In my childish attempts to protect myself, I almost lost her forever. Tomorrow, we start over. And unlike Manda, Sarah has a second chance, and I fully intend to help her take it.

Chapter
EIGHT

Emma

ME: HEY, you know anyone with a truck up there?

Caleb: Sure do! What's up?

Me: I found a two bedroom apartment, and I need to move all Sarah's stuff over there.

Caleb: Oh.

Me: Oh. What?

Caleb: Oh, I just thought you were getting your own place. That's all.

Me: Nah, I'll need to be close to her, but her place is a one bedroom.

Caleb: Gotcha. My buddy Eli has a truck. I'm sure he'll help.

Me: Great! Oh, and I also booked my flight to Chicago!!!! :)

Caleb: Now this I'm interested in. When?

Me: Thursday!!!!!! :)

Stolen Course

Caleb: Wait, this Thursday or next Thursday?

Me: As in, you should probably call and make dinner reservations for two days from now, Thursday.

My phone immediately lights up with an incoming call.

I pick up immediately. "Hey, you!"

"You'll be here in two days?" he asks, and I can hear the smile in his voice.

Caleb and I have been playing this long-distance game for a few weeks now. It's taken me a lot longer than I expected to get my life tied up in Georgia. Moving across the country is not exactly an easy feat. It's worked out though, because they did eventually move Sarah to a court-mandated rehabilitation center. Her trial was rushed due to the questions around her mental stability. I didn't even have time to get up there before it was over. Jesse actually spoke on Sarah's behalf. I love that tiny woman.

Sarah was sentenced to ten months in a rehabilitation center. It specializes in traumatic brain injuries, but they will also be working with her through her grief over Manda's death. Honestly, this is the best thing that could have ever happened to her. I freaked out when Caleb sent the text to tell me.

Hunter tried to convince me to stay in Savannah while Sarah is away in rehab, but I refused. I need to get up to Chicago and start a new photography business. I have a few leads on companies that are looking for photographers, but I'm determined to start my own business again. Plus, I'll be close enough to visit Sarah on the weekends. This decision has nothing to do with Caleb.

Okay, I'm totally lying. It has a lot to do with Caleb. I love every minute of our nightly conversations. I can't wait to get to know him in person.

"Yep. Two days and you get to take me to dinner. Seriously, you are a freaking lucky man."

"I am." He laughs at my sarcasm.

"I'm so excited to see you," I breathe.

"You should be. I am pretty amazing. Seriously, you are a freaking lucky lady." He throws my sarcasm right back at me.

I love the banter I have with Caleb. He's sharp and can keep up with even the most sarcastic of conversations. Don't get me wrong. He is sexy as fuck, and I've had many of dreams about him without his clothes on. But there is nothing sexier than a man with a sense of humor and a quick wit.

"I get in at noon. You think you could pick me up?"

"Of course! I'll take the day off. I'll make Brett cover for me or something."

"Speaking of Brett… Have you told him that we…talk?"

"No. Have you?" he asks with a shocked curiosity.

"No, but I've only talked to him a few times since I got back. Mainly just stuff about neighborhoods and stuff in Chicago. I was thinking about calling Jesse and seeing if she wanted to go out for drinks when I got back though."

"Jesse? Really? Won't that be weird?"

"Why? Oh God, do you think she will think it's weird?" I ask, embarrassed. I just assumed, but now that he mentions it, I can definitely see how Jesse might feel weird about hanging out with Brett's ex-sister-in-law.

"No. Knowing Jesse, she is already baking muffins for your 'Welcome to Chicago' basket."

"Ohhhhh, I get a welcome basket! Even more reason not to miss my flight on Thursday."

"Hey, am I not enough to keep you from missing your flight?"

"Caleb, are you searching for reassurance? Wait, do you have a secret welcome present of your own for me?"

"Actually, I do." He starts laughing, and I realize I walked right into that one.

"But the real question is, can it compete with Jesse's muffins?" I say with a huge grin, knowing this will only making him laugh harder.

"Oh shit, Emma. I have laughed more in the last three weeks than I have in years." He pauses for a second before finally responding to my earlier comment. "I can't wait to see you, too."

"Good," I breathe.

"So Thursday at noon?" he asks.

"Yes, Thursday, but don't think you are getting out of talking tomorrow night."

"I would never dream of it. Goodnight, Emmy."

"Night, Caleb."

Caleb

I TOSSED and turned in bed for hours thinking about Emma. Usually when I can't sleep, I head to the box locked away in the closet, but that didn't even feel right tonight. I'm excited to see her on Thursday, but at the same time, I'm terrified. Emma and I have been getting along really well. I've loved every second of our nightly conversations. She's smart, funny, and witty. And as much as I want to see her and fuck her senseless, I'm not looking forward to the shitstorm that will surely follow her arrival. She is Sarah's little sister. Of all people for me to decide to start dating, it had to be her.

I know that there is only one place that will bring me any peace tonight.

"Hey, love." I walk up to Manda's grave and settle into my usual position next to her headstone.

I take the small black velvet box out of my jacket pocket and rest it on the ground next to me. My fingers glide over the indention of her name. I hate this fucking headstone, and not just because it has the date signifying the end of her life. I hate it because it says 'Manda Baker.' No matter how many times I see it, it always burns.

Manda and I had a very tumultuous relationship. She was feisty as hell, always giving me shit about something. For the first year of our relationship, I swear we broke up biweekly. She'd storm out of my house and go back to her place. We wouldn't speak for a full day, but one of us always gave in. We couldn't stay away from each other. I showed up at her apartment more times than I care to admit with an apology, a.k.a. sushi and wine. When it was her turn to apologize, she always brought burgers and beer. The food was usually always cold and the alcohol always warm because the minute the door opened we couldn't keep our hands off each other.

This on-again-off-again process worked for about two years. Then one night on my way to pick up the customary sushi, after a two-day breakup, I finally broke. I was done with the bullshit games. I wanted to settle down and start a real life together. I was sick of the back-and-forth. We both knew we were in this for the long haul, even if we did fight like cats and dogs. Manda was my life, and I was more than ready for it to begin.

That night, I took a detour, and instead of sushi and wine, I showed up with a diamond ring.

Six Years Earlier...

"WILL YOU marry me?" I ask, kneeling on her front steps just as she pulls open the front door.

"Um, no," she says shortly, staring down at me in disbelief.

"What do you mean, no? I'm not joking. This is serious, Manda. Marry me!" I give up on asking and start telling her.

"Yeah, still no," she says as she turns around and walks into her apartment, leaving the door open behind her.

"I just proposed to you!" I shout.

"And I said no. You didn't even bring any wine." She frowns then gives me a smile and wink.

"Are you fucking with me here? I brought you an engagement ring and you're pissed I didn't bring wine? Manda, I am very, very fucking serious about this. So please, if you are joking, stop."

"I'm not joking!" she yells at me.

"Manda, I love you. I'm sick of this on-again-off-again game that we play. I don't want to do this with you for the rest of my life. I want more— I want you."

"Caleb, we can't get married," she sadly whispers, suddenly becoming serious.

"Why not? I have a ring. I have you. I don't need anything else."

"We fight all the time! What kind of marriage is that going to be?"

"We fight. So what?" I let out a loud frustrated groan. What I hoped would be some fucking magical moment has turned into the shittiest proposal known to man. I'm standing here, yelling at her to marry me. I take a deep breath and try to calm myself down. "Look, I'm sorry. I have no idea what we were even fighting about the other night, but I'm sorry." I roughly run my hands through my hair.

"I'm not mad about that anymore."

"Then come here, beautiful."

She shakes her head, but I can see her resolve start to slip. I storm across the room and pull her into my arms.

"What if we get a divorce?" she asks, and it makes me stumble.

"Is that what you're scared of—a divorce?"

"No, I'm scared that if we get married things will change. Then we will get a divorce, and then I'll lose you forever. At least the way things are now, I know you'll always come back."

"Manda, I want to spend the rest of my life with you. We can make crazy little redheaded baby girls who are sure to land me in jail for killing their high school boyfriends. I want to grow old and wrinkly with you."

"I'll never get wrinkly," she interjects, but I just keep talking.

"I know we fight, but it's always about stupid shit. We are two stubborn people. We're always going to argue. But this, right here, is what I don't want anymore. I don't want you to disappear for a few days every time we disagree about something. I want you to get pissed and march your hot little ass back to our bedroom and pout for however long you would like."

She starts laughing and pinches my stomach.

"Manda..." I pull away and place a kiss to her lips. "I'll apologize with sushi and wine every night for the rest of my life if that is what it takes. I just want to be with you, fighting and all."

"You want to move in together, too?"

"I've heard most married couples live together, but I could be wrong. I've never really done this before," I say playfully.

"No, jerk. I mean like...you want to live together now?"

"Say the word and I'll start packing your bags tonight." I squeeze her tighter, and she quickly melts into my body.

"I love you," she mumbles into my chest.

"I love you too." I release a content sigh. "Was that the word?" I ask while resting my chin on the top of her head.

"No," she replies, causing me to let out an impatient growl. She laughs for only a second before looking up into my eyes. "Okay."

"Okay?" I ask in shock.

"Yeah. That was the word," she says, causing me to burst out laughing. I can't even begin to contain my excitement. "Can I see that ring

again?" She steps out of my grasp with a huge smile on her face.

"No, sorry."

"What? Why not?" she shrieks.

"See, my fiancée was pretty pissed off when I showed up with a ring instead of wine, so I need to head out and exchange it. You know, got to keep the old ball and chain happy." I shrug then turn to head for the door.

"Caleb, give me my ring!" She jumps on my back before I get even a few steps away.

We wrestle around for a few minutes before I pin her to the ground. Reaching into my pocket, I pull out the emerald-cut diamond ring and slide it onto her tiny finger. It's so big she probably could fit two fingers inside of it—but she doesn't take it off.

That one night was the happiest moment of my life. Manda and I never got married. Don't get me wrong. I tried. She moved in with me the following week, but she would never set a date for the wedding. We fought almost weekly about it, including on the way to the restaurant the night she died.

When Manda died, she didn't just leave me alone. She left me to grieve. Amanda Baker. *Fucking Baker.* I've never hated that name more. Her headstone should read Jones. She was mine, and the entire world should know it.

Chapter NINE

Emma

AFTER A long six a.m. flight from Savannah, I finally arrive in cold-ass Chicago. I'm sure the city is beautiful, but when I left, it was seventy-four degrees. It's the middle of March, and the snow flurries are still floating through the air in my new city. I have no idea what I've gotten myself into by moving up here. I'm just glad I at least have something—or more specifically, someone—to look forward to.

While riding the escalator down to baggage claim, I'm trying to keep my excitement at bay when I catch sight of the gorgeous wide shoulders waiting at the bottom. I wouldn't be able to tear my eyes away even if he weren't waiting for *me*. His jeans ride low and his dark green button-up clings to his body. Shit, is this the way guys feel when checking out girls? Because I'm not just staring right now—I am straight-up ogling him. As I step off the escalator, dragging my large suitcase behind, he flashes me a bright smile. I give myself away as I jog over to meet him.

I'm not exactly positive how you greet someone you have met once but have been talking to every single night for weeks. I'm usually all about the hug, but I can't figure out what to do with Caleb. If you ask me what I want to do? I would throw him down, right here and now, on the cold airport floor. I'd lick every inch of his defined body, but I'm classier than that—at least in public.

Instead, I stop just in front of him and say, "Hey, you." It's kind of my go-to phrase at this point. I shove my hands in my jacket pockets to keep from touching him.

"Hey, Emmy." He smiles a breathtaking grin before pulling me against his hard body. I guess Caleb is a hugger, too. I go all too willingly into his arms, and he squeezes me tight before releasing me.

"You have more bags?"

"No, just this. The guys are driving up the rest of my stuff in a few weeks."

"The guys?" He lifts a questioning eyebrow.

I roll my eyes and shake my head at his jealousy. "Oh hush." I gently slap his chest but immediately wish I hadn't. I have to turn and look away to keep from moaning when my hand meets his firm pec. Oh shit. Caleb is even hotter than I remember.

"Come on, sweetheart." He throws a casual arm around my shoulders and guides me outside.

We stroll through the parking lot, chatting about the trip, when suddenly we stop next to a shiny black…truck.

"You drive a truck?" I ask, surprised and even slightly confused.

"I figured a Southern girl like you would appreciate it. Why the surprised face?" He leans over to lift my bag into the back.

"Uh, because some guy named Eli is using *his truck* to help me move in a few days," I say with a little more attitude than I needed, but I can't help but feel like Caleb pawned me off on someone else. If he didn't want to help, that's fine, but he could have just told me that. Now I feel awkward for even having asked him to pick me up today. Perfect—he probably felt obligated.

"No, my *friend* Eli is helping *Sarah* move," he says very calmly but still manages to pack some unexpected asshole into it.

"What? That's the same thing! She's in rehab—*I'm* moving her stuff."

He leans his back against his truck, and I can tell that he is trying to choose his words. And he'll probably even apply a little sugarcoating too.

"Caleb?" I demand a response. "Can you enlighten me here? If you didn't want to help, that's fine, but you could have just told me that. I don't want to be a burden on you just because you are trying to sleep with me. Jesus." I throw my hands in the air and head back toward the airport. "Forget it. I'll call a fucking cab!" I shout, walking away. Yeah, I'm acting like a child, but I can't help but feel a little put off.

"Jesus, what the fuck, Emmy?"

"Emma," I correct over my shoulder just to be a bitch.

Caleb doesn't follow me, but he doesn't let me get very far before he shouts, "I'm not helping Sarah! You can ask me for whatever you want, but I flat-out refuse to help *her*."

I freeze as his words penetrate my mind. Then I quickly swing back around to face him.

"Wait, you still hate her?" A lot of things suddenly make more sense.

"Was that ever in question? Yes, I fucking hate her! She killed my fiancée!"

Oh damn, this is bad. Really fucking bad. I slowly walk back over to his truck when I realize that we are slinging cusswords across the airport's short-term parking lot.

"I just thought… I mean, Brett said you carried her out that night she broke down. And you were at the hospital, and you kept me updated for the last few weeks. I just assumed you had…gotten over it."

"Gotten over it?" he asks incredulously before laughing. "Emma, she killed my fiancée!" he repeats, you know, just in case I didn't hear his declaration before.

I shake my head in frustration. "She didn't kill her, Caleb."

"Oh really?" He once again laughs humorlessly.

How the hell did Caleb and I never have this conversation in the four weeks we have been talking? We've talked about Manda, we've talked about Sarah, and while it was never really in depth, I just figured it was an understandably sensitive subject for him. I'm not stupid. I knew he was never going to love Sarah or anything. But hating someone is a totally different ballgame than just disliking them. I can't help but feel a little duped.

"Why am I just finding out about this now?" I ask.

"It was never a secret!" he yells before dropping his voice again. "You knew I hated her that day at the hospital. Nothing's changed. It's not some magical feeling that comes and goes. Damn it!" He once again starts yelling, and this time I feel the hate seeping from his voice.

"You carried her out! You stayed overnight at the hospital just so she wouldn't be alone! That's a hell of a way of showing you hate someone!" I shout back.

"I did all that for Manda, not Sarah!" He sucks in a deep breath, regaining his calm. "I hate your sister, but Manda loved her. And that night,

I just did what Manda would have wanted."

"Shit," I whisper.

"Yep. 'Shit' covers it. And, Emmy, the updates? Those were for you. Again, not Sarah. You can't expect me to help her. Not after everything that's happened. You just can't."

"Well, this is going to be one hell of a problem then, Caleb." I step closer now that things have slowed down. "I just moved all the way across the country to devote myself to helping her."

"I know you did. And I know she needs it." He lets out a frustrated growl. "Damn it, I knew this was going to be bad. I fucking knew it." He bangs his hand against the side of his truck.

And he's right—this is bad. It really sucks to have to let Caleb go, but I know what I have to do. As excited as I was at the prospect of starting something with him, this move was about Sarah.

"I can't get involved with someone who doesn't support me. I've fucked up enough when it comes to Sarah. I really have to make it right this time."

"I know," he says, taking in a resigned breath.

"I mean, look at us. We're already fighting over her. As much as you hate her, I love her more."

"I get it. Fuck, Emmy. It sucks, but I get it." He offers me a sad smile before reaching for my bag again. "Come on. I'll drop you off at Sarah's place."

And just like that, twenty minutes after landing in Chicago, whatever Caleb and I had ends.

THIS. SHIT. Sucks.

I'm not sure if it's practiced skill or just a God-given ability, but Sarah Erickson always manages to fuck things up. Even when she's not around, she stills screws with my life. It's been five long days since I've talk to Emma.

It's funny. I've been on my own for a long time, but the last month with Emma has changed me. It might be a stretch, but I might even dare to say that I've been happy. It doesn't even matter that we spent all of that month long distance and on the phone.

I knew it was a dangerous game she and I were playing. One that would eventually blow up on both of us. I just never thought it would be so soon. I figured we'd at least get to hang out for a while, maybe even have some mind-blowing sex before it all crashed and burned. Instead, I got a hug and a fight in the airport parking lot. All courtesy of Sarah.

Let's be honest here. It's not like my life is over without Emma or anything. I get along just fine during the days. But it never fails. Every night since I dropped her off, I sit on my couch, staring at my phone. Hell, I haven't even been out looking for the distracting orgasm, and that says a lot more than I'm even willing to admit at this point. It used to be a nightly occurrence, but even the random encounters don't fill the void anymore.

I just miss Emma. I miss our time spent talking about anything and everything. We used to laugh for hours. God, it felt so good to laugh again. Worst of all, now she is just a few minutes away but I still can't see her. It's pure torture, and judging by the text that just popped up on my phone, I'm not the only one who feels that way.

Emma: Editing pictures and thinking of you.

Attached is a picture of one of the parks downtown. She turned the entire image black, white—and brown. The leaves on the trees are grey, but the trunks remain their natural color. The older woman in the image has been changed to black and white, but the jacket and shoes she is wearing and the bench she sits on are all various shades of brown. It's an amazing picture alone, but what she did with the color is stunning.

Me: Wow. That's beautiful.

Emma: I know! Brown is starting to grow on me.

Me: See? I told you.

Emma: I still stand by orange though.

Her response makes me laugh, but that only makes me miss her all the more. I don't text anything else, and even though I know I shouldn't, I devise a plan.

The next evening, after a few stops, I drop a gift bag off on Emma's front porch. She's staying at Sarah's, and I'll admit that it makes my skin crawl to go there, but I'm too excited to leave this for Emma to give it much thought. See, I spent the last few hours putting together an orange feast. I started with a bouquet of orange tulips. Those were the easy part.

Then I went to three different restaurants to piece together the rest of my surprise. I ended up with smoked salmon, steamed carrots, and a sweet potato with butter and cinnamon. I even found a restaurant that had orange citrus cake on the menu for dessert. I topped it all off with a bottle of citrus vodka and a gallon of orange juice.

After dropping the bag off on her porch, I went back to my truck and sent her a text.

Me: I just remembered that I still owe you that dinner. Check your front porch. Enjoy.

Me: By the way, orange is starting to grow on me too.

I drive home, not even sure if she got the message. But just as I pull into my driveway, the phone chirps on my lap.

Emma: One, this might be the sweetest thing anyone has ever done for me.

Emma: Two, I can't believe you just dropped this off without saying hi or anything.

Emma: Three, Thank you.

I begin to text her back when it chirps again.

Emma: Four, I just finished an amazing (and a random) dinner and suddenly, I'm in the mood for a drink. Want to join me?

I stare at my phone for a minute. Of course I want to grab a drink, but I know I shouldn't. There is no changing the fact that Emma's last name is Erickson. I don't blame her for anything, including wanting to finally step up and take care of her sister. However, that doesn't mean that I should be hanging out with her. I never should have started things with her to begin with. Maybe this is just the way out. One day, I'm going to prove that Sarah was drunk and driving the car that night. It's probably best for everyone involved that I'm not dating her sister when I do it. But damn it to fucking hell, the idea of hanging out with Emma excites me. Whatever. I've made far shittier choices than this, and the truth is, I can't stop my fingers from typing.

Me: Absolutely.

Chapter
TEN

Caleb

EMMA AND I decided to meet at a bar in downtown Chicago. I only thought I had fun with Emma on our nightly phone calls. In person, she is even more entertaining. I swear my face hurts from laughing nonstop since we met up about three hours ago. Emma is a people watcher, and holy shit, her commentary is fucking hilarious. She's not mean about it, but she was very quick to point out the juiced-up bodybuilder who was sporting a fanny pack and the emo guy who paid the bartender with cash from his Care Bears wallet.

I learned that she also has a bleeding heart. When we left the first bar and headed to the second, she gave money to every single homeless man we saw. At one point, she chased a man down the street, only to find out he wasn't homeless after all. I almost collapsed in hysterics at her face when he refused her money.

Emma and I played pool—or more accurately, she played pool while I stared at her ass while she was leaning over the table. She's only wearing jeans and a little T-shirt, and her hair is in a ponytail, but I've never seen a sexier woman. Yeah, this was a horrible idea coming here tonight. There is no question in my mind that I'm going to end the night inside her. And even though it's fucked up, I'm going to do my damnedest to get her on the same page. She's been more than flirty all night. She held my arm as we walked around the city and even squeezed in tight against my back as we weaved through one of the more crowded bars. I don't exactly think it's going to be a hard sell.

"I need to go to the bathroom," she says, standing up from the high-top table.

I watch her long legs as she stands. She is so fucking tall. I love it. I can't wait to drag my tongue up those thighs tonight. Fuck, I'm getting hard just thinking about it.

I, along with every guy in the room, track her perfect ass as she walks across the bar. Just before she disappears around the corner toward the bathrooms, I catch a glimpse of one guy tapping his buddy on the arm and nodding toward her. I don't blame them. She's smoking hot.

The best part about Emma is that she's not some stuck-up snob who expects men to worship her. Hell, the fact that she didn't get all dressed up to come out tonight is proof. Emma is comfortable in her own skin, and that confidence is sexier than anything she could ever put on. I laugh to myself at the poor guys.

No sooner than Emma clears the corner, both guys both rise to follow her. Yep, that's my cue. I head back towards the bathrooms just to find her. You can never be too careful. At least that's what I tell myself. It has nothing to do with the idea of those pricks hitting on what's mine. Nope, not at all. I'm just making sure she's safe. *Right.*

"Savannah," I hear Emma say as I get close to the corner.

"Oh yeah? What brings you all the way to the Windy City?" Douche-bag One says.

I wait for a minute, listening, very aware of how big of a creeper I look like while eavesdropping. I'm really curious how Emma is going to handle this though.

"I just moved up here last week," she says, and I can hear the smile in her voice.

"How are you liking it so far?"

"It's cold. I'm not going to lie. I'm ready for bathing suit season."

"I think we are all ready for that, baby," Douchebag Two says very suggestively. It almost has me turning the corner to interrupt, but Emma's response keeps rooted.

"Well not everyone. You should probably stick with jeans and a sweatshirt," she says in such an exaggerated Southern accent that she almost makes it sound sweet.

I bark out a laugh but quickly try to cover it. Luckily Douchebag One also laughs are her catty reply.

"Just ignore him. How about I show you around town? You want to grab some dinner tomorrow night? I'll give you the grand tour."

"I don't know how my guy would feel about that. I can ask though." She perks up. "Hey, Caleb!" she shouts around the corner.

Fuck! Oh yeah. Emma's not stupid. She knew I was standing here all along. I shake my head at myself and round the corner to face the group.

"Do we have dinner plans tomorrow night?" she asks with a huge knowing smile. "This friendly Chicago man just asked if he could show me around." Then she bites her lip to keep in the laugh. Emma is fucking with me right now just as much as she is these guys.

Game on.

I walk over and suddenly pull her hard against my body. I drag my nose up her neck, breathing her fruity scent as I go. I should have left it at that, but I can't help grazing my teeth across her ear before pulling away.

"No, sweetheart, we don't have dinner plans. So if you'd like to go out with these guys, that's fine." Her lust-filled eyes go wide with surprise. "You want me to give them your number?" I ask, dropping my hand to splay across her ass. I give it a tight squeeze before leaning away to give her a questioning look.

"Yeah, sorry, boys. I've got plans tomorrow night," she says breathlessly.

"Whatever," Douchebag One says before walking away.

I stand there for a minute before releasing her. I don't back away. Instead, I take a step forward, forcing her back against the wall. It's a small hallway right outside the bathrooms. There is a steady flow of traffic around us, but I have a point to prove. Starting at her hips, I slide my hands up her sides. I'm careful to touch the curve of her breasts on my path, but not enough for it to be a full-on grope. I push her hands up over her head, intertwining our fingers as I pin them to the wall.

"Emmy, I don't play games," I whisper into her ear. Her breathing quickens, and she lets out small moan as I circle my hips into hers.

"Yes, you do," she says, tilting her head to the side. I don't lean in to taste the exposed neck that might as well be screaming my name. But that doesn't stop her from leaning forward and dragging her tongue up the side of mine. She pauses at my ear. "You play games the same way I do—hard." And with that, she pushes her breasts against my chest and rolls her hips into mine.

Fucking hell. I've met my match. Things just got dangerous for a completely different reason.

"We need to go home," I say, barely restraining myself from fucking her right here.

"Yes, we do," she responds, and thank God for that. I don't have to patience to try to convince her right now.

"I'll close the tab. You grab our jackets. We're going back to my place. You good with that?"

"Yep. Sounds like a plan." She pulls her hands from my grip, straightens her shirt, and walks away seemingly unaffected.

I wish I could say the same, but the raging hard-on threatening to break my zipper keeps me standing here and reciting basketball stats for a few minutes longer.

Emma

CALEB AND I ride home in silence, but he holds my hand the entire way. Thankfully the cab ride is short, because there is a very serious chance that I am going to spontaneously combust if I don't get him naked soon. After that little display at the bar, we both know where this is headed. So when we arrive at his house, it's all I can do not to sprint to the door.

His house is a ridiculously cute, old brick one-story. The yard is perfectly manicured, even despite the piles of snow that are just now melting. He leads me inside to a surprisingly clean and organized living room. There are a few wooden frames scattered across the walls. The whole place is very well decorated, but there are no knickknacks or mementos filling the area. The only thing that even resembles a knickknack is a clay pot sitting in the corner. I'm assuming it used to hold a flower, but the plant is long since dead and gone.

The furniture is nice, brown leather, and while it does look like a bachelor pad, it also has a warm, homey feel. I look around the room, trying to take in everything that is Caleb Jones. The stripped wood coffee table has a few magazines strewn across the top, but everything else is perfectly in its place.

"Wow. I figured there would be dirty clothes everywhere. I've lived with two guys and neither one of them was this neat." I run my finger over his bookshelf, pretending to check for dust.

"I'm a neat guy, but I also have a cleaning lady who comes once a week."

"Ah! Makes more sense, although the idea of you with a vacuum and feather duster was really doing something for me."

He begins to laugh. "I guess I could clean something if that's what gets you off," he jokes but begins to roll up his sleeves, revealing some very unexpected tattoos.

"Holy shit!" I say breathlessly as I visually orgasm.

"What?" he asks, staring at me like I'm crazy.

"You have ink!"

"Do you have a problem with that?"

Sweet Mother of Hotness. "No. I love them." Are there seriously woman out there who have issues with tattoos? Because they shouldn't be allowed to run loose in society.

"That's probably a good thing. I've got a few."

"You have more? Let me see!"

He laughs at my excitement but confidently pulls off his shirt, revealing more mouthwatering art.

The tattoos on his forearms are actually full sleeves. They are made of different shapes and patterns all pieced together to form one perfectly flowing design. Over his heart, he has the name Manda. The top of the "M" is broken off and appears to be a bird flying away. There are eight other birds flying up toward his shoulder, growing increasingly larger as they drift up his sculpted chest.

Above and beyond the spectacular designs, his body is to die for. Caleb is gorgeous, no denying that. He's tall and lean, but every inch of his body is covered in hard muscle. I have no idea what the hell those muscles are called just above his pants, but they make me want to trace them down to the sure-to-be-amazing package below. I struggle to keep in the moan that is desperately trying to escape my throat. Shit, he's hot. He remains still while I ogle his body, but a barely there smile tips his lips.

"You want a beer?" He reaches to put his shirt back on.

"Don't do that!" I yell, exposing my sopping-wet panties. *Real smooth, Emma.* I never was any good at playing coy.

"Well, well, well. Does someone have a thing for tattoos?" He struts over to me in a way so ridiculously sexy that only Caleb could pull it off. It's also annoying as shit because he so obviously has the upper hand here—something I don't share very well.

"Are we going to do this or what? We have been dancing around this for weeks on the phone. Now that I've seen you without a shirt, I won't need the foreplay you were probably going to skip anyway," I blurt out then offer him a sarcastic smile.

"Of course we are going to do this, Emmy." He reaches forward, pulling my ponytail down to force my eyes to connect with his. "But you're wrong about that whole skipping-the-foreplay thing. I've been waiting for weeks now to taste you. I have a seven-course meal planned for this evening. If you're lucky, I might even let you taste too." He drags one quick swipe of his tongue across my parted lips. I'm unable to move as my head swirls with thoughts of this so-called feast. "So I'll keep the shirt off if you want me to. I would have sent you shirtless pictures weeks ago if I'd known it would have had this effect on you." He brushes his fingers over my hardened nipples. They have probably been showing through my shirt all night. *Note to self, wear padded bras when hanging out with sex-personified Caleb Jones.*

Unable to keep it in any longer, I moan and sway forward to finally connect with his mouth. He dodges my kiss and instead licks up my neck and whispers, "Patience," into my ear.

A tidal wave of chills spreads across my body.

"So, was that a yes to the beer?" he asks before taking a step away.

It takes me a few seconds before I'm actually able to clear my lust-filled head enough to form a coherent response.

"Yes, and I agree. You should have sent me shirtless pictures weeks ago. The tattoos are hot. And who knows? I might have reciprocated by sending a few topless pictures of my own." I smile, knowing that I just took back control of this situation—Caleb's groan confirms it.

He lets out a sigh and scrubs his hands back and forth over his face. "Okay, beer," he reminds himself. Taking another step away, he gives me a wicked smirk. "Just so you know, I'm not responsible if you melt into a puddle," he says oddly, causing me to tilt my head in confusion.

"Huh?"

Without another word, he turns and walks away, revealing the pièce de résistance. His back is covered completely from the base of his neck to the just above his waistband with the body of a blackbird. It's created from the same patterns and shapes his sleeves are done in. It's so beautiful that it's staggering. The head of the bird is turned so you can only see one menacing emerald-green eye—the only bit of color on Caleb's entire body. Its body is placed so that Caleb's arms appear to be the wings of the massive bird. If he spread them to the side, I have no doubt it could take flight.

"Fuck," I hiss as he walks away laughing.

He knew I liked the tats, and he knew exactly what that work of art would do to me. He wasn't completely wrong. I didn't melt, but there was definitely a puddle.

My fingers begin to twitch for my camera. I could take pictures of his back for hours—well, right after I lick every inch of it.

Caleb comes back into the room carrying two beers and a bottle of water. "Thought you might be thirsty."

"So tell me about your tattoos," I ask, taking the water from his hand. I've had a lot to drink tonight. I'm not drunk anymore, but I'm definitely dehydrated.

"Not tonight." His sparkling blue eyes flash dark as he turns away and places the drinks on coasters on the table.

I don't push him. It's probably for the best. I'm sure they are about Manda, and the less we talk about her, the less we will have to talk about Sarah.

When Caleb showed up at the bar tonight, I couldn't contain my excitement. I jumped up from the table and hugged him. I pretended it was just to thank him for my orange dinner, but it was mostly because I've missed him. It'd only been five days since we'd talked last, but I have become quite addicted to our nightly conversation. This has been a very transitional time for me, and it was nice to have someone to lean on. I just wish we had spent those nights talking about things that actually mattered instead of laughing and telling old stories the whole time. Maybe then we wouldn't be in this mess. I have no idea what's going to happen to us tomorrow, but I fully intend to make the most out of tonight.

I walk over to Caleb, pull the beer he has tipped to his lips away, and place it on table behind us.

"Hey, you." I place a kiss to his collarbone and run my hands over his hard chest and shoulders, tracing up his neck and into his thick hair.

"Hey, sweetheart." He licks his lips while staring at mine.

"I missed you this week."

"Jesus, Emmy. I missed you, too," he says dropping his forehead to mine.

"You're not wearing a shirt," I teasingly remind him, and it causes a small smile to cross his lips.

"Nope."

"But I am." I place a soft kiss to his lips.

"We really should remedy this situation," he says, gently brushing a finger over my stomach and under the edge of my shirt.

"I agree." I cross my arms between us and lift the shirt over my head, discarding it on the couch beside us.

His eyes immediately flash down to my chest. Using his index finger, he traces the line of my cleavage.

"You're cheating." He drags his finger over the fabric of my bra, biting his lip as he once again watches my nipples become hard.

"Oh, sorry. I definitely wouldn't want to cheat." I reach back and unclasp my bra.

Chapter

ELEVEN

Emma

AS I drop my bra to the floor, my eyes return to Caleb's. With that damn sexy smirk on his face, he stares into my eyes. Gradually, he slides them down to my breasts and thankfully doesn't keep me waiting. His hands immediately lift and begin exploring the swells of soft flesh. I sway and shudder when his rough fingers brush over my hard nipples. A moan forces its way from my throat, and I boldly push my chest into his hands.

My body may know what it wants, but I want to have some fun with this sexy man first. Ice sounds like the perfect addition to this undeniable heat.

Standing on my toes, I peck his lips and quickly turn towards the kitchen. I add extra sway to my hips as I move away from him, offering nothing but a flirty glance over my shoulder. Just before I cross into the kitchen, I spin around to face him. I pull my hair loose from the ponytail and enjoy watching him squirm as I back away. I can see his chest heaving and the promising bulge against the zipper of his jeans. Licking my lips, I turn and head toward the freezer.

I don't make it far before I feel a warm, solid body press up against my back. My hand hurries to grasp the handle of the freezer door, but just as quickly, his fingers close around mine.

"Whatcha doing, Emmy?" he asks with a devilish tone.

"I'm about to make you beg." I stare over my shoulder into his entrancing blue gaze.

"Shit. That's too bad, because I was about to fuck you right here in

Aly Martinez

the middle of my kitchen."

A slight shudder runs through my body as I anticipate what's to come. As he circles his strong arms around me, his hot breath is at my ear. He glides his hands up my stomach but stops just below my breasts.

The power struggle has officially begun.

"I like my idea better," I lie, pressing my ass into his cock.

He groans into my neck and the vibrations from his throat tickle my shoulder. Grabbing my wrist, still holding the freezer door, he effortlessly spins me to face him. When his lips meet mine, I can't stop the trembling that pulses through me. I hang on tight to Caleb's strong shoulders as he begins to devour my mouth. I am so lost in this man that my mind barely registers his fingers flipping open the button of my jeans.

What seems like only a breath later, his hand is inside my panties, rough fingertips circling my sensitive clit. He quickly shoves down my jeans, and wantonly, I spread my legs to help him. He wastes no time dipping one long finger into my wetness, then another. An audible moan escapes from deep inside, and Caleb brings his mouth to mine—swallowing my cry.

"Caleb," I exhale against his mouth.

"There's no one else here, Emmy," he says, sweeping his tongue against mine.

I can't let him take charge of this. I want him, but I want to control it.

As my hands slide down over his broad chest, my fingers map the planes of his muscles all the way to the clasp of his pants. I undo the button and make quick work of spreading the fabric wide. It's not exactly a secret that I'm eager to feel what's hidden behind his denim. Nipping along his neckline, I reach inside his jeans and am met with the smooth, and surprisingly hairless, warm skin of Caleb's hard cock. If it was promising in clothes, it's revolutionary unsheathed. I wrap my hand around him just as I feel a hiss linger over my skin.

Hallelujah! He's freaking huge, smooth, and oh so hard against my palm. I can't even begin to check off all the boxes on my sexual wish list that Caleb has filled tonight.

Slowly, I begin to stroke him from base to tip. Groaning in protest, he slides his fingers in and out of me harder and faster than before. I can almost see his patience escaping him just seconds before he lifts me up and forcefully wraps my legs around his waist. It's not exactly like I was

70

fighting him though.

He carries me to the counter and gently places my ass on the cool granite. With one arm wrapped around my hips and the other inside me, Caleb doesn't miss a beat. I once again moan into his mouth and push my hips to meet the thrusts of his hand. I have no idea nor do I care what I look like at this moment. All I can think about is the rhythm of his pistoling fingers.

When I drop my head back, my hair cascades down my back, sending even more tingles over my sensitive skin. My body is thrumming with the intensity of unexpected emotion, but just before that feeling can shut me down, Caleb grabs my attention.

"Why do I feel like I just lost you?" He sucks hard against by bottom lip, his teeth roughly raking over it.

"There's no one else here, Caleb." I throw his words playfully right back at him— biting his top lip in the process. "Now stop talking and get to work."

He smiles, and it burns like I'm looking at the sun. So. Fucking. Perfect. I hate his cocky ass sometimes. That's what I want to think, feel, and say. However, one look at that confident grin and I know I'm here to stay. Fortunately—or unfortunately—Caleb must feel it too.

His lips slide down to my neck, over my collarbone, and back up my neck to the tip of my chin. His mouth is soft and wet, and it's slowly driving me wild. I lift my head, eyes closed, lost in the emotion and overwhelming pleasure that I secretly knew he would bring to me.

"Open your eyes. I don't want you to disappear again," he breathes.

I have no choice but to obey his command and slowly open my eyes.

"I never left." I blink, focusing my hazy gaze on his strong, handsome face.

Caleb's rhythm slightly falters as his eyes meet mine. I try not to read into that small reaction, but I'm shocked by the intensity staring back at me.

"You're fucking beautiful," he says in a voice so rough and deep it sounds—and feels— like liquid sex sliding over my body. As he presses his thumb to my swollen clit and curling his fingers inside me, I feel the ache starting to build. He ghosts his lips over my neck, wetting my skin with his hot mouth. "Come on, Emmy. I need to get inside you, but I want you to come first." His words and the feel of his breath on my skin are enough to light the blaze that is burning inside me.

Never taking my eyes off of his, I come so hard that, if Caleb weren't holding on to me, I might have fallen off the counter. I ride his fingers until my orgasm begins to subside. With lust still roaring in my eyes, he brings his fingers to his mouth and slowly slides them in one by one, licking and sucking every last drop of my release.

My orgasm-induced fog is thick, but my eyes still drift down his hard body and land on his cock. The corner of my lips tip up an inch at the very thought of him moving inside me.

"I believe I owe you a little something," I say, placing a hand on his hard stomach. I give him a slight push and hop off the counter.

"You don't owe me anything, but I'm sure as hell going to take it anyway," he says, grabbing my ass and pressing against me.

His eyes have grown dark, and his skin is flushed and damp with sweat. My legs are a little wobbly, and I pause a minute to make sure they still work. Giggling under my breath, I grab him by the waist of his jeans and turn towards his bedroom. With a wink, I drag him after me down the hall. Caleb doesn't complain and remains quiet behind me, but his facial expression hits me right on the clit.

That. Fucking. Smirk. It's going to be the death of me.

Oh yeah. It's my turn to play now.

When we reach his bedroom, I push Caleb in front of me and close the door with a loud click. He stands still, watching my every move with hooded eyes.

"Condom?" I ask as he stands frozen in the middle of the room—clearly enjoying the show.

He doesn't utter a word, but his eyes point to the drawer on his nightstand. I walk around him and open it to pull out a condom and—what do you know—a brand-spanking-new bottle of lube.

"You won't be needing that," he says, licking his lips.

Dirty fucker. I am going to wipe that smirk right off his face.

"Who says it's for me?" I offer him a sexy smile of my own.

He shakes his head and silently laughs while staring at the ceiling.

Moving in front of him, I place my hands on his stomach and slide them inside of his jeans. I push his pants down his muscular hips and over his very eager erection. I've been with men before…but fuck, I already know Caleb is going to be amazing. Even if he just lies there, I could ride my way to multiple orgasms with what he's packing. My pussy is so wet I can feel it drip on the inside on my thigh, reminding me of my nudity. I squat, forcing his jeans all the way to the ground. I look up commandingly, urging him to step out.

Before he follows my unspoken directions, he reaches forward to tug my nipple.

Was that a fucking challenge?

I lock my legs and rise, strategically dragging my breasts over his dick and up his chest. His resounding groan matches the moan caught in my throat.

"Hey, you," I say, pausing as we both stand completely naked in the middle of his bedroom.

He swipes his tongue out and across my lips before responding. "Hey."

Curling his arm around the small of my waist, he pulls me a step closer. But I place my palm against his stomach to keep a fraction of an inch between us. What's the saying? Good things come to those who wait? Apparently Caleb missed that memo, because his hand comes up and grips my wrist, pulling it aside and closing the invisible gap. My eyes meet his, and my legs almost give out from his smoldering look. I wonder if he can see that I'm vibrating, because I have zero doubt that I am right now.

This is the hottest sex I've ever had and he hasn't even been inside me yet.

Taking a deep breath, I move a few inches in his direction, forcing him backwards and his legs to hit the bed. With less than a gentle shove, I push him down on the bed. I quickly straddle his thighs and push his shoulders down to follow his body.

"Move to the top of the bed," I demand with a sexy purr.

His muscles move and tighten as he follows the order. He pauses for a brief second during his ascent. Rebelliously, his hand snakes forward, gripping the back of my hair, and pulls me in for a borderline painful kiss. I melt into him as his tongue skillfully plunders my mouth. Unable to fight it any longer, I begin to climb the bed—and his body—to take what his hard-on clearly states he is offering.

"No, carry on. I'm enjoying this." He pushes me away, his thick cock slapping his stomach as he shifts all the way to the top of the bed.

I watch him for a minute to see if he is patronizing me, but his hands clenching the sheet beside him give him away.

Carry on. My. Fucking. Pleasure.

I stalk up his body like he's my prey. Stopping at his cock, I slide my tongue over my lips—making sure my breath hits him, but nothing else. Just as I hoped, it twitches, and he lets out a groan. Darting my tongue, I slide it up his hard shaft and back down the other side.

"Fuck, Emmy."

Caleb's muscles tighten under my legs, and I smile as I wrap my mouth around the tip of his cock and quickly devour him—sliding him all the way to the back of my throat. I hear a strangled, "Fuck," growled from above me. He tastes so good that I hum my approval around him.

"Emmy, fuck..." Like a flash, he reaches down and grabs me under the arms. He slings me up the bed and rolls so he tops me. "I get it. You want to run this…and as sexy as that is…that's not the way it's going to happen."

"Really? I beg to differ." I sling a leg over his hips and forcefully roll him over to his back.

He lets out a quick laugh but goes over easily. "Oh, Emmy. I love to hear you beg," he says, humorously submitting to me as I push his hands over his head.

I grab the condom off the nightstand and tear it open with my teeth, I roll it down his strained erection like a pro. With one hand wrapped tightly around his dick, I run the fingers of my other hand between my legs and through my folds. My fingers slide back and forth with ease—looks like I won't need that lube after all. I position him at my entrance and slide his hard cock over my wet slit just for good measure. Catching his eyes with mine, I press his tip inside me and we both moan as I slowly sink down on top of him. I take a minute and let my body adjust to his size and catch my breath. All the moisture in the world couldn't have prepared me for this. *Fuck.* Caleb Jones just claimed me without even moving.

His hands come up and grip my hips, pulling me off balance. I fall forward, catching my body with an arm by his head. My hair falls like a curtain around us. I don't take my eyes off him as I start to ride. His hands stay on my hips, flexing his fingers every few strokes. The burn starts within, and I know with this man it won't take long for my orgasm to take over. Seeking out that spot where my world falls apart, I move faster above him. His eyes go from hooded in lust to some other emotion I can't I figure out with my foggy brain. *Whatever. I'll worry about it later.*

I fuck him hard, forgetting the whole screwed-up world around us.

"Damn it. Slow down, Emmy. This isn't a race," I hear him whisper hoarsely, but I'm so lost in feeling that it sounds a million miles away.

"No, don't stop. I'm close," I moan and greedily grind down on him. I hear him chuckle, and I flash my eyes to his. He's smirking at me. *Of course he is.*

"You've had your fun, sweetheart, but let me show you who's really in control here."

With a yelp, I'm picked up and flipped over. Caleb somehow magically manages to stay in me the entire way over.

"Hold on to the headboard, baby." The look in his eye has me complying without question.

Fucking me hard, fast, and deeper than I ever thought possible, he shows me exactly who's in control, and as much as I want to hate it—I fucking love every second.

A sheen of sweat covers his body, and I rake my nails down his back as I quicken.

"Oh God, Caleb!" I writhe under him.

I hear him growl as I tighten around his dick. With one last thrust, he stills and shakes as he empties his release inside me. It feels like he is coming forever, but he finally drops on top of me with a sigh. With a sated smile, he kisses my lips several times before looking into my eyes.

"That, Emmy, was one hell of a good time."

I give Caleb my best sexy smile and pull him down so he hovers just over my lips. "You are a fucking asshole, Caleb Jones, but I think I love your cock."

I feel him as he laughs out loud. His whole body shakes, and the movement sparks something inside me anew.

"Round two?" I ask, rolling my hips as he softens inside me. My words only cause him to laugh harder.

"Shit. As much as I'd like to say hell yeah, I think it's wiser for me to start a cold shower for you, because it's going to be a few minutes before I'm up for more. Jesus, woman. That was amazing."

He steals the words right out of my mouth. Although I would have used an exclamation point.

Chapter
TWELVE

Caleb

STARING UP at Emma's flawless body, I know that another round is a few minutes down the agenda right now. Round one…I mean…shit. That. Was. Incredible. She drained me, and I can't even begin to take inventory of the feelings that were flying off me. Shit. What is it about this woman that has me stumbling? Watching her try to gain control alone almost got me off. I'd love to say that I'm only interested in her for sex like I have been with every other woman since Manda, but there is no possible way for me to pretend that's all it was. I need to take this somewhere else. Somewhere where my dick isn't a pussy that's getting all moist and sappy.

I quickly roll to the side, forcing her to the mattress beside me.

"How did we never meet?" I ask, entwining our hands. *Yeah, real manly.* Thankfully it's dark, because I'm forced to roll my eyes at myself.

"I don't know! I didn't come up here much. Sarah and Brett always came to Savannah. My mom was terrified of flying, so they came down so they could visit the whole family at one time," she answers, dragging her nails gently over my abs. I flinch at the sensation.

"I still think it's crazy." I brush her hair away from her face, punctuating it with a soft kiss on her swollen lips. Pulling her snug against my body, I roll onto my back. She immediately relaxes into me, and the feelings that wash over me—because of something so simple—taunt my already muddled heart.

"You weren't at their wedding." She smiles. "I was only sixteen, but I would have definitely remembered you." She snuggles even tighter into my side.

"I didn't know Brett until he and Sarah were already married. And don't remind me how young you are," I tease, rolling to face her. I tuck her long blonde hair behind her ear and gently stroke her cheek. Fuck it. I'm willing to admit it. *God, this feels fucking good.*

"I'm only six years younger than you are." She leans forward, kissing my lips. "You're not exactly robbing the cradle."

"You're staying the night, right?" I trace the curve of her hip up to her breast.

"Of course. I'm a cuddler." She nuzzles in close and yawns into my neck.

"We'll talk in the morning, okay? But we need to figure this out. I don't know how we are going to do it, but Emmy, I'm not going another five days without you."

"Mmm, I agree," she mumbles sleepily. It doesn't take more than a few minutes for her breathing to even out, and she never rolls away—not that I would have let her even if she'd tried.

I watch my arms covered with black tattoos glide against her creamy white skin as I stroke her sides. The stark comparison is not lost on me. My dark soul is filled with hate and revenge, while Emma is filled with hope and promise. I honestly can't even begin to figure out how we are going to make this work, but I know that I have no choice. I'm not losing Emma, and I sure as hell am not letting Sarah take her from me too.

I WAKE up to the sound of knocks on my front door. It's probably only been a few hours, but it was the best sleep I've had in years. Emma is still curled tightly into my arms, and before I get up to answer whatever asshole is disturbing us, I take a minute to breathe her in.

The knocking doesn't stop, so I try to quietly roll away. I don't make it very far.

"Who the hell is making all that noise?" she asks, stretching like a cat before curling back into a ball.

"I'll be right back." I kiss her forehead and move to my feet.

"I need coffee." She sits up, trying to pull her hair back into a pony-tail.

"Kitchen. Coffee is over the stove. Make a whole pot." I say as she stands to get dressed. I walk over to stop her from pulling on her shirt. "Whoa! What are you doing?"

"Can I get dressed?" She laughs, snatching the shirt back out of my hands.

"Um, I'm going to say no."

"Well you're just going to have to live with it." She pulls on her shirt, not even bothering with a bra. I can see the faint outline of her nipples through her white shirt, and if it's possible, this might be even sexier than Emma naked.

"Let's compromise." I pull her into my arms. "Shirt and panties only." I reach between her legs and drag a finger through her wet folds. Her soft sigh has me desperate to toss her back into my bed. Just when I'm ready to ignore the door completely, I hear another loud knock.

"Coffee. Shirt. Panties. Nothing else. We'll continue this in a minute," I inform her as I pull on a pair of jeans and head to the door. I listen to her whispered curse as I walk away.

I fucking love that she likes my tattoos. And just to make sure she is ready for round two, I throw in a back flex as I walk out of the room.

"Now that's cheating!" she shouts.

My smile is huge but quickly wiped away as I snatch open my front door.

"About damn time!" Eli barks, shoving past me into the living room.

"What the fuck are you doing?" I growl, getting ready to close the door when Brett rounds the corner behind him.

"What took so fucking long?" He also busts in uninvited.

"Well, by all means, come on in!" I say roughly, slamming the door behind them.

"You're not even dressed yet?" Eli asks. He flops down on the couch and props his feet on the coffee table.

"Hey, asshole. Feet off the table. Dressed for what?" I look down, noticing that they are both dressed for the gym.

"It's a table, jerk-off," Eli says dryly, ignoring me and leaning back against the couch.

"No, it's *my* table. Get your damn feet off it!" I shout, turning back to Brett. "What's going on this morning?"

"You were supposed to take us to your boxing gym. Get a few spars in and see about getting us signed up."

Fuck! All thoughts of commitments disappeared last night. I knew I had to work today, but I fully intended to call in late. Emma's more than worth whatever shit the boss would dish out.

"Fuck, I completely forgot." I run a hand through my hair.

"Hey, did you make this?" Eli asks, running his hand over the table where his feet once sat.

"Yeah. I finished it a few weeks ago."

"Damn, this is nice." He leans in to get a closer look. "Oak?"

"Uh, no. That's Bubinga. And it's highly figured so don't put your feet on it. Or anything for that matter." I scoff.

"Highly fingered? Jesus, Jones. Do you ever think of anything other than sex?" Eli responds jokingly.

"No, dumbass. Are you twelve? It's highly *figured*. See the wavy lines. That's called figuring. And the closer together those lines are, the more expensive the wood is. So like I said. Get. Your. Feet. Off."

"This is really fucking nice!" he says, inspecting even closer.

"I could have done better, but I love that table. Look at the joints. There aren't any screws or nails like that cheap shit you buy at Walmart and put together yourself. I used mortise-and-tenon joinery," I explain to Eli, who is looking at me like I'm speaking Greek. I start to elaborate when Brett's shout from the kitchen interrupts my thoughts.

"Emma?" he says, and my eyes go wide when I realize what he is just finding out.

I had big plans of talking to Brett about Emma. Looks like that won't be necessary anymore. Fuck. And she's half naked, too.

I quickly make my way to the kitchen to find Emma hauling ass out down the back hall toward my room.

"Em, wait." Brett tries to follow her, but I catch his arm first.

"Let her get dressed."

He may act like her big brother, but he's not related to her, and he most certainly is not going to see her in a T-shirt and panties. Besides, it will give me a minute to talk to him alone.

"You son of a fucking bitch!" He turns to face me with a murderous glare. *So much for talking.*

"Jesus Christ, calm down." I walk to my hall closet and pull on a hoodie. If Brett and I are going to brawl like high schoolers this morning,

I should at the very least be dressed.

"Calm down? Calm down?" he says, following me. "What the hell is Emma Erickson doing half naked in your kitchen at seven a.m.?"

"Oh, fuck!" Eli joins the conversation.

"Well, she was fully naked at two a.m. if that helps at all," I say just to be a prick.

Truth be told, I'm pissed. I'm pissed because Brett and Eli showed up, ruining my morning with Emma. I'm pissed that her last name is Erickson. And most of all, I'm pissed off that I don't have a single explanation for him. A week ago, I would have had a whole story to give Brett, but now, things are so up in the air with me and Emma. What do I even tell him?

Brett's eyes go wide as he steps up into my face. Eli quickly moves to get between us, but it's Emma who stops it from escalating.

"Caleb, shut the fuck up!" I hear from behind me. "And, you!" She directs her attention to Brett. "Chill!" She is once again dragging her hair up into another ponytail even though the one she had moments ago was perfect.

"What the hell are you doing here?" Brett snaps at her, causing me to go on alert.

"Brett, watch your fucking mouth. That's your only warning, so I really suggest you heed it."

Brett and I have had our fair share of blowouts since we lost the girls five years ago. Almost every single one of them revolved around Sarah. They are almost always resolved quickly and usually my fault. He's still my best friend. I love the guy—I really do—but I don't need any other obstacles when it comes to Emma.

I reach over and pull Emma into my side, making it very clear that this isn't one of our usual fights. This is real—or at least I fucking hope it is.

His eyes immediately flash down to my arm around her waist. "Are you fucking kidding me? Jesus Christ, this is a joke. Right?"

I don't say anything, and Emma just shrugs before shaking her head.

"All right, big man. Let's get out of here. You two can talk this over, maybe over the phone…on a long-distance call…with at least twelve hundred miles between you." Eli tries to move Brett toward to the door.

"Fuck you, Eli," he snaps.

"Eli?" Emma squeals, causing us all to look at her. "You're the one who snuck Sarah a phone, right?"

"And you're the crazy-ass woman who screamed at me," Eli says with a devilish smirk.

"Eli," I growl in warning.

"Yep, that's me," Emma says proudly before releasing me and throwing her arms around his neck.

"For Christ's sake! Can someone fucking tell me what the hell is going on? You have been in town not even a week, yet somehow you and Jones have already hooked up?" Brett booms.

Emma immediately releases Eli and resumes a protective stance at my side. It's almost cute to think that she's protecting me. I bite my lips to keep my smile hidden. I have a sneaking suspicion that it would be highly underappreciated right now.

"We've been talking every day for over a month now," Emma quickly explains, and I can't help but close my eyes and look up at the ceiling, hoping for divine intervention. I know exactly how well that little bit of information is going to go over with Brett.

"A month?" he whispers. "A. Fucking. Month."

Like I said, I've known Brett for a while now. These fights are nothing new, so I know exactly how this is going to go down. While he stands there stunned, I walk to my den and grab my prized coffee table, pulling it into the corner. I grab one wooden picture frame with a picture of my niece off the wall and the clay pot from the corner, tucking them safely out of the way next to the table. Just as I turn around, Brett is already storming toward me.

"Start talking," he says, stopping directly in front of me.

Emma starts to head toward me, and I know Emma too—she's about to get all up in this shit, and it won't have a positive ending.

"Don't let her go," I say to Eli.

He rolls his eyes and lets out a frustrated groan but grabs her arms.

"Get your fucking hands off me!" she screams, becoming suddenly aware where this is going.

"Caleb?" Brett says again, oblivious to all the activity going on around him.

"Well, jeez, sir, I've been dating your daughter for…oh wait. You're not her daddy at all!" I smart off. It's habit. Really, I can't even control it.

I shouldn't have kept this from him, but I knew he was going to over-react. I figured as soon as Emma got back in town, we could sit down and tell him together. Maybe go out for drinks with him and Jesse. She can usually keep him from freaking out completely. I guess it's out there now though.

"Don't give me that shit. Don't act like I'm the fucked-up one in this situation."

"Am I the fucked-up one? I met a girl, talked to her on the phone, built a relationship, and then brought her home. I'm pretty sure that's how dating works these days."

He barks out a laugh but never backs away. "A relationship? You're fucking delusional! She's no more than a passing obsession for you, and the fact that you kept this from me for over a month proves it." He takes in a deep breath before roaring, "That's my family!"

"No, she's your ex's family. Is Sarah still your family?" I say as Brett leans in even closer.

"God damn it, let me go!" Emma screams, but thankfully Eli does his job and keeps her back.

"Fuck. You," Brett says slowly.

"Get out of my house. What I do with Emma is none of your fucking business."

"Oh, I believe it is very much my business. I have watched you fuck every woman who has come within a ten-foot radius of you for five years now. You get your fill then walk away. The only woman who ever managed to get you to commit was Manda, and you have made every woman since her pay for the fact that she wouldn't commit to *you*."

The truth in his words stings. I don't necessarily agree with him, but that doesn't mean his words don't hit me hard.

"Fuck you, Brett," is my very uncreative response.

"Can you please stop them?" Emma yells at Eli.

"It's okay, sweetheart. He won't hit me. He never does," I tell Emma while smirking at Brett. "Right, *brother*?" I say with a wink.

I'm not lying. He won't hit me. He never does. He likes to think he will, but he's just a good guy who has a jaded asshole for a best friend. He's used to this shit by now. The only time we have ever come to actual blows was the day of Manda's funeral. And I think he only hit me that day because he knew I so desperately needed some sort of distraction to keep myself from losing it completely.

Brett never drags his eyes away from mine as he addresses Emma behind him. "Em, you might want to ask Caleb when the last time he was in a relationship was. You might also want ask him when the last time he fucked Lisa was. I know it wasn't very long ago that she came to me, concerned about his nightmares." Brett offers me a wink of his own. "Lastly, make sure you find out who he really thinks should have died in the wreck."

"Well, shit, Brett. Your lack of faith in me is *almost* insulting. Emma already knows the answer to every one of those questions and then some. You see, you clearly were not listening. I have spent the last month *talking* to her. Not fucking her. Should I have told you this? Probably. Is it really any of your fucking business? Absolutely not. Now you and I can talk about this later, once you calm down and without an audience. But for now—get out."

Brett stares at me for a minute before turning on a heel to walk away. I glance over at Eli as he begins to release Emma and raise a hand for him to wait. I never expected a fight with Brett, but I did expect his next move. Not two seconds later, Brett snatches up the lamp off my end table and throws it against the wall. He walks right past Emma, who stands stunned, and out the front door.

Eli just shakes his head before asking Emma, "You going to be all right here, babe?" She nods, and he follows Brett out the door.

I head over to comfort her. I know that couldn't have been the easiest thing to watch. I know she loves Brett, but he was being a total—

"You dick!" she screams, surprising me.

"Me?" I ask, stunned by her accusation.

"Yes, you! Couldn't you let me talk to him? Maybe explain it so he would understand? He didn't do anything wrong, and he sure as shit didn't deserve to be treated like an ass because he was trying to protect me. I don't have much family left, but I consider him to be a part of it." She turns, snatching her purse and coat off the rack.

"Emmy, wait."

"Emma!" she corrects me, slamming the door behind her.

I watch from the window as she marches out and stands on the curb. I have no idea where she thinks she's going. We took a cab back here last night. I can only assume that she's doing the same now when she digs her phone out of her oversized purse. I've never in my life claimed to be the easiest person to get along with. I'm a hot-tempered dick sometimes. I know it, but apparently Emma didn't.

I walk to the coffee maker and pour two travel mugs of coffee. I leave mine black, but I have no idea how she takes hers. She is a chick though, so I add a bunch of cream and sugar to it. I pull on a jacket and head to the curb.

"Here." I offer her the mug. "It's a peace offering."

She tries to ignore me but finally gives in to the temptation. Without a word, she snatches the cup from my hand and takes a sip. She makes a horribly disgusted face as she barely chokes it down.

"Shit, are you trying to kill me now?" She hands it back to me and snatches mine out of my other hand. She takes a sip and her shoulders instantly relax. "Ah. Much better."

I can't help but laugh. Of course she takes her coffee black. It wouldn't be Emma if I'd expected it.

"Look, I'm sorry. I'll talk to Brett. You and I have a lot going on right now, and I just felt like he was one more problem for us to overcome."

She doesn't reply, and we stand in silence, sipping coffee on the sidewalk. Less than two minutes later, a cab pulls up. She hands me back the mug and reaches for the door.

"Maybe you are the only problem we are going to have to overcome. Ever think of that?" She opens the door and slides into the cab.

"Sweetheart, come on," I plead, trying to get her to stay—or at least talk to me for a minute longer.

"I'll call you when I'm ready to talk."

Chapter
THIRTEEN

Emma

I HAD to do something to get my mind off Caleb. Sure, I'm pissed. He was a dick this morning, but I'll get over it. That doesn't mean I'm not going to make him sweat it out a little bit first though. I also need to make amends with Brett. He didn't answer my calls this morning. I know he's upset, but I'm not sure what exactly to say. *Sorry I was talking to your best friend?* One thing is for certain—I need to get out of the house.

> *Me: Hey, it's Emma. Any chance you want to grab a drink tonight?*
> *Jesse: Sure! Brett came home in a crappy mood today. I heard you might know something about that.*
> *Me: Ugh! Yeah. I do. Sorry.*
> *Jesse: No worries. It happens. Do you care if I bring my friend Kara?*
> *Me: Of course not! I could use a girls' night.*
> *Jesse: Well you are in for a treat then. Kara is well…Kara.*
> *Me: Can't wait. Shoot me the place and time. I'll be there.*
> *Jesse: See you then. Again, I'm warning you about Kara.*
> *Me: Lol Trust me. She will be fine.*

I hang up and begin to get ready to go out. I'm a jeans-and-T-shirt girl most of the time, but tonight, I'm in the mood for something a little sexier. After dragging on a pair of tight black pants and a low-cut pink shirt, I top it all off with a pair of black heels. I spend an hour flat-ironing my long blond hair and applying just enough make up to highlight and cover my sleepy eyes.

Just as I walk out the door, I shoot Caleb a text.

Me: Going out with Jesse. Can we talk tomorrow?

He instantly replies.

Caleb: Yep. Be careful. Catch a cab. No driving.

His message is short yet bossy. Maybe I'm not cracked up to be with someone as moody as Caleb. No matter what I may think, my heart tells me something completely different.

I WALK Into the bar that Jesse said she and Kara frequent regularly. I scan the room, immediately feeling overdressed. There are probably ten tables filled with guys who all pause and look over at the door when I walk in. Apparently my idea of *girls' night out* is very different than Jesse's. This is a restaurant/sports bar, not a martini bar or dance club like I was expecting. My boobs are half exposed and I swear there is a twelve-year-old in the corner who is drooling. *Shit!*

Thankfully I locate Jesse sitting at a table with another small brunette and quickly head their way.

"I need a sweater to cover up," I say, sliding into the booth across from them. Her friend is staring at me with her mouth hanging open.

"Holy shizzle, you are hot!" she shouts, causing Jesse to elbow her. "You did not tell me she was this hot," she says to Jesse while rubbing her arm. "I'd totally become a lesbian for you. Damn it! I should have dressed up tonight."

"Um, thanks?" I can't help but smile as I look over at Jesse, whose cheeks are bright pink.

She offers me a slight shrug before looking down to take a sip of her drink, clearly embarrassed. I don't want her to be uncomfortable. I need friends, and Jesse has been sweet enough to reach out to me even despite our awkward circumstances.

"Well you're pretty smoking too. I'm glad you didn't dress sexier. I'd hate for us to both to switch teams tonight. The male population of Chicago would suffer a great loss."

Kara doesn't even try to hide it as she whispers to Jesse, "She thinks I'm smoking." I can't control the laugh that escapes.

"Kara, this is Sarah's sister, Emma Jane. Emma Jane, this is my ex-best friend, Kara."

Kara's head snaps over to Jesse. "Ex?"

"I told you not to embarrass me," she says then starts giggling.

"No, you told me not to mention Caleb—" Kara's hands snap to her mouth. "Sorry," she mumbles from behind them.

Now I'm full-on laughing. This chick is hilarious. Awkward, but hilarious nonetheless.

"No, it's cool," I say, reassuring them both. "I need some drinks. Then we can talk Caleb and all things moody hot guys. Just promise me we can get out of here in a little bit and go somewhere where we can dance."

"I love you!" Kara screams.

My eyes get wide at her enthusiasm. Jesse just shakes her head and finishes off her beer.

"Shots?" I ask when the waitress stops to get my order. Both girls nod enthusiastically. "Three Blow Jobs and three Titty Twisters please. And I'll take a vodka cranberry."

"She even orders sexy shots," Kara once again openly whispers to Jesse.

"Would you shut up?" Jesse snaps back at her, and we all begin laughing like old friends.

"So when we get drunk, will you give us the vegetable report?" Kara asks, momentarily confusing me.

"Kara!" Jesse shouts.

"What? This is need-to-know information! She's sitting right here. You know I had to ask."

"What's a vegetable report?" I ask, even more curious based on Jesse's red face.

"It's just a little thing Jesse and I do where—" Kara starts, but Jesse quickly interrupts.

"Oh, no you don't. This is something *Kara* does. Leave *Jesse* out of it!" she yells.

"Um, okay. My traitorous best friend is now pretending like she didn't tell me a large zucchini for Brett. It took quite a few beers, but she eventually spilled. Anyway, it's just where you compare your man's business to the vegetable it most resembles." She finishes with an unabashed grin.

"One, ewwww! I did not need to know that about Brett." I pause and lean in close. "But congrats to you, girl!" I laugh, and Jesse wrinkles her nose, completely mortified. "Two, oh, I'll tell you this now. I don't have to be drunk to talk vegetables." I laugh at my new term. "Butternut squash."

"Noooo!" they both breathe out at the same time.

"Yep! And not one of those just short and fat ones. I'm talking a genetically engineered, agriculture-experiment-gone-wrong butternut squash."

"Shut. Up," Kara says with a dazed look on her face, which has me laughing all over again. She is entirely too excited about this vegetable report. But even Jesse looks a little interested.

"I mean, really. It's just wrong for a man that hot to have one that big." I toss back a shot the second the waitress sets it down on the table. "Oh, and don't get even get me started on his tattoos."

"What!" Kara screams.

"Caleb has a tattoo?" Jesse asks.

"Oh yeah! Two full sleeves, a few on his chest, and his entire back is covered."

"I've never seen that. I guess he always wears long-sleeve shirts. I can't believe I've never noticed that before." Jesse almost sounds a little hurt that she didn't know this about Caleb

"I didn't think it was possible for him to get any hotter. But now? You're telling me he's a tatted-up butternut squash. I think I need a cold shower...and a vibrator," Kara says before she promptly chugs the rest of her drink.

We all burst into a fit of laughter and fall into an easy comfort with each other. Jesse might not be the normal type of girl I would hang out with, but she is sweet. Kara is another story altogether. I kind of want to steal her from Jesse and make her my new BFF. She is awesome! Back home, it's usually just me and the guys, so this girl time feels really good—

and long overdue.

Three shots and two drinks later, the topic of Caleb finally comes back up.

"So you're really sleeping with Detective Hot Ass?" Kara asks.

"Hey, I thought that was Brett's nickname," Jesse slurs. Poor little thing is already pretty toasted. It's obvious she isn't a big drinker.

"Yeah, but he's taken now. I need to move on."

"Oh, Caleb's taken too," I tell her matter-of-factly.

"Really?" Jesse asks, shocked.

"Yep. How much did Brett tell you?"

"Not much. Just that he found you at Caleb's this morning. And they got into one of their tough-guy staring competitions—my term, not his."

I nod at her accuracy. That is pretty much exactly what happened.

"So here's the deal…"

I spend the next fifteen minutes telling them all about my relationship with Caleb. Jesse is obviously in shock, while Kara continuously fans herself with a menu.

"Wow," Jesse says when I finish. "So are you going to call him?"

"Yeah," I groan, knowing that, even though I'm more stubborn than I care to admit, I won't be able to stay away from Caleb for long. "So how pissed is Brett?"

"He's pretty upset, but I think it's because he's worried. He loves you, Emma. You know Caleb's never been with anyone since Manda."

"Why does everyone feel the need to keep telling me that?" I ask in frustration. "Is it supposed to be a bad thing that he hasn't been in a relationship in the five years since his fiancée died? I think it's a compliment that he's willing to give this a try with me."

"Caleb is a really good guy. I love him a lot. But you have to know he hates Sarah to his core. I'm worried this is going to blow up and be bad for both of you. Caleb has already been hurt enough. And if he's acting this way with you, it means he's finally moving forward. I think it's great. I just wish you two didn't have so much between you. Caleb needs easy, Emma."

"Shit. I know," I say, resigned. "I just don't think it will ever be easy for us. Not with how much he hates Sarah. But I definitely don't think it's impossible either. He and Brett have managed to stay friends and move past it for all these years."

"No, he and Brett just avoided the Sarah topic altogether. Brett is really good with denial. The few times they did talk about her, it was always explosive."

"Fantastic." I slump down in the booth.

"I think Brett's worried he's just sleeping with you. Although I can almost guarantee you that is not what it is to Caleb."

I wave her off. "Oh please. He's not just fucking with me. There is something really special between us. Ugh, I hate that word. But that's what it is. Caleb and I just click. However, just out of curiosity, how exactly can you guarantee that?"

"Because he just strolled in the door," she says, nodding to the front of the restaurant.

"What!" I scream, sitting straight up and turning to look at the door. Sure as shit, sexy-ass Caleb Jones is strutting in the door with Brett right behind him. My head snaps back around to Jesse. "Did you set me up?"

"What? No! I had no idea they were coming. Last I heard, they weren't even speaking."

"Hey, sweetheart," Caleb purrs when he stops beside our table.

"I believe I said I'd call you," I snap. Half of me is more than a little irritated that he followed me here tonight, but the other part is stoked to see him.

"You did, but I'm not a patient man. Especially when it comes to you, Emmy." He slides in the booth beside me, forcing me to move over. He brushes the hair off my shoulder and whispers in my ear, "And don't even try to correct me to Emma just because you're pissed. It's Emmy." His hot breath sends chills down my body.

I no longer trust my intoxicated words at this moment. There is a very good chance an invitation to go home and ravage his body will tumble out. So I cross my arms and pout like a child.

"What are y'all doing here?" Kara slides out so Brett can sit next to Jesse.

"We need to talk," Brett says, looking directly at me. He kisses Jesse and throws a protective arm around her shoulders. I really like Jesse, and I'm really glad Brett moved on. But it is *really* fucking weird to see him this way with another woman.

"Butternut squash," Kara says in complete awe while staring wide-eyed at Caleb.

Jesse and I both burst into drunken laughter. Caleb looks confused for a minute before looking down at me with a knowing smirk.

"I finally made the infamous vegetable report, huh?"

"Yep, congratulations! Now can I see your tattoos?" Kara asks, and her already wide eyes get even wider.

"I see Emma has been talking about me. I guess she's not too pissed after all."

"I told them you had ugly tattoos and a weird squash-shaped dick," I say, trying to keep up my bitch mode.

"No, you didn't." He calls my bullshit as he rolls the sleeve up on his shirt and shows Kara his arm. Jesse even gets in on the action by standing up and looking at the black bird down the back of his shirt.

"All right, ladies and cocks. I'm going to see if I can find a squash of my own. I'll be back in a few," Kara says, heading toward the bar.

"I like her a lot," I tell Caleb, who is looking down at me with warm eyes. I know I'm pissed, but I'm also drunk, so I lean up and place a lingering kiss to his perfect lips.

"Ehm." Brett clears his throat across the table, and Jesse begins to giggle.

"Talk. Do it quick, because I'm taking Emma home—very soon," Caleb informs Brett, never taking his eyes off mine.

"Jesus Christ. Fine." Brett lets out a groan. "Look, we talked. Caleb assures me that he's not using you. I have been very honest with him and told him that I don't necessarily believe him. However, we both agree you are an adult and can make your own decisions."

"Well, gosh. That was really kind of y'all," I say sarcastically.

"Emma, I'm serious here. I don't want you getting hurt. I know shit didn't work out with me and Sarah, but you're still a sister to me. My problem is I also consider Caleb family. So you two...doing whatever you're doing...is just an awkward situation waiting to happen when you break up."

"But what if it works out?" I question, and Caleb leans down and kisses my hair in apparent agreement.

"Well that's up to you two. But I'm out of this. Do whatever you want. Just don't drag me in the middle when it falls apart."

"It won't fall apart," Jesse chimes in from beside him.

"Right, I mean *if* it falls apart," he corrects.

91

"Okay. Everyone cool? Emmy, get your purse," Caleb says, rushing me out of the booth.

"Wait! I'm still pissed at you."

"No, you're not," he replies, pushing me to my feet.

"Yes, I am. I'm going to have another drink with my friends, and you are just going to have to be patient. That is your punishment." I wave down the waitress as he groans beside me.

I'm not mad anymore. I'm actually really glad he took the initiative to make up with Brett and have an actual conversation rather than a dick show. I'm just having a really good time hanging out with everyone, and Caleb's being here now only makes it better.

Chapter
FOURTEEN

Caleb

TWO HOURS. Two. Fucking. Hours. That is how long Emma has been 'punishing' me for. It hasn't really been punishment at all, but she has definitely been making sure that it's been torture. I've had fun hanging out with everyone, but Emma's gently stroking my cock under the table has made it virtually unbearable.

Brett and I apparently have the same plans for the end of the evening, because the minute a round of shots that Kara sent over from the bar arrived, we both ordered a table full of food. Tipsy sex with your girl is fucking hot, but there is a fine line between tipsy and hammered. I need a replay of last night with Emma, but I have to keep her sober enough to get it.

"Eat," I say, pushing some fries into her face.

"No. I'm full. Leave me alone. I'm not drunk, Caleb." She bats my hands away.

"Good. Stay that way. You need to eat, Emmy. I have big plans for tonight, and none of them involve you passing out on the drive back."

"Oh yeah? What are these plans of yours?" she asks.

I glance up at Jesse and Brett across the table. They are quietly talking, and by the slight blush on Jesse's cheek, I can tell that they are carrying on a secret sexy conversation of their own. I'm ready to go, and now is my chance to make sure Emma is ready too.

"You want to know my plan?"

She bites her bottom lip and nods enthusiastically.

"Okay, but if I tell you this, it's only good if we leave right this very second. Even a minute longer and the plan is void."

"Oh! I like the sound of this. I really want to see if Kara hooks up with that bartender, so you better make this a good plan."

"Oh it's good! See, I'm greedy, Emmy. I'm going to make that tight cunt of yours come on my hand, my mouth, *and* my cock tonight. I want it all." I pause for a second as her breath catches. "So my plan is to get in my truck and peel those tight-ass pants off you. Normally, I would want to watch you come, but I'm in a rush to get you home tonight. So as we drive back to my place, I want you riding my hand. I only need one to drive." I place a damp kiss to her neck. "You only get one in the truck though. That's all I'm willing to sacrifice. I loved the way you tasted when I licked my fingers last night. I haven't been able to think about anything else today." I lean in close and whisper even more quietly, "Tonight, you're coming on my mouth. I'm going to lick that pussy until you can't come anymore. Then, and only then, will I slam into you, nice and rough, giving you one last impossible orgasm. It's going to be hard…fast…and deep. That's my plan, sweetheart."

"That's a really good plan," she breathes with need building in her eyes.

"I thought so." I lick my lips and give her a sexy wink.

"Well, I think it's time Caleb and I call it a night," she announces, jumping up from the booth to collect her purse.

"Here." I hand her my keys. "You go ahead to the truck. I'll get the bill and meet you out there. You should probably *get ready* while you wait." I glance down to her pants.

"Okay, but hurry up or I might have to start without you." She snatches the keys. "Night, y'all. Jesse, text me Kara's number when you have a chance. Maybe we can all get together for lunch next week."

"Sounds good. Goodnight, Emma."

She waves over her shoulder as she heads to the door. Just as she breezes past me, she quietly warns, "Two minutes."

I search the bar for our waitress but quickly give up. I pull out my wallet and toss a stack of cash on the table. It's way more than enough for whatever we had and anything Emma could have possibly ordered before I got there.

"Let me know if that doesn't cover it," I tell Brett as I turn and head to the door.

"Night, butternut!" Kara calls across the bar.

I flash her a quick smile but keep moving toward the door.

When I reach the truck, I can see Emma calmly sitting in the passenger's seat, and my dick instantly goes rigid. I yank open the door and my eyes flash to her naked legs. Fuck, I love this woman. Or at least my cock does.

"That's a good look for you," I say, climbing in.

I openly stare for a minute. How could I not? Emma sitting naked from the waist down is enough to make lesser men cry. Hell, it's more than enough to steal my breath.

"I thought you'd approve."

She slips the cup holder up, converting the front into a bench seat. I watch as her glistening pussy slides across the leather, and I silently vow to never wash it again. She crushes into my side as her mouth finds mine. It's been twenty-four fucking hours since I was last inside her, but my kiss is desperate. This woman is going to ruin me.

For just a moment, I hold her close, forgetting all *plans* but rather just embracing this moment, making love to her with my mouth. I want this with Emma so God damn badly. I have no idea what this is, but I know for certain that it's real. That's a feeling I'm not used to these days. I've had sex with more woman since Manda than I ever did before her. But Emma isn't a score or an empty orgasm. She is so. Much. More.

I'm nowhere near ready to use L-word. I mean, who the hell knows what page Emma is on right now? What I do know is that I'm addicted. And she is the absolute best kind of addiction. Emma is life.

My hand dives between her thighs and I roughly push two fingers inside her.

"Oh God!" she screams, lying back across the seat, exposing herself completely

"Jesus Christ, sweetheart. I'm going to fuck this tight little pussy tonight. This"—I curl my fingers inside her—"is mine." She lifts her hips into my hand with a moan. "We are officially together. I don't care about the rest of this bullshit we have going on. We're going to figure this out one way or another. No one comes near this but me. Yeah?"

She moves her bare foot to rub over my rock-hard cock, which is currently straining desperately against my zipper. "Does that make this mine?"

"Exclusively," I say with another finger curl that has her sitting straight up. "Say you got it, Emmy. We make this work and this is mine."

"I got it," she says on a moan.

"No, say all of it."

"We'll make this work," she whispers.

"And?"

"And this is mine." She makes another swipe over my hard-on that makes me groan.

"Emmy," I warn.

I rub my thumb over her clit. Lying back down, she begins furiously rolling her hips into my hand. She could care less that we are in middle of a parking lot. Emma is a sexual beast. I've been with her exactly once, but I could have told you that from our first night on the phone. She's not timid or shy. She bares it all in every aspect—especially in bed.

I tear my eyes away from her writhing body long enough to make sure no one can see what's going on. I may have talked a big game inside, but I need to get her home. And I was wrong before. There is no way I can concentrate enough to drive while she's riding my fingers.

"Okay, sweetheart. We need to go so I can fuck all those little jokes out of you. I promise, you're going to be screaming that this cunt is mine by the end of tonight."

I quickly twist my fingers inside her. I lick the thumb on my free hand then use it to make fast circles over her clit. She claws at the door above her head as I pump into her. Her muscles begin to clench as her orgasm draws near. With one last twist of my wrist, she explodes around me.

"Caleb!" she shouts, and it echoes off the windows.

"Jesus Christ." I remove my hand. I would love to enjoy the moment of watching her come down, but even as it stands, there is no way I'll get her home quick enough.

With the turn of a key, my truck roars to life and I carefully speed out of the parking lot. Emma doesn't bother to put her pants back on, but she does turn and crawl over, resting her head in my lap. She doesn't even reach for my zipper, but it all feels so fucking right. The warmth runs through my chest, and this moment of closeness fucks even further with my head.

I don't know the what, when, where, or why about my life, but as I stroke her hair on the way home, I suddenly know the who.

"Thanks for talking to Brett today." She sits up and curls under my arm as I drive.

"He's my family too. I treat him like a dick a lot, but I never let it linger long. I swear I've apologized to Brett more than any woman in my life," I joke, and thankfully she laughs along with me. I was worried that this would be yet another sore subject—one I can't afford to have between us.

"How'd you know where I'd be tonight?" She snuggles in close and finally drops a hand over my zipper. *Thank Christ.*

"You said you were going out with Jesse. That woman is a creature of habit. I would have been there earlier, but Brett gave me the what for."

"Mmm, good. After this morning, you deserved hell." She begins licking her way up my neck.

At the very first stoplight, I grab her head and crash my mouth into hers. Palming her bare ass, I—

Beep

The wussy horn of a Prius sounds behind us, snatching me back down from my Erickson intoxication.

"Home," I mutter to myself as Emma begins to giggle beside me. "Laugh it up now. You only have about two more minutes before this is mine," I say, darting a quick finger inside her. She sucks in a breath, but I don't take my eyes off the road as I bring my hand to my mouth.

Emma loves to challenge me, and I feel like I just won the World Series when she whispers, "Drive faster," before sucking my earlobe into her mouth.

Pulling into my garage, I click the button on my visor to close the door behind us. As soon as the darkness cloaks the garage, she climbs into my lap. With her round ass pressing against the steering wheel, she attacks my mouth. I immediately rise under her, pushing my hardening cock against her core. The sting of her hand pulling my hair sends a spark directly to my balls.

"What the hell are you doing to me?" she asks, fiercely attacking my neck in the best possible way.

Somehow I know she isn't talking about this moment. Maybe I'm fraying her wires as well. None of this instant connection with her makes sense, yet somehow, as she physically assaults me in my truck, it strengthens me. Like rain from the sky, a million emotions randomly fall over me. I'm down, done for, lost, and ensnared. There is no going back from Emmy.

"Funny, I could ask the same question." I move my mouth to her covered breast.

"Condom," she demands.

"Let's go inside."

"I won't make it that long." She grinds down against my erection, causing us both to moan.

"Wallet," I relent, lifting my hips an inch to pull it from my back pocket. As soon as my ass is back on the seat, I reclaim her lips.

We fumble around as I try to push my jeans down and Emma tries to roll the condom over my length, but finally all the stars align. I move my tip to her wet entrance and begin to glide inside.

"Shit!" I exhale as she quickly begins to move over me. This isn't enough, but then again, with Emma, it never is. I give her a few more strokes before stopping her completely. "Wait, sweetheart. Wait."

"No," she answers, continuing her rhythm.

"Damn it, stop." I force her hips to still. "I'm not fucking you in my truck like a horny adolescent. Let's go inside where I can take my time with you."

"Too late." She smiles, and it's magnetic, pulling more than just my body to hers.

What I wouldn't give to not be wearing this fucking condom right now. There is something so wrong about having something between us. I hold her down with my dick buried completely inside her. I won't let her move until she says it.

"Tell me you're mine."

"You're mine," she says, struggling to rise—desperate to find her release. But what she doesn't understand is that hearing her say those words would be mine.

"Emmy, I'm not fucking around with you anymore," I growl. "We make this work. It's exclusive. No one touches you but me. Stop playing and tell me you get it."

"I got it." She gives up her fight and kisses me breathless.

"Tomorrow, I want you to get on the pill. I'm clean, and next time I'm inside you, I want to really feel you."

A small twinkle lights her eyes. "I'm already on the pill," she says, running her hands up my chest.

"Tell me you're mine," I repeat.

"Take off the condom," she says, moving her hands into the back of my hair.

I chuckle and shake my head, knowing, as usual, that she's still screwing with me. However, the idea of being bare inside her forces me to let it go.

Emma pushes up on her knees, allowing me just enough room to snap off the rubber barrier. No sooner than my hands are out of the way, she slams down, rejoining us completely.

"Jesus!" I shout, and she moans.

She rides me in the front seat of my truck until I honestly can't take it anymore. I turn, depositing her on the seat beside me, and slide out the door before she can protest.

"I'm not finishing this here." I pull my pants up then reach in and sling her over my shoulder. "My turn." I slap her naked ass, and she lets out a loud laugh as I carry her into the house.

For over an hour, I make good on my 'plan.' I take my time, touching every inch of Emma's body before finally, and truly, making her mine. Sated, we silently lie in bed while I try to figure out a way to keep her. I need some magical fix-all that can help us both overcome our bullshit. And what I really mean is for *me* to overcome *my* bullshit.

"I meant it, Emmy. We're going to figure this out," I whisper against her neck. "Something is going on here, and I know you feel it too. I want this. I want to see where it goes and what we can be together."

"What if we just keep Sarah separate from *us*?" she asks, confusing me.

"She's your sister. How do you propose we do that?"

"Yes, she is my sister, and I love her. I know you don't like her, and while I adamantly disagree with your reasons, I'm not too blind to see why you would feel that way. You know I'm going to see her and talk to her, and I'm not going to lie to you about that. However, it also doesn't mean you need all the details."

"No, I really fucking don't," I snap a little too harshly.

"And you know what I don't need?" she says, suddenly sitting up and cocking her head at me. "Your attitude about it. If you want this to work, you are going to have to figure out a way to keep your hatred to yourself. I know it's there. I definitely don't need you to remind me about it every single time her name happens to come up."

Feeling like an ass, I sit up also and drag her across my lap. She quickly moves to straddle me, not even willing to relinquish control for a minute.

"Fair enough. You don't talk about her and I'll keep my shit to myself?"

"Yep," she says shortly, but I can feel her body begin to relax.

"Deal. Now tell me you're mine."

"You're definitely mine, Caleb," she says with a smirk that has me growing hard all over again.

Chapter
FIFTEEN

Emma

IT'S MOVING day, and Eli just picked up the last load of Sarah's stuff. True to his word, Caleb has been completely absent today. It doesn't hurt. I understand his reasons, and after our little discussion, we both agreed that distance between him and Sarah is the best answer. I can't keep them as separate part of my life forever, but for now, this seems to work.

Eli Tanner is my new pal. He showed up bright and early this morning to help me move all of Sarah's stuff into our new two-bedroom apartment. Without even asking, he walked in and immediately started packing boxes. We didn't think it was right to ask Brett to help. His opinion of Sarah isn't any better than Caleb's right now. So Eli brought along another friend, Ty Stephens, to help. He's a big quiet guy who has probably only said ten words to me all day. However, he's been working his ass off. Between the two guys, they have made quick work of this move.

"Hello?" I answer my phone. "Eli, no! That's my room. Sorry…hello?"

"Miss Erickson?"

"Yes?" I say, pulling the phone away from my ear to look at the caller ID on the screen.

"My name is Dr. Preston Clark. I work at Building Foundations. I'm currently treating your sister, Sarah."

"Oh, hi! Is she okay?" I quickly ask as guilt and panic settle in my stomach.

I haven't talked to Sarah since that day in the hospital. I've tried, but she just rejects my calls. I get updates from the center, but it's always from her the patient coordinator, Judy. This is the first time I've actually heard from one of her doctors.

"Yes, Sarah is fine. I was wondering if you would be available to come in for one of her therapy sessions this week?"

"Really? Does Sarah know you're calling? Does she want me there? Will she talk to me?" I rush out a million miles an hour, causing the good doctor to laugh a little.

"Yes, she does. We were hoping you could come in tomorrow?"

"Can I come today?" I can't contain my excitement. I've been wanting to talk to her for weeks now.

"Sarah's session is in thirty minutes. Perhaps tomorrow—"

"I'll be there!" I jump to my feet, scanning the room for my keys.

"Miss Erickson, really, tomorrow—" He starts, but I once again cut him off.

"Please, please just let me come today! I've been dying to talk to her, but she has been avoiding me. Please. I can be there in twenty-five minutes."

He lets out a resigned sigh but finally answers. "Don't speed."

"Thank you!! I'll see you in a few." I quickly hang up the phone. "Eli!" I scream, and he pokes his head around the corner.

"What's up, babe?"

"Can you finish this up on your own? I hate to do this. I really, really appreciate your help, but I just got a call and I can see Sarah if I get there in the next half hour."

"Yeah. Yeah, of course. Go ahead and get out of here. I'll drop the key off with Jones when we're done."

"Thank you!" I shout over my shoulder as I sprint to my car.

Thirty minutes later, I walk into a large medical building.

"Hi, I'm Emma Erickson. I'm here to see Dr. Clark."

"Please have a seat. I'll let him know you are here," a sweet older lady says from behind a glass window.

I sit in the waiting room, frantically trying to figure out what I'm going to say to Sarah. I have so many things to say, but I don't want to set her off. Damn it, I really should have waited until tomorrow to figure out the best way to approach her.

I nervously wait. I must redo my ponytail twelve times before they finally call me to the back.

"Mrs. Erickson?"

"That's me." I jump to my feet.

"Hi, I'm Dr. Clark." He extends a hand.

"Hi. Please just call me Emma."

"Okay, Emma. Sarah is waiting for us in my office."

He guides me through the winding halls. This place is definitely more hospital-like than it is celebrity resort. I guess that's what you get for a court-mandated treatment facility though.

He stops just outside an office door. "Today is going to be you listening. I wish we could have had more time to discuss things on the phone, but it is what it is. This is not the time for you to tell Sarah how you feel. This is the time to listen and ask questions. Got it?"

"I can do that," I say, more eager than ever knowing that Sarah is on the other side of the door.

Slowly, the good doctor swings open the door, revealing a woman I barely recognize. She sits in a chair, chewing on her nails and shaking her leg with nervous anticipation. Her hair, which has always been well below her shoulders, is now chin length. It's blond, but not our natural white color. It's fried and frizzy from overprocessing. She must have been dying it weekly to cause that kind of damage. She's entirely too thin, and her clothes hang off her body.

Tears immediately spring to my eyes as the guilt from not being there over the last few years twists a knife in my heart. Her eyes never rise to mine, and as my chin begins to quiver, Dr. Clark gently soothes a calming hand over my back.

"Please have a seat, Emma." He guides me to the loveseat sitting beside Sarah's chair.

I quickly run my fingers under my eyes to remove any stray tears that might have escaped. I'm heartbroken, but she doesn't need to know that.

"Hey, sis," I say, reaching over to squeeze her hand.

She doesn't pull away, but she doesn't reciprocate either. Avoiding me with her eyes, she looks up at Dr. Clark.

"Are okay with Emma being here, Sarah?" She doesn't respond but offers him a quick nod. "Don't be nervous. Emma loves you. She was so excited when I called. She insisted on dropping everything and coming straight here." He smiles at both of us.

"That's true. I was moving your stuff into our new apartment," I say, and her eyes immediately flash to mine.

"New apartment?" she questions with wide eyes.

"Yep, two bedrooms with a balcony and everything. It's really nice."

"You really moved up here?" she asks with an unreadable expression.

"I told you I was. Besides, I kind of like it here."

Sarah barks out a laugh. "Just wait until the winter. You'll be hauling ass back to Savannah," she says jokingly, and my eyes light up as I get the first true glimpse of my sister.

"It was snowing when I got here. It's freaking March. What the hell is that all about?" I joke, trying to hold back my happy tears.

Sarah laughs, and it's a beautiful sound. One that I've missed so much over the years. My hands are aching to hug her. I quickly drag the elastic band from my hair and redo my ponytail just to keep from reaching out to grab her.

"Okay. So, Emma, Sarah and I have been discussing quite a few things over the last few weeks. We were in agreement that it was time to bring you in and fill you in on where things are at in her treatment."

"Oh, yeah. That sounds great," I rush out, rubbing my hands back and forth over my jeans.

"As you know, Sarah is being treated medically for her brain injury suffered during the accident, and I am helping her emotionally move past it as well. Currently, we are focusing on her guilt over Manda's death and her role in the accident. During one of our chats, we pinpointed why she has so desperately tried to separate herself from those who love her. Sarah, care to elaborate?"

My eyes move to focus on her, but her eyes frantically jump around the room, looking at anything but me.

"Hey." I try to catch her attention. "You don't have to be nervous. There is nothing you could say that would make me think less of you. I love you." I try to encourage her, but she leans even farther away from me and begins knotting her fingers in her lap.

The doctor tries to prompt her. "Sarah?"

"I killed Manda," she whispers. "I was driving that night, and I feel guilty that I lived and she didn't."

"You remember?" I ask, shocked.

"No." She finally looks up at me. "I don't remember. But based on the proof, I've accepted it. It doesn't do me any good to play the what-if game. The only way I will ever truly move on is to own it and figure out how to get better."

"That's a really brave thing to say. I respect you for that," I say, trying to let her know that I'm on her side.

She just laughs though. "I definitely don't deserve respect."

"Why do you say that, Sarah?" Dr. Clark cuts in.

"I just don't."

I look at him to see if he is going to push the subject, but he just nods and moves on.

"Why don't you tell Emma what we talked about on Monday?" he says, causing Sarah to let out a groan.

"You have to know this therapy bullshit is driving me crazy." She turns to look at me. "It's like he has all the answers, but he still makes you guess before he gives them to you."

I smile at her logic. I love these sarcastic flashes of my sister—my old sister.

She takes in a deep breath and very calmly, with no trace of sarcasm, bares her soul. "I have pushed everyone away for years because I don't feel like I deserve anyone's love after what I did. I still miss Manda every single day, and sometimes it's crippling. It's bad enough to know that I lost my best friend, but knowing that I had a role in her death slices me deep. I've wanted to escape that feeling for years, so I tried to kill myself. I just needed a way out of the pain."

"Okay, I need to say something here. And I probably should just be listening but I need to say this for *me*." I look at the doctor, but he doesn't try to stop me. Turning back to Sarah, I rush out, "I'm sorry I left you to deal with all this on your own. I was terrified of losing you, and I know that is a shitty excuse, but I couldn't stand by and watch you try to kill yourself. So I took the coward's way out. I'm sorry. That's what *I* feel guilty for."

"I wouldn't have let you help me even if you tried." She finally reaches out to grab my hand.

I can't hold myself back anymore. I dive across the chair and throw my arms around her neck. She's stiff at first, obviously not having ex-pected me to assault her with hugs, but a second later, she relaxes and wraps her arms around me too. We stay like that for a few minutes, both of us silently dripping tears and sniffling.

"I've missed you so much," I say, and the moment is immediately ruined.

She goes stiff and awkwardly releases her hold on me. "I'm not who you miss," she says with a cold chill to her voice.

The forgotten Dr. Clark speaks from across the room. "We didn't get to this part, Sarah. Give her a break."

"What did I say?" I frantically look back and forth between them.

"Go ahead. Tell her," she says to the doctor.

"But then you wouldn't have to guess." He offers her a fake grin that has her rolling her eyes.

"I'm not the person you remember anymore. Shit changed after the accident. My 'care team'"—she makes air quotes around the words—"says it's because of my brain injury or whatever. But I'm not that woman anymore. It's weird. It's like I remember who I used to be, but I hate pretty much everything she used to love. Remember how much I used to read and write?"

"Of course. You were always such a geek when it came to books." I laugh, but she doesn't even smile.

"I hate them now," she says matter-of-factly, like her sudden anti-reading status is going to run me off.

"Okay?"

"Oh and remember my obsession with cooking?"

"Yep," I say, knowing where this is going.

"I would order takeout every day for the rest of my life if I could," she says, and it once again makes me laugh. "What's so funny?" she asks in a bitchy tone I definitely recognize.

"You!" I exclaim. "I'm not laughing at you per se, Sarah. I do, however, find it funny that you think your reading and cooking habits have any bearing whatsoever on how I feel about you."

"Okay, let me interject here. I think Sarah might be not be explaining this very well," Dr. Clark says, placing his notepad on the table beside him. "What she's trying to say is she is not the same person you might remember. People who know her have expectations of who she is, but she feels that the person she is now will never be able to live up to those expectations. Is that accurate, Sarah?"

I look to her as she nods.

"She's my sister!" I shriek at the doctor. He uses his pen to point over to Sarah, reminding me who I should be talking to. "You're my sister!" I repeat to her.

"I'm not the person you remember though."

"I don't give two shits who you are now. You could turn into a purple flying monkey and I'd still love you. You're my family." Her eyes get wide and fill with tears. "Jesus, Sarah, is this why you pushed everyone away? Oh my God, is this what happened with Brett? You didn't want to disappoint him?"

"No!" she screams and jumps to her feet at the very mention of his name. "Brett is my biggest change and regret. I just don't love him anymore, and he wouldn't fucking accept that!"

"Let's everyone calm down."

"Wait, do you still love me?" I jump to my feet alongside her as fear floods my veins. If she fell out of love with Brett, maybe she hates me now too.

"No. I mean yes! Yes, I love you." She looks around the room before repeats my words back to me with a timid smile. "You're my sister."

"Well okay then," I say, flopping back down onto the couch, filled with relief.

Instead of sitting in the chair, she moves to sit next to me. I'm done with the seriousness of this conversation. I quickly collect myself then whip out the old trusty humor.

"Look, we're in this together. I'm not going anywhere. I don't care how much you have changed. It looks like we have a lot of catching up to do. Good thing we live together now." I give her a wink. "I see many 'get to know you' wine nights in our future."

"I don't drink anymore," she whispers.

"Okay, well you can watch me drink while we talk." I pat her leg and offer her a crooked grin. We both start laughing, and she leans her head on my shoulder.

Finally, fucking finally, something feels right with Sarah. It's crazy how one hour-long conversation can change everything. I still feel guilty as hell for not having been there for her, but we are at least on the right track now.

"Those jeans make your ass look big," Sarah pulls me into one last hug before I leave.

"Your hair looks like shit," I tease back.

She leans away and gives me a huge smile. "Next week?"

"I'll be here. Maybe you can call me if you get a chance?"

"I'll try," she replies, looking down at the floor.

"Thanks, Dr. Clark." I extend a hand but at the last minute go in for a hug. I'm really fucking happy, so he can suck it up and take it.

"All right, Emma. We'll see you next week." He quickly pushes me away, and Sarah quietly laughs behind him.

Today has been amazing.

As I walk to my car, I pull my phone out to text Caleb. I toss it around for a minute, trying to decide what to say. Separation. That is what we agreed on when it came to him and Sarah, but this is something I want to share with my boyfriend. I know that by now Eli has dropped off my keys and probably told him where I went. I'm not going to let Mr. Broody ruin this for me.

> **Me: I'm on my way back. I'm in a really good mood. Please don't ruin this by acting like an ass.**
> **Caleb: Um. Okay? Thanks for the vote of confidence.**
> **Me: I'm sorry. I'm just really fucking happy right now, and I wish I could share it with you.**
> **Caleb: Good visit?**

Holy shit! Is he asking about Sarah? I'm not giving him the details that I know he doesn't want. So I decide to keep it short and simple.

> **Me: Yeah. It was great! Can we go out to dinner?**
> **Caleb: Sounds like a plan. See you soon.**

And just like that, I kept up my end of the bargain and Caleb did the same. It looks like he and I might actually be able to make this work. This day just got even better.

Chapter SIXTEEN

Emma

I WOKE up early this morning and decided to surprise Caleb with coffee at work. Poor guy got stuck working two Saturdays in a row. I know I've only been in town for five weeks, but I've missed our weekends together. Recently, I've been busy doing some free shoots for local magazines to try and get my name out there. So between my running around town at odd hours for work, visiting Sarah two afternoons each week, and Caleb's work schedule and woodworking hours, the last two weeks have had us running in different directions.

Saturday is usually our lazy day. No work or Sarah between us, just the two of us spending quality time together. This basically consists of lying in bed naked all day. Half the day, we make love. The other half, we just chat or watch funny movies. Thankfully he has a four-day next weekend, and he has already informed me that I'm not allowed to wear clothes the entire weekend. That makes days like today slightly bearable.

I'm patiently standing in line, waiting to order Caleb's coffee and my scone, when I see a familiar face out of the corner of my eye.

"Casey?" I catch her attention, and when her eyes meet mine, for a brief second, they fill with surprise before immediately returning to a flat expression.

"I'm sorry. Do I know you?"

"It's me. Emma—"

"Erickson," Eli finishes, walking up behind her. "What's up, babe?" He nods to me while rubbing his hand over Casey's back.

I've seen Eli probably two dozen times since moving to Chicago. He is always with Caleb or some combination of Brett and Caleb. But I don't think I've ever noticed how attractive he is before now. Sure, he's got a nice body. I'm not blind. But he's wearing a tight baby-blue button-down that really makes his toffee-brown eyes stand out. His hair isn't the usual shaggy mess I've seen. It's perfectly styled. It's obvious he is trying to impress her, but it honestly confuses me.

"I didn't realize you two knew each other," I say, motioning between them.

"Yeah, we go way back," Eli answers, pulling her into his side.

"Hi, Emma. Sorry I didn't recognize you. You've grown up a lot since I last saw you." Casey gives me a forced smile.

"Yeah, it tends to happen. How the heck have you been?" I ask her.

I've only met Casey three or four times, but I knew her better than Manda back in the day. After the accident, Casey went off the map. Sarah wouldn't speak to her, and Manda was gone. She essentially lost her two best friends that night, and it broke her. I heard she'd moved to Ohio and never looked back. Seeing her with Eli now makes me smile. She deserves a good man, and what I know of Eli says that he more than fits the bill.

"I'm okay. Living in Ohio. I'm just here visiting family and decided to catch up with Eli." His nostrils flair, but if possible, he pulls her even tighter against his chest.

"Look, I know things have been crazy over the last few years, but Sarah is finally getting help and dealing with her demons. Maybe I can talk to her doctor and see if you could go visit her? She really is getting better, and I bet she would love to see you."

"I don't know. I think it might be best if we just leave it as water under the bridge."

Shit. She must have really done a number on Casey the last time they spoke, because those three were inseparable.

"Okay, but just know she really is a different person these days. She's come a long way from how she was after the accident. If you change your mind, here's my number." I dig through my purse to find her one of my business cards.

"Yeah, okay. I'll think about it." She nods, but a small tear threatens to escape her eye.

"She's not the same, Casey, but she's still there."

"I miss them," she chokes out, and Eli pulls her completely into his chest.

"Shit, I'm so sorry." I didn't mean to upset her. I thought maybe she might be happy to see Sarah again. "I'm going to leave now. I'm really sorry. I'll just grab Caleb's coffee and be out of your hair before you even know it."

"Caleb?" She suddenly perks up.

Eli lets out a curse, and I suddenly realize that I've said too much. I steel myself, ready for the reaction everyone gives when they realize Caleb and I are dating, but it never comes from Casey.

"Are you dating Caleb?" she asks with a quick swipe under her eyes.

"Yeah. For a few months now. I shouldn't have said anything. I know this must be awkward as hell."

"No. Not at all. Is he happy? I mean, are you two happy? Is it serious?" She asks a barrage of questions.

Her reaction completely confuses me, until it dawns on me—Casey doesn't have a vested interest in this. She just wants to see someone in this whole mess moving on and finally happy again.

"Yeah, we are doing really well. I think he's happy—or I at least I hope he is." I laugh. "I'd say we are kind of serious. Maybe?" I laugh again.

Her lip begins to quiver as she nods. "That's good. That's really fucking good." The relief floods her face.

Eli leans down and kisses her long black hair. She offers me a genuine smile, but that damn tear finally escapes the corner of her eye.

"Well, we're going to head out, Emma," Eli says to me as Casey begins to blankly stare into the distance.

"Yeah, okay. Sorry if I ruined y'all's morning."

Casey speaks up. "You didn't ruin anything. I just don't talk about Sarah or Manda very often. It's still hard. I'm glad to hear Caleb is doing well though. He's a really good guy. Loyal to a fault. I'll let you know if I change my mind about visiting Sarah, okay?" She leans her head back against Eli.

"Yeah, that would be great." I smile then head back toward the counter.

A few seconds later, Eli leads Casey out the door. A small sense of peace washes over me as I remember that simple smile on her face. I can't help but hope she takes me up on the offer to see Sarah.

Caleb

"DETECTIVE JONES," I hear spoken in a sultry voice behind me. A smile immediately spreads across my face as I spin in my chair to see Emma carrying two large coffees.

"Oh, I love you, woman!" I say teasingly as I reach forward to grab one of the cups from her hand.

"Wait! Who said that was for you?"

"Excuse me! Do you have another man working here today?" I glance around the office. The only other man in the room is Bob Stein, a fifty-year-old man with a potbelly. "Huh?" I lift a teasing eyebrow. "Hey, Bob, were you expecting any coffee?" I shout across the room.

"Oh my God, stop. Here. Take it," she says, annoyed, but she still leans in to give me a kiss.

All is right with the world if Emma is still giving me kisses.

"Thanks, sweetheart." I take a long, much-needed, sip. The sludge they call coffee here is terrible, and after the late night I had buried inside Emma, I need caffeine to keep me going.

"So I ran into Casey earlier."

I almost choke on my coffee at her announcement. "Casey Black?" I need to clarify. None of us have seen or heard from Casey in years.

"Yep. She was with Eli."

"No. Shit?"

"Nope. I had no idea they knew each other."

"Yeah, Eli and Casey had a relationship long before the accident. And trust me. I use the word relationship loosely. Eli was in love, and Casey thought they were just fucking. When Manda passed away, it left Casey so brokenhearted that she took off, leaving everything behind—including Eli."

"Damn, that's rough."

"I didn't know he and Casey kept in touch."

"Oh they definitely have. I would wager they are even seeing each other again. She got upset and he was comforting her."

"Really?" I ask surprised.

"Mmmhmm."

"Wow. Well good for him. Casey's a good girl. Eli just needs to fight a little harder this time."

"Anyway, how's work going?" She walks over to my desk and plops down on the corner.

"It's going. I'd rather be at home in bed with you." I trace a finger down her jean-covered thigh.

"I'd rather you be there too."

"You didn't schedule any shoots for my days off, did you?"

"Nope. I'm all yours." She leans forward, begging for a kiss. Who gives a shit if I'm at work? I will never miss an opportunity to take my woman's lips.

"Good. I told Lindsey we would come over for dinner on Thursday night. Then I'm chaining you to my bed until Tuesday morning."

"Chains, huh?" she questions with a sexy smile pulling at her lips that goes directly to my cock.

"Oh, Emmy, you need to leave. I'm about thirty seconds away from bending you over this desk. I'd probably lose my job for cuffing you then fucking you in the middle of the office. But if you throw another one of those smiles my way, I might be willing to choose a new career path."

Emma chokes out a surprised laugh. "Well we can't have that. I'm too high maintenance for you to be unemployed." She tries to cover it with a joke, but judging by her nipples suddenly peaked under her shirt, she's turned on. The mental image of those beautiful pink nipples gives me an idea.

"Give me a hug then get out of here." I pull her hard against my body for what any outsider would assume is an innocent goodbye gesture. I squeeze her tight then whisper into her ear, "Your nipples are so responsive to me, and tonight, we are going to do a little experimenting. See, I like a challenge too. It just dawned on me that I've never made you come without touching your pussy. I have no doubt it *can* and *will* be done tonight though. It's just going to be my hands, mouth, and these." I bring a hand between us and gently brush over her nipple.

I quickly release her and step away. She sways, almost tipping over at my sudden departure. She can't hide the lust behind her eyes any more than I can hide my hard-on.

"You always do make the best plans." she breathes, straightening her un-messed hair. "I'll be at your place at six. Don't be late." She leans forward for a light peck then walks out the door.

I watch her ass as she walks away. I don't know what I did to deserve a woman as amazing as Emma. It sure as hell wasn't being kind or forgiving. But regardless of why, I silently thank the Lord for whatever it was.

Chapter SEVENTEEN

Caleb

"HUNTER!" EMMA squeals.

I watch as some asshole picks up my woman and spins her around like they are in the middle of some atrocious romantic comedy.

"Hey, sugar," he says, putting her back on her feet.

It's been six weeks since Emma moved up to Chicago, and "the guys," as she calls them, are just now dragging their lazy asses up here with all her stuff.

Emma and I have been doing really well at balancing our lives together. We acknowledge Sarah but never discuss her. Emma goes to visit her twice a week at rehab, and on those nights, I lock myself in the shop and catch up on my woodworks. Yeah, it's my way of being a bitter dick without taking it out on Emma. It never gets easier, knowing that Emma is spending time with the woman I hate most in this world. I did, however, agree to make it work. And if it means I get to keep Emma, I can bottle that hate up. I'm just terrified it will eventually explode.

Emma and I spend more time together than apart. I'm not falling in love with Emma. Oh, I've more than passed that. I am unquestionably in love with Emma Jane Erickson. And while that feeling usually elates me, some days it scares the ever-living shit out of me. I never thought I would feel this way again after Manda, and I am constantly on the edge of my seat waiting for it all to be snatched away from me again. That alone is the only reason why I haven't told her how I feel yet. I think Emma loves me too, but I want to give it some time before I drop the L-bomb on her. That shit changes everything—for better or worse.

So I stand here watching her fawn all over these two guys, and it isn't sitting well with me. I'm not usually a jealous guy, but no other man should be looking at her the way this "Hunter" guy is right now.

"Caleb Jones." I extend a hand, forcing him to release her in order to shake it.

"Hunter Coy," he answers, giving my hand an unnecessarily hard squeeze.

Oh yeah, this asshole is challenging me.

"Caleb, these are my best friends Hunter and Alex."

I extend a hand to the big guy who towers over me. Alex is huge and, thankfully, a bit standoffish with Emma. He gave her a hug when they first got here, but he quickly released her. Unlike this Hunter prick, who ran into her arms with his ridiculously tight nut-huggers and frat-boy-pink polo shirt.

"I can't believe y'all are here!" Emma jumps around, and both of these jerk-offs' eyes glance down at her boobs. Yeah, this little visit isn't going to end well.

"All right, let's get this unloaded so you guys can get some rest. I'm sure you're tired from the drive. What hotel are you staying at?" I ask the big guy.

"Caleb! They're staying with me. You know that. Quit being a dick," Emma says, calling me on my bullshit.

I roll my eyes and head to the back of the U-Haul, wanting to get this over with as quickly as possible. *Three days. They are only in town for three days.*

"I want to go out tonight," Hunter states, once again pulling Emma against his side.

"Yes! Let's do it. Hey, babe!" Emma yells. "You want to go out with us tonight? I bet they would love that bar we went to in the city."

"Yeah, sounds good," I lie. It sounds like a shit idea, but I'll be damned if I'm going to let Emma go out with these two alone.

"You grab the back. I'll get the front," Alex says, pointing to the dresser at the opening of the packed truck.

"Yep. One, two, three." We both lift the dresser and carry it toward the door.

Hunter and Emma are still talking and laughing on the sidewalk.

"Little help here?" I shout pointedly at Hunter.

"Shit. Yeah. Sorry, man." He leans forward and kisses her on the forehead before running our way.

It's all I can do not to drop this dresser. He kissed her—right in fucking front of me.

And just in case that alone didn't have my blood boiling, he finishes it off by saying, "I've really missed you, sugar."

Hunter and I will be having words tonight. I don't care if it does piss Emma off. She'll have to get over it.

Emma

"HELLO."

"Hey," Sarah says flatly.

"Hey!" I squeal back at her.

I love when Sarah calls. Things have been going great since my first visit with Dr. Clark. I get to see her twice a week, and she usually calls once, but it's always at random times. We've been spending this time getting to know each other all over again. She's really not that different, but I let her pretend that she is.

"What are you doing?" she asks, trying to strike up conversation.

"Just moving in."

"So the guys finally brought all your shit up?"

"Yeah. It probably took this long just to pack the truck. I did not realize how much stuff I have."

"You never were a minimalist," she jokes.

"Oh and you are? You forget I moved all your stuff too."

"Where do you want all your photography stuff, sweetheart?" Caleb says walking into the bedroom I'm currently hiding in.

"Who was that?" Sarah quickly asks even though I can tell by the tone of her voice that she knows exactly who it is.

Sarah and I are doing really well, but I still haven't broached the whole Caleb topic. I just figured it would be a topic better saved for later in her treatment and recovery.

"Oh just one of the guys helping me move."

Caleb lifts a questioning eyebrow, but I shake my head and try to push him out of the room. He doesn't budge though, but he suddenly becomes very interested in my phone call. He crosses his arms and leans against the doorjamb. All I can do is roll my eyes and go back to the conversation.

"So what are you up to?" I try to ignore the hot, tattooed elephant in the room.

"Why is Caleb Jones helping you move?" she asks, obviously recognizing his voice.

I flat-out lie to her. "Um, he offered to help."

"You know he used to call Manda sweetheart?"

"What?!" I shout, whipping around to face him.

"What's going on, Emma?" she asks.

"Shit, Sarah. I…" I stumble over my words. Caleb's eyes go wide, and the veins in his neck begin to strain. "We've been seeing each other since I moved up here."

"What. The. *Fuck!*" she screams.

"I'm sorry! I should have told you sooner. I just didn't want to upset you. I mean, I'm not even sure how serious it is." I lie again, frantically trying to backtrack out of situation that might hinder her recovery.

"No, what you should have done is not started fucking my best friend's fiancé!" she screams so loud I have to pull the phone away from my ear.

Fantastic. I've downplayed it too much and now she thinks we are just sleeping together. I glance up at Caleb, whose wide eyes have turned murderous.

"Sarah, it's not what you think."

"What is it then?" she yells back at me.

"We started talking a couple of months ago when I first came up." I begin to explain everything so that hopefully she will understand, but she quickly interrupts me.

"Did he tell you that he hates me? That he blames me completely for the wreck and killing Manda? That he thinks I should pay for it?"

"Sarah, no one blames you for the wreck."

The lies won't stop coming out. I once again glance up at Caleb, who might as well have flames shooting from his ears. I'm trying to talk my way out of this, yet I only seem to be digging myself deeper.

"Caleb does! For fuck's sake, Emma. You can't be this stupid. He is going to use you to get to me. He is hateful and calculating and will do just about anything he can to hurt me. And in this case, he is doing *you!* Wake the fuck up!" she screams before hanging up on me.

"Shit!" I quickly begin looking through my numbers to find one for Building Foundations on speed dial. "Hi, Judy, this is Emma Erickson. Can you have someone go check on Sarah? We just had a pretty big argument. I just want to make sure she doesn't do anything rash."

"Sure thing. I'll call you if anything is wrong," she says reassuringly.

"Thank you."

"No problem."

I hang up the phone and turn my attention back to the man who is damn near exploding in the doorway.

"What?" I scream, becoming increasingly pissed off by his over-the-top reaction.

"Where do you want me to start?" he hisses.

"Oh God, stop the dramatics. Just tell me what you're pissed about already."

"You never told her about us, but then again, why would you? It's not like we're serious or anything." He doesn't say another word before he turns and heads for the door.

"Caleb, you're acting like a baby!" I shout at his back.

It's probably not the smartest thing I ever could have yelled, but I'm pissed. If he doesn't understand why I didn't tell her or why I tried to downplay it, then he isn't as smart as I thought.

"Fuck you, Emmy," he says over his shoulder, charging for the front door.

"Hey, dickhead. Don't talk to her like that," I hear Hunter say from the other room, and I know this just got a hell of a lot worse.

I rush into the den and find Caleb standing nose to nose with Hunter, with Alex pushing into the middle to separate them.

"Enough. Everyone just quit!" I yell, trying to break up the chaos.

Caleb's chilly gaze swings to mine. "Gladly," he says before walking out the front door, slamming it hard behind him.

I'm so mad right now—at him, at Sarah, at myself—but Caleb is the only one close enough for me to take my anger out on. I immediately head out the front door, catching him just steps away from his truck.

"You recycled 'sweetheart,'" I say accusingly.

He freezes and slowly turns to face me. "What does that even mean?" he snaps, anger seething from his body.

"You used to call Manda sweetheart."

"And?" he asks with genuine confusion on my face.

"Well, you call me sweetheart! I thought it was something special. But now I find out it's just a generic term you use for people you sleep with."

His already pissed eyes turn dark as he steps in close. "First of all, since apparently you think I *recycled* the word sweetheart, you need to know a few things. One, I was no more 'just sleeping with Manda' any more than I am with you. Two, I was with Manda for years. I also called her babe, baby, honey, love, beautiful, gorgeous, honey buns, sweet cheeks, darling, dear, hot ass, and most recently, angel. Should I also strike all those words from my vocabulary as well?" He lifts an eyebrow while staring down at me. Suddenly I feel like an ass, but Caleb keeps going just to drill that home. "However, never in my life have I called another woman Emmy. Focus on whichever name you would like, but I know the only one that counts."

How the fuck did I just go from anger to guilt in three sentences? I try to pull myself together and give a bitchy response, but damn. He has a point.

"Caleb."

"No. Listen to me, Emmy. I'm the type of person who gives the women in my life pet names. It's what I do. I call Jesse baby girl, my niece Lulu, and my sister bubbles. I'm sorry if that bothers you, but that is what I do for the women I love. I think of disgustingly silly names to make them special. You are and have always been Emmy."

I suck in a stunned breath. Thank God we are standing outside, because if we were inside, I have no doubt that I would have sucked all the oxygen out of the room. Did Caleb just say that he's in love with me?

"You're in love with me?"

"No," he says very shortly, and the sudden pain in my chest surprises me. "I am absolutely not *in* love with you. Because that would imply that I could ever be *out* of love with you. But, *Emmy,* I do love you. Plain and simple."

"What?" I breathe as shock settles over me.

"I get it. Obviously we're on different pages. I didn't know 'we weren't that serious,'" he says, being sure to throw the air quotes my way. "Somehow, I mistakenly—"

I have to cut him off. When Caleb gets on a roll, there is a very good chance he will never come up for air.

"Stop! Just shut up for ten seconds and let me process this!"

"I don't want you to process it. I want you to *feel it*!" he yells, turning back toward his truck.

"I love you too, Caleb. I also hate you because you are a broody ass who hates my sister. Don't think I don't notice that you head to the shop every night I visit her. I deal with it because I love you too—no matter how fucked up that huge detail in our relationship may be. You are not exactly the easiest man to love, you know? I may have Sarah, but you have a shit-ton of baggage of your own.

"So far, I have been warned off of you because they either think you are using me or that we are going to destroy each other or some screwed up combination of the two—that you are only using me to destroy Sarah. At this junction in time, I happen to believe neither one of us will be left standing when this ends."

"Well, I've been on my knees for a long time, Emmy. I'm ready to fucking stand again, even if it means I have to fall when this ends."

"Caleb," I whisper as the anger ebbs from my body.

He runs a defeated hand through his hair and begins to once again head to his truck.

"Please wait." My feet become unstuck from the ground and I quickly close the distance between us. I slam into his back just as he pulls open the door to his truck. I wrap my arms around his waist and bury my face between his shoulder blades. "I'm sorry."

"Emmy, what the fuck are we doing here?"

"Currently? I'm physically restraining you while begging you not to leave."

"I'm serious," he says, turning in my arms but keeping me pulled tight against his chest.

"Well, you were overreacting as usual, and I was acting kind of bitchy—again, as usual. Sounds like par for the course for us."

"Please. Just be serious for a minute."

I let out a frustrated growl. "Look, I didn't want to tell Sarah and set her back in treatment. I knew she wouldn't approve. I just thought maybe it would be easier to tell her when we were a little more established and I knew where our relationship was headed. Like maybe…now."

"I get it. That's the same reason I didn't say anything to Brett at first. This is just really hard, sweetheart…I mean, Emmy."

"No, I like sweetheart." I look up and catch his mouth in a soft kiss. "So you love me, huh?" I smile.

He holds up his fingers about an inch apart and says, "Little bit."

"Oh, come on! I love you at least this much." I spread my fingers about three inches.

He gives me a smirk that Caleb should be famous for. It's bad-boy sexy but still warm and tender. "Tell me you're mine."

I lean into his chest and take a deep breath of his scent. He's sweaty and sticky from working hard at moving all of my stuff, but he still smells amazing. Part sweat, part soap, and one hundred percent Caleb.

"I'm yours," I whisper into his neck, giving him the one sentence he asks for daily. It's true, and it always has been.

"Fuck!" He quickly lifts me off my feet and pushes me against the side of his truck. I wrap my legs around his waist just as his hand roughly moves over my breast and up the back of my neck. He looks deep into my eyes and demands, "Say it again."

"I'm—" I begin, but I'm interrupted.

"You all right, Emma?" Hunter yells from the doorway.

"I'm fine. We'll be there in a minute."

Caleb lets out a string of curses while staring up at the sky. "Fucking prick!"

"Oh, stop it. He's a good guy. Give him a chance. Will you please still go out with us tonight?" I beg, being sure to add my pouty lip that never works on him.

"Fine, but here is how it's going down. Tonight, I will put on my best happy face. But I swear to God, if he touches you, I'm going to lose my shit. I'll try to keep in under wraps, but you're going to have to help me out a little too. Don't encourage him, and for the love of God, stop bouncing your tits in their faces. Alex is a big dude. That fight would not end well for anyone involved."

I let out a loud laugh. "Okay, no touching and no shaking. I think I can handle that."

"Then, you are coming home with me. They can stay here alone. I want to be inside you where I can say I love you properly." He leans his forehead against mine.

"I like the sound of that."

"You always do." He rolls his hips into mine.

Chapter
EIGHTEEN

Caleb

"HEY, ANGEL," I say as I walk up to Manda's grave.

The familiar weight settles in my stomach the way it does every time I come here. I miss her—there is no denying that—but it's just different these days. Emma has filled the darkness surrounding my heart. She has rejuvenated me and pieced me back together. It's been just over three months since we met at the hospital, but Emma Erickson has changed me, and as rough as it is going to be, it's time I told Manda.

"Sorry. It's been a few days since I was here, but I wasn't exactly sure what to say. I'm treading in new waters right now." I settle down on the ground next to her name. "I finally met someone who makes me feel again. It's been a long time coming, and to be honest, I wasn't sure I'd ever be able to move on from the holes you left in my soul."

I glance around the cemetery, very aware that I'm talking to the wind. *Fucking hell, Manda is the wind.* No matter how long it's been, it still cuts me deep.

"I've been seeing Emma Jane Erickson for months now, and last weekend, I finally grew a pair of balls and I told her I love her." I let out a loud sigh. "Jesus Christ, I was scared to death at first, Manda. This whole thing with Emma has been a whirlwind. It's been fast, but it's the realest thing I have felt since I met you. I know she's Sarah's sister, but no matter how fucked up it is for me to be with her, I couldn't stop myself from falling in love with her. I even feel like you may have had a little something to do with that—which is why I'm here today.

"I loved you, angel, but this thing with Emma is something completely different. I don't know where it's going for sure, but I know where I want it to go eventually. So I hope you understand that I need to leave this with you." I spin the black box around in my hand. "I don't feel right about carrying it around with me anymore. It's time. Jesse has told me repeatedly that I should leave it here, but I just couldn't let go." My voice chokes in my throat at the admission. "It's just that we never talked. I never knew your reasons, but I hope you know there is nothing you could have said that would have changed my mind. Nothing.

"You were right. We didn't need a piece of paper or this"—I hold up the box—"to bind us together. You were my wife the first time you said yes. We both knew it in our hearts."

My head falls into my hands as a single tear rolls down my face.

"I'll still visit. You can't get rid of me that easily. But that belongs to you now. It always did."

Five Years Earlier...

"IT'S A super small detour," I say, turning down a side street.

"Where are we going?"

"You'll see soon enough."

"Caleb!" she screeches in frustration.

"Manda!" I yell back, squeezing her leg with a teasing smile on my face.

"We're going to be late. You know Brett gets pissy because we are always late."

"He'll get over it. He always does." I brush off her excuse as I pull up in front of Hip Huggers—the club we met at almost exactly three years earlier.

"Um...you may have to wait until later if you are planning to get your dance on," she says, running her hand through her hair, flipping the red curls out of her face.

"I don't want to dance, but this will only take a second." I jump out of the car then open her door, dragging her out to join me.

"What are you doing?"

"Just come on."

I lead her to the front door of the club. After I knock twice, the door finally opens. I nod to the bald bouncer named Mick. I've known him forever, and thankfully listening to his stupid hunting stories has finally paid off.

"Hey, Mick!" Manda calls over her shoulder as I drag her down the short hallway and into the bar area.

Just as Mick showed me last night, I walk to the DJ booth and press the flashing red light. With the press of one button, Daniel Bedingfield's If You're Not The One *blares over the sound system.*

"What are you doing?" she asks, stepping away from me as the white lights begin dancing around the floor.

"What I should have done months ago. I'm re-proposing."

"You're repro-whating?"

"We only have ten minutes, but I'm not leaving until you agree to be my wife." I intertwine our fingers and tug, forcing her to collide with my body.

"I already did that."

"No, you said yes, but based on the last six months, we both know you have no intentions of actually marrying me."

"That is not true." She pulls away, suddenly aware of where this conversation is going.

"Oh, it's very true, beautiful. However, that all ends tonight."

She shakes her head and turns to walk away. She always gets so pissed when we talk about this. "I'm not having this conversation again, Caleb."

"I believe we are, because it's obvious we have conflicting ideas about how it's going to end."

False confidence rolls off me. I've been having this argument with Manda for a while now. She never budges, but I'm not letting it go tonight. I want answers, and I want her to give them to me. I reach into my jacket pocket and pull out a velvet black box containing a wedding band covered in diamonds.

"Manda, I met you here three years ago, and that night was the most amazing night of my life. I walked into this stupid club looking for a girl, but what I found was the woman I want to spend the rest of my life with. Funny how one night can change everything, huh? I'm not going to play

this game with you anymore. I love you. Marry Me."

"I've already said yes!" She begins to chew on her top lip and pace a circle around me.

"No, I'm asking you to actually commit to marrying me this time. Don't just say it—do it."

"I said yes, damn it!" she shouts again, continuing her nervous pattern.

"Manda, stop. What the hell are you doing? We share a house and a bed. The only thing we don't share is a last name."

"Why is this so fucking important to you? Can you just give me a little space? I love you. Forever. Is that not enough for you?"

"No!" I scream, rising to my feet. "It's not enough. It won't be enough until I have all of you. And I'm not even sure if that will be enough, Manda. I love you. I want you to be mine, but more than that. I want to be yours."

"Damn it! This is ridiculous. I'll marry you eventually, just not right now. It's not a big deal. Just let it go!" She stops in front of me, throwing her arms out to the side

"Just like that, huh? You want me to let it go? If it's not that big of deal to you, why don't you just wear the God damn ring and sign your name on a fucking piece of paper. Because this is a really fucking big deal to me." I shove the black box back in my jacket pocket and storm past her and out the door.

I get in the car seething with anger and frustration. For the life of me, I can't understand her hesitation about getting married. She never offers an explanation. She might be wearing my ring, but she isn't my fiancée. She has no intentions of ever marrying me. She will also never leave though. Maybe it's time I give up on this power struggle and just accept the fact that she won't ever be my wife.

Fuck, that idea burns. Damn it! I can't make her see how much I want this. Manda is my everything. I want it permanently. How am I just supposed to move forward with her, hopefully have children and build a life with her, when she can't even commit completely to me?

Manda doesn't immediately follow me out, but a few moments later, she opens the car door and slides in. "I love you."

"Yeah, I can tell," I say dryly.

"How important is it to you that we get married?" she asks, causing

my eyes to snap over to hers. A small tear is running down her cheek, and the anger fades from my body.

"I just want you, Manda. I'm not trying to force you into this, I swear." I reach over and dry her tear with my thumb.

"I don't want to lose you when you finally get sick of waiting for me."

"I'm not going anywhere. This sucks, but I won't walk away. I'd rather have you as my fiancée for the rest of my life than not have you at all." I lean in and kiss her, pouring every bit of my love into her mouth.

"How about this? We go to dinner with Sarah and Brett. Then we go home and figure this out. I have a few things we need to talk about, and if we're on the same page after that, we can set a date."

"Don't fuck with me about this Manda. Are you serious?" I ask, and she offers me a nervous smile.

"Yeah, I'm serious."

"You're going to set a date? Tonight?"

"No, I said after we talk and figure out a few things, we can set a date."

"That's a yes." I kiss her again.

"No, that's a maybe," she says sternly, but it does nothing to wipe away my smile.

"No, that's a yes." I wink and start up the car.

"Please don't get excited until we talk, I need you to hear me out and listen to my reasons."

"Sure," I say, completely ignoring her warning. I reach into my jacket pocket, pull out that black box, and place it on her lap. "Here. Hold on to this. You'll be needing it soon."

"I can't believe you bought a wedding ring." She flips open the box to get a good look at it. "It's beautiful, Caleb." She never takes it out or even touches it, but she looks up at me with a hopeful glow in her green eyes.

"It's going to look amazing on you, Mrs. Jones."

"If I put it on, I'll never take it off. But I need to make sure you really want to give it to me first," she says with an eerie edge to her voice.

"Manda, I've been asking you to marry me for six months now. I think it's safe to assume I want to give it to you."

"Yeah, I know. Let's just go to dinner. I could use a drink." She places the box in the cup holder and straightens to pull on her seatbelt.

"Not too much. I need you sober when you set a date tonight." I smirk and pull out of the parking lot.

Chapter
NINETEEN

Emma

"TELL ME about your tattoos," I ask, sitting on Caleb's lower back.

He is sprawled out across the bed as I massage his body. He had a tough workout at the gym tonight—or at least that is what he said. I'm pretty sure he just wanted me to rub his back. I'm okay with that though. He always returns the favor, right after he rolls me over and really loosens me up a few times.

"Manda's favorite song was Sarah McLachlan's *Blackbird*. I swear she used to listen to it on repeat all day every day."

I freeze at his answer. I must have asked him this question a dozen times, but he always finds a way to get out of answering. I never push it. I know it's some sort of tribute to Manda. I just don't know the details.

"Oh," is all I say.

I continue to scratch my nails down his back as silence fills the room. This is a giant tattoo. There is no way it was a simple request or impromptu decision. He had to have put a lot of thought into it, but I don't want to dig too deep and make him uncomfortable by prying.

"I got it piece by piece every month for the first two years after she died. It was therapeutic for me. It made me feel like I didn't just have to hurt on the inside anymore."

The idea of Caleb hurting so much breaks *my* heart. I quickly give up the massage and lean down pressing my chest flush with his back. I hold my weight on my knees and elbows but snuggle in as close as possible to his muscular shoulder, looping my arms under his.

"Did you design it?

"Yeah." I know he's not done with just that one word, but it takes him a little while to continue. "She can't fly anymore, so I decided I would do it for her."

"Tell me about it." I sit up and click on the lamp next to the bed.

"Are you sure you want to hear this? I know you don't have an issue with my past, but listening to me drone on about another woman is a different story. I know I wouldn't be able to handle listening to you talk about someone else."

"I'm sure. I love you. I want to know it all."

He lets out a loud sigh but begins to talk. "Two months after she died, I decided to get her name done. I was in a bad place back then. She was gone, Brett and I weren't speaking, and I was filled with anger and hate for…" He pauses for a second, but we both know who he was going to say. Thankfully he leaves it at that. "Anyway, I knew I wanted a blackbird, so I drew up the one on my chest and took in the very next day. The burn of that needle felt so fucking good. It reminded me that I was alive. I was walking through life emotionless and numb, and I began to crave that burn and all that it symbolized. The next month, I had entirely too many beers one night and sat down and started drawing on the back of an envelope. The first draft of my blackbird was born."

I begin to inspect every curve of the dark black ink. I've seen it a million times, but as he talks, I feel like I'm looking at it for the very first time. This is the story of Caleb's life those first two years after the accident, and it fascinates me. It's a timeline of his grief and pain—so hauntingly dark yet beautiful.

"Where did you start?"

"On the sleeves. The tattoo artist laughed at me when I brought in that drawing. He never thought I would finish it. It took forever, but I was determined." I trace my fingers over his shoulders and down his arms, causing goose bumps to pebble his skin. "I got *fly free* because I hope that's what she is doing these days. She isn't weighted down here on earth the way I am. She's soaring, I'm sure. Manda never knew how to do anything else."

A tear finds its way from my eye and drips onto his back. Like a bolt of lightning struck him, Caleb quickly rolls under me. I remain straddling his body, but it's now his stomach instead of back.

"Don't cry, Emmy. It was a really dark time for me. I'm okay now."

"Roll back over! I don't want you to see me cry." I slap his chest to try to lighten the mood a little bit. The expressions of concern and heartbreak mingle on his face.

"Please stop," he says tenderly, gently pushing my hair back behind my ears. I offer him a quick nod, but I continue my tattoo investigation on his chest.

"These are really amazing." I trace my fingers over the blackbirds rising up his shoulder. "But I wasn't done with your back."

He lets out a groan but rolls back over underneath me. I lift my finger and glide it down his spine to the small of his back.

"Did you start with the head of the bird first?" I ask, curious about the various stages.

"No, we did the entire outline and the shading first, then filled it in one section at a time as the months passed."

My fingers trace over the word *stolen* weaved into one of the patterns in the bird's body. But before I have a chance to ask about it, he quickly stops me, "Don't ask. You know the answer. My words will only be bitter."

I know he thinks Sarah stole Manda from him, and that guts me, but if I want to make this work with Caleb, I have to bite my tongue. I say nothing, but my hands never stop roving over his back. Finally, I reach the head of the bird. The menacing green eye staring at me. Once again, anticipating my question, he answers.

"Manda had the most beautiful green eyes. I met her in a dark dance club, yet I can still remember her eyes from across the bar."

"How long were y'all together?" I have to ask. I know the basic story, but I want to hear it from Caleb.

"Three years. Engaged for six months of that."

I lean down and kiss the back of his neck just above where his tattoo starts. "When were y'all supposed to get married?"

"I don't know." His answer honestly surprises me, but judging by his rough voice, it's not something he wants to talk about anymore.

Suddenly, Caleb rolls, flipping me to the bed beside him. I let out a scream, but seconds later, he has me pinned against the bed with his upper body.

"I told her about you today." He leans in for a brief kiss.

"You told her?"

"Yeah. I stopped at her grave on the way home from the gym. I used to carry her wedding ring around with me. But, Emma, I love you. I want this to go somewhere with us, and that ring was a symbol of my past. I want you to be my future. So I left the ring with her where it belongs."

"Wait. You left it at her grave?" I ask, trying to sit up.

Shit, that is a really big deal. I love Caleb, but he just left his dead fiancée's wedding ring at her grave because he wants a future with me. That is fucking huge for a man who has been carrying it around for five years. What if this doesn't work out and I have to live with the guilt that he gave everything up for me? He can't get that back once it's gone.

"I love you. I don't need that ring anymore. I just need you."

I squeeze my eyes shut to hide the uncertainty and panic. I knew things were moving fast with Caleb, and up until now, I was completely on board. However, I don't think I'm quite ready for him to make life-changing decisions around me yet.

"I love you, too." I briefly kiss his mouth. "But I need to go home and get my camera and stuff for my shoot tomorrow."

"What?" he yells, leaning back to look me in the eye.

"I have that thing for the magazine in the morning," I lie.

"I thought that was next week?" It is totally next week. Damn Caleb for actually listening to me when I talk. "Why didn't you bring your stuff over tonight? I haven't gotten to return the massage yet." He smirks, and it almost makes me want to stay.

I lie again. "I forgot."

"I'll wake you up early. You can stop on your way."

"I can't. I have to clear a memory card, and that will take a little while. I need to do it tonight." Jesus, I'm not even sure if I remember how to tell the truth anymore.

"Ugh. You are killing me," he says, releasing me and rolling to his back.

I stand up and grab my shoes, before heading back to sit beside him on the bed.

"Would it make you feel better if I just run over there and grab my stuff and come back here?"

"Hell yeah it would. Give me a second. I'll get dressed and drive you over there," he says, pushing to his feet.

"No, I'm okay. How about you cook me some dinner while I'm gone? I'm starving."

"Oh, I could use some dinner too." He rubs a finger across the seam of my jeans between my legs. The heat in his eyes has me wishing I could abandon this mission altogether.

"I'll be back. Give me an hour and you can have whatever you want." I press a deep kiss to his lips, pulling away just before his tongue has a chance to find its way into my mouth.

Caleb lets out a groan but lets me go. "One hour, Emmy!" he yells as I head to his front door.

"I love you!" I yell back, shutting the door behind me before he has a chance to respond.

I get in my car and immediately pull out my phone.

Me: Where is Manda's grave?
Jesse: Oak Terrace Cemetery. Why?
Me: Thank you.
Jesse: Caleb is going to kill me now, isn't he?
Me: Probably. Just don't tell him I asked.
Jesse: Oh this does not sound good, Emma.
Me: Trust me. I'm doing the right thing.

Caleb

THE WORLD rushes around me as I watch Emma walk out my door. I know she's coming back, but if I have learned anything in my life, it's that there are always the what-ifs. You can't live by them, but you can't forget about them either. But with Emma, I have to consider it all.

When I'm with her, I'm a different man. She sets me free. I never even realized I was trapped until she forced her way into my life. I've spent years trying to fly for Manda, but with a smile and an intoxicating laugh, Emma somehow managed to release *me*.

I'm not a jealous guy—usually. You live, you love, and you don't stray. If you do, you failed at the first two. But with Emma, it's a horse of a different color. I hate her best friend just because I think he wants to see her naked. I can't even see past the green to trust *her*. All rational thinking flies out the window when it comes to her. I've never wanted anything so much. But I'm a fucking hypocrite. I have a body full of tattoos dedicated to my past, including her name across my heart. I don't think I could be with Emma if the tables were turned. But when she lies in bed with me, I don't feel like I'm fucked up. She erases it all. And for that alone, she has stolen not only my heart, but my entire soul.

Chapter
TWENTY

Emma

I CAN'T even begin to explain how excited I am right now. I just picked up the pictures I printed of me and Caleb. They turned out amazing. I couldn't even bring myself to touch them up in Photoshop. We don't look perfect, but that is more fitting than anything for us. While they were all great, I fell in love with one particular picture. It's a selfie I snapped while we were lying in bed. The smile on Caleb's face and my wide open-mouth laugh have all the makings of a picture that would usually make its way to my recycling bin. But this picture caused my heart to skip a beat. It perfectly encompasses our relationship, and the glimmer in Caleb's eye as he watches me laugh sends warm chills over my body every time I look at it. I had two copies printed—one for Caleb's place and one for mine.

He's at the boxing gym tonight, so I'm going to surprise him by hanging it in his room. I found an empty natural-wood frame—one he no doubt made—in his bedroom. I hope it's okay that I use it. He has these scattered all over his house. If I bought a new one, it would completely clash with the rest of his decor.

I know he keeps his tools somewhere. Just last week, he had them out when he and Eli were hanging his new TV. I'm pretty sure he left them inside. His workshop is locked, so I begin to dig through the closet. On the top shelf is a big cardboard box. I drag a chair over from the kitchen to pull it down. Surely he will have a hammer and maybe a nail in this heavy-ass box.

I lift off the top of the box only to find that it's filled with paperwork.

Just as I'm about to put it back, I see a picture that all but stops my heart. I slide out the tattered image of Sarah's car wrapped around a tree. The immediate sickness I feel in my stomach knocks me to my ass. I know I shouldn't, but I can't stop myself from dragging the box to the floor beside me. Piece by piece, I empty its contents. I carefully arrange picture after picture of that horrible night in a circle around me. From close-ups of the seatbelts inside the car to the skid marks that start just before the grass, this disturbing box has it all. But it's not the pictures that bother me most. It's the pages upon pages of witness statements with Caleb's notes scrawled out to the side. Some dated as recently as two weeks ago.

If my heart stopped when I found this box, it shatters when I realize what this is. Caleb doesn't just hate Sarah. He is actively trying to prove that she caused the wreck. Printed reports about her blood alcohol content stapled to the doctor's statements about when the test was performed make it obvious what he thinks happened.

"Oh my God." I cover my mouth as anger rolls though my body.

I continue to sift through the files and eventually find three full notebooks of Caleb's handwritten notes. His words are, not surprisingly, filled with hate, but they hurt no less. It isn't until I come across a page detailing his plans to prove that she was drunk and his ultimate goal for her to end up in prison that I become physically ill. Choking down my dinner, I rush to his kitchen to grab a garbage bag.

Fuck him. He thinks he's protecting Manda and doing right by her. Well, it's my job to protect Sarah, and apparently I'm sleeping with the enemy. I rush back into the hallway and frantically start shoving everything into a trash bag.

"What are doing?" Caleb asks when he walks through the door. At first, he looks confused, but the moment he recognizes the box, an icy glaze slips over his eyes.

"You are still investigating the accident!" It's not a question. I look at him for only a minute before I continue my cleanup effort.

"So?"

"So? Are you fucking kidding me?" I ask, becoming even more pissed off at how nonchalant he is acting. This is a big fucking deal, and he has the audacity to give the "so" bullshit.

"Don't act like this is news to you, Emmy. We agreed not to talk about her, yet here you are, going through my shit." He remains frozen at the door with his gym bag still slung over his shoulder.

"I knew you hated her…but Jesus, Caleb. This"—I throw a picture of the car at him—"is a whole new level of fucked up. Do you expect me to lie in bed at night while you pore over old dead ends to help you prove that Sarah screwed up? You're delusional!" I go back to shoving papers in the bag.

"That's mine," he says, grabbing my wrist to halt me.

"That's funny, Caleb. I thought I was yours." I look into his eyes, and for a second, his mask slips. "Get your fucking hands off me. I'm throwing this shit out with the trash where it belongs."

"No, you're not." Caleb leans down and starts repacking the box.

"You're trying to prove that Sarah was responsible. Why? What good will come from this?" I beg for an answer.

"For Manda," he says simply, pulling the trash bag from my hands.

My heart breaks at his answer, but it's not breaking for him this time. It's breaking because I realize that this is the moment where all our cards will finally be on the table. I have an overwhelming fear that Caleb will choose his hate for Sarah over his love for me. I take a deep breath and choose my next words very carefully.

Caleb

AFTER SUCKING in a breath, Emma stops yelling and calmly begins to talk. "So you think Manda's best friend sitting in jail will bring her back? You think that is what she would have wanted? Damn it, you are stubborn. Caleb, you have to forgive her. Don't you think Sarah has paid enough for what may or may not have happened that night?"

I wish I had her calm. I wish those weren't the words she'd picked. I wish she weren't related to Sarah at all, but I learned years ago that there is no magical genie to grant my wishes.

"No, she hasn't paid enough!" I scream at the top of my lungs. "She should be dead, not Manda!"

Before I have a chance to utter another word, Emma rears back and slaps me.

"That's my fucking sister." She leans into my face, screaming, tears rolling down her face. "You're an asshole! I get it! You hate her, but I *love* her! Would you rather I feel the pain from that night? Because that is essentially what you are saying."

"It's not the same, Emma! She's your sister. I lost my wife!" I yell right back into her face.

Emma's next words cut so deep that I'm not sure there is any way to repair the damage. "She wasn't your wife!" she spits out, her chest heaving.

I can't even begin to contain my rage. "You're a bitch! She would have been, but your nut job of a sister killed her first!" This whole conversation has become more than just an argument, and it's quickly spiraling past the point of no return.

"Sure, it's all Sarah's fault. Who the fuck leaves two drunk women alone at a bar anyway?"

I actually stumble backwards from the verbal blow. Emma's eyes immediately go wide and she throws her hands over her mouth, but the damage has been done. She begins to apologize, but I'm officially done listening. I storm past her into my bedroom. I don't care if it's rational or not, but to insinuate that the car accident was my fault is the lowest blow someone could ever hit me with. And for the woman I love to throw that bullshit in my face is more than I can handle.

I grab her bag off the dresser and start shoving in her clothes as fast as I can, desperately trying to erase her from my house the same way I'm trying to erase her words from my mind.

Seconds later, I walk through the den and head straight to the front door. I yank it open and hurl all of her belonging into the front yard.

"Get out," I calmly say in her direction.

"No." She wipes the tears off her face

"Emma, get the fuck out of my house. I should have seen it all along. You're no better than Sarah. We are done."

"Caleb, please just stop for a second and listen."

"Get the fuck out of my house. Leave!" I yell as loud as possible. The intensity in my voice has her heading for the door. And just because I need to hurt her the same way she hurt me, I say words I'll never be able to take back. "Emma, while you are pointing the magical finger of blame, you might want to take a look in the mirror. Your sister tried to kill herself four times before you decided to get off your ass and actually try to help. Who knows? Maybe it would have only been one attempt if you had done something instead of pawning her off on Brett. Yeah, it's obvious how much you love her." Just as the pain of my words cross her tear-stained face, I slam the door.

I only make it a few steps before the realization of what just happened hits me. I just lost Emma. The only woman who has managed to make me feel since Manda, and now she's gone too. I reach a hand out to balance on the wall, needing something to support me. My eyes cross the room and see a picture propped up against the wall. I have no idea where she got it from, but Emma must have found one of the frames I used to make for Manda. Inside is a picture of us smiling and laughing, and it breaks me.

I have no control as my legs carry me across the room. I grab the picture and shatter it against the wall—the very same way both of those woman did to me. First Manda, now Emma. I was only half of a man to begin with, so losing Emma should completely destroy me. But there is no way I can put my pride aside and chase her down now that I know that she blames me for the wreck. I've blamed myself for leaving that night for years, and Emma's words just confirmed my guilt.

Emma

"PICK UP, pick up, pick up," I chant into the phone as I pull out of Caleb's driveway. As soon as I started the car, I burst into full on tears and dialed Hunter. He didn't answer though. I know he and Alex are probably out at the bar, so I dialed Alex next.

He answers on the third ring. "Hey, hun."

"Where's Hunter?" I choke through my tears.

"Shit. Are you okay?"

"No. Where is he?" I hear him pull the phone away from his ear and call for Hunter.

"What's up, sugar?" Hunter says sweetly.

"It just exploded. Really fucking huge explosion."

"Fuck."

"I'm coming home. Is that okay?"

"Of course. I'll change my sheets and everything." He tries to make a joke, but it only makes me cry harder.

"I blamed him for the wreck."

"Oh fuck, Emma! That's pretty harsh."

"Then he blamed me for not being there for Sarah after her first attempt."

"God damn. This must have been some fight. Just come home. We'll figure it out."

"I'm on the way to the airport now."

"You want me to buy you a ticket? We're just next door at Murphy's. I can run home and do it now."

"Could you please? I'll be at the airport in twenty-five minutes. Oh God, Hunter. This is so fucked up."

"Just get your ass on the plane. I'll see you in a little bit."

"I love you, Hunt."

"Love you too, Em."

Chapter
TWENTY-ONE

Caleb

NOTHING PREPARED me for the way I would I feel when I lost Emma—not even losing Manda. To know she's just down the block going about her life—a life that no longer involves me—makes my chest ache. I keep telling myself this is just a fight and together we will move past it, but I don't think there is any getting past this. We aren't just on different pages with the whole Sarah thing—we are in two totally different libraries. I've spent days walking around lost in my thoughts, replaying that argument, her words that slayed me, and my words to punish her. It was a vicious circle of hate, pain, and guilt.

I pull into my driveway, hopeful that she will be there waiting for me. It's been two weeks, and I would give anything to feel her right now. I fell for Emma. I told her I was ready to stand again, but I was wrong. I was nowhere near ready for this. I'm not just on my knees these days. I'm flat on my ass. It's been two weeks without her, and the image of her face as I slammed the door that night still shreds me. But we both said words that can never be taken back or explained away.

Sitting on my front porch is a small package. It's not unusual for my mailman to leave them there. It's probably a drill bit or something I ordered online. I scoop it up and walk inside, dropping it with my keys on the kitchen table. I grab a beer from the fridge and prepare myself for another night alone in the workshop.

Just as I pass the package, I catch a glimpse of the sender's name—Emma Erickson. My heart jumps to my throat, and I quickly rip it open. A small, familiar black box falls out along with a handwritten letter.

Caleb,
I couldn't let you give this up. If you want to leave this with
Manda, do it for yourself—not me. I couldn't have that on my
conscience. We both knew from the start where this would end.
But I'm not sorry we tried.

Love always,
Emmy

I stare at the paper for a minute, blinking and trying to figure out how the hell Emma ended up with Manda's ring. I think back to the night I put it there and remember Emma's sudden departure to go home and get her camera. Fucking hell. She was planning our breakup weeks ago. We weren't even having problems when she went and got this. Maybe she knew where this was going to end from the start, but I apparently thought it was heading somewhere completely different.

She couldn't live with what on her conscience? The fact that I was willing to give up everything for her? I take a sip of my beer, knowing that that's not true. I would have given up everything...except for my vendetta against Sarah. Which just so happens to be the only thing she ever asked for. *God damn it!*

I immediately grab my phone even though I'm not completely sure why.

Me: I'm coming over. We need to talk.
Emma: I moved back to Savannah. That's a long drive.
Me: You what?
Emma: I'm moving on. You should do the same.

What the fucking hell kind of response was that? I know it pisses me right the hell off though. I grab my keys, ready to call her bluff. I stop for only a second to get an honest answer.

Me: Did Emma move back to Savannah?
Brett: Yep.

Damn! I hurl my keys across the room. I feel like a mental patient right now. I keep flipping from being pissed that it seems she was planning for this all along to just wanting her back and willing to do anything to make that happen. But no, Emma said her goodbye on a stupid piece of paper. She had the balls to lie to me and go steal something so personal from Manda's grave but not enough to return it in person? *Fuck that!* My spinning wheel of emotions finally lands on asshole.

Me: I hope that works out for you. And for the record, I AM sorry we tried.

I stare at my phone for a minute, daring her to respond. But as the minutes pass, I realize that no response will come. That was it. That was the end.

I find an old bottle of scotch in my cabinet and throw back shot after shot until the burn in my throat completely disappears. I long for the numbness I have tried so desperately to get rid of over the last few years. And as the scotch begins to do its job, that familiar feeling slides over me.

I stumble to my den and not-so-gracefully flop down on the couch. I start to prop my feet on the coffee table but pause, hovering just inches above it. I love that fucking table, and not because it's perfect. It's not even my best work. It's flawed. The polish would not go on smoothly no matter how hard I tried. But no, I don't love that table for its perfections. I love it because I finished it the same night I called Emma for the very first time. I'm such a sentimental bastard. Well, Emma and I are torn to shit. It only seems fitting for this God damn table to match. I jump to my feet, flipping it over, and begin to, one by one, rip the legs off the motherfucker.

"I'm usually the one who breaks shit."

My eyes fly to the door to see Brett standing in the hallway.

"What the hell are you doing here?" I shout, trying to catch my breath from the exertion of destroying the table and the surprise of someone standing in my house.

"You should lock your door." He turns to walk toward the kitchen.

"Right. I'll be sure to jump right on that. Now, what the hell are you doing here?"

"I brought you some scotch, but it seems you already found the emergency stash." He grabs a beer out of the fridge and turns back to me. "So what's going on?"

"I thought you didn't want to be involved?" I say, leaning up against the doorway to keep myself from swaying.

"I don't. But Jesse was threatening to withhold sex if I didn't come over here and talk to you. I'd really like to get her naked, so if you could hurry up and spill it so I can get home, that would be great." He tips the beer up to his lips.

"She left."

"Knew that two weeks ago." He walks past me to the den.

"She found out I was still actively investigating the accident," I rush out, grabbing his beer from his hand and draining it.

"Jesus Christ, you're still doing that?"

"Never stopped." I look down to find a place to put the empty bottle but only find splintered wood covering the floor. I drop the bottle into the pile of scraps where a coffee table used to sit and head back to the kitchen to grab the bottle Brett brought over.

"The table?" he yells.

"Reminded me of her."

"Gotcha."

"So yeah. That's it. You can go tell Jesse we talked. I'm fine. Go home and get some." I try to force him to leave, but Brett only leans back, crossing his legs knee to ankle.

"Do I need to plan to work doubles for when you call out and rush to Savannah and try to caveman-style drag her back?"

"I don't think so. She told me tonight that she's moving on. It fucking sucks, but I think she's right."

"You think she's right or you don't know how to fix this?"

"Could you fucking leave now?" I ask, avoiding the question.

"Nope. Put something on the TV. If I go home now, Jesse will never believe we talked. She'll just send my ass right back over here—or worse, come herself."

"Oh God, I can't handle the Jesse inquisition tonight."

"Exactly. See if there's anything on ESPN."

Brett and I stare at the TV in silence, but I've known him long enough to know that he's not watching it either. Finally, I say the most honest thing I've said since Emma ran into my life.

"She scares the motherfucking shit out of me."

"Good," he says, never dragging his eyes off the TV.

"Good? Thanks, dickhead."

"Jesse scared the shit out of me too," he admits, still not looking at me.

"Oh, I remember that. I witnessed that train wreck firsthand."

His eyes finally swing to mine. "I'm going ask her to marry me."

"No shit?" I ask, surprised. I always knew Brett would do it, but it still surprises me.

"Few months from now, when she graduates. I rented out the bowling alley we went to on our first date. I never thanked you for that, by the way."

"Yeah, you're welcome," I say dismissively.

"Caleb, get off your ass and do something. Don't sit there drowning. She's in Savannah, not another planet."

"And do what? Nothing has changed."

"Now that part is up to you. You can continue to hate Sarah or you can let it go and choose Emma. That's a choice you have to make."

"Don't you think if it were that easy I would have done it a long time ago?" I say, rubbing a hand over my tired eyes.

"Then *make* it that easy." He leans forward like he just unlocked the secrets of the universe when in actuality he just said the equivalent of Nike's "Just Do It" campaign. I can't help but start laughing at him. He rolls his eyes and heads for the door. "I'll let Jesse know I'll be covering for you in a few weeks."

"We'll see," I respond, but I know he's right.

Emma

"WHAT DID he say!?" I scream at Hunter while trying to snatch my phone out of his hand.

"Nothing you need to worry about," he answers, dodging me.

"Tell me!"

Caleb got the ring today. I got the UPS alert on my phone the minute it was delivered to his house, and I've spent the entire day freaking out about it. Finally at five, I started drinking. I have no idea how Caleb is going to react to getting Manda's ring back, but I know I'm not strong enough to deal with it right now. So two glasses of wine in, I gave Hunter my phone. And now, a whole bottle later, I'm pretty sloshed and begging for it back.

"Who said he even text?"

"He text, I know he did. Delete it. Please just delete it," I say, sobering for only a moment.

"Already did, sugar."

"Stop calling me sugar!" I scream at him yet again. "Did he sound happy? Sad? Pissed off?" I ask, nervously pulling my hair into a ponytail.

"He sounded like an asshole," Hunter says, sitting down beside me.

"Yeah, he always sounds like that." I sigh, defeated. "I really love him." I lean my head down on Hunter's shoulder.

"I know you do. If it's any consolation, I think he loves you too."

"What?" My head springs up off his shoulder. "Oh my God, what did he say?"

"Nothing. I'm just saying, when I saw y'all together—when he wasn't glaring at me—he was always staring at you."

"Don't tell me shit like that." I smack him across the chest. "You are the worst best friend in history." I lean my head back down.

Hunter throws an arm around my shoulders and takes a deep breath. "He said he was sorry y'all tried."

My whole body stills as the pain of those words slice through me. I nod against his chest and try to fight back the tears but fail miserably.

"That definitely sounds like Caleb."

"I know this shit hurts. I still remember it like yesterday when Lacey and I fell apart. I'm so sorry, Em."

"Yeah, me too."

Chapter
TWENTY-TWO

Emma

Six Weeks Later

"NO. NO. No. No. No. This is not happening."

"Emma, calm down."

"No, you calm down."

"I am calm!" Hunter laughs beside me.

"I swear to God, if you laugh again, I will castrate you while you sleep."

"Jesus! That is not even funny," he says, appalled.

"Neither is this," I hiss through clinched teeth.

"Emma, we're having a baby." He gives me a huge smile.

"Um, no. I am having a baby with a man who freaking hates us both. He hasn't spoken to me in two months, and I can guarantee if he ever hears you call this your baby he will kill you on the spot. Oh my God, how is this even possible?" I settle my head back against the table and stare up at the butterflies painted on the doctor's office ceiling.

"When a man and woman love each other—"

"Get out!" I yell just as the ultrasound tech comes walking in.

"I can come back." She turns to walk back out.

"No, wait. I was talking to my friend. I'm sorry. Please come in."

"I didn't mean to interrupt," she says, walking in with a warm smile.

"No, I'm sorry. I'm just a little nervous and he was cracking jokes."

"The dads are always more laid back than the moms. Well, at least until delivery." She winks then starts typing into a computer.

"We really are more relaxed." Hunter chimes in with a teasing smile.

"He carries a gun for a living. At this point, I won't even try to stop him," I say pointedly.

I should have brought Alex, but when he found out that there was even a slight chance he would have to see any part of my body naked, he immediately had to work.

"So let's see what we have here," she says, squirting warm jelly on my stomach. "Now keep in mind, if we don't see anything, don't worry. It might just be too early to see on the abdominal ultrasound."

I nod nervously.

She rolls it around on my slick stomach for a few seconds while black-and-white images blur across the TV mounted in the corner of the room. Suddenly, a small image comes into view.

"Oh my God," Hunter breathes beside me and reaches out to grab my hand.

"Is that her?" I barely squeak out as tears fill my eyes.

"Yes, that's her *or him,*" she clarifies, smiling over for only a second before she goes back to taking measurements.

"You okay?" Hunter leans down, resting his head next to mine and kissing my hand.

"Nope," I answer honestly.

"You will be." And no sooner than he finishes that sentence, a fast thumping fills the air.

"Baby has a perfect heartbeat of 136," she announces, hanging the wand back up. "You are measuring at ten weeks, two days. He or she looks great! Here are some paper towels for you to clean up with. I'll be right outside with some pictures for you to take home. Okay?" She heads for the door, and I know I must look like a deer in headlights.

"Holy shit," I whisper as the door clicks behind her.

"That was the most intense two minutes of my entire life," Hunter says, bringing my hand to his mouth again.

"I'm pregnant," I announce as if he hadn't just been sitting there. "With a gummy bear," I add.

"It will be the most beautiful gummy bear in the world," he says reassuringly.

"What the hell am I supposed to tell Caleb?" Tears once again fill my eyes.

"I'll go with you," Hunter offers as I wipe the goo off my stomach.

"No. He really hates you." I pull down my shirt and stand from the table.

"Whatever. He'll have to get over it." He pulls me against his chest and holds me while I try to dry my eyes. "Hey, regardless of how he responds, we've got this, okay? Uncle Hunt is not going anywhere."

"I'm know you're just trying to help, but please never talk in third person again."

"Creepy, right?" He pulls back and offers me a tissue.

"Very." I wipe the makeup from under my eyes, grab his hand, and head out the door.

Caleb

I ANSWER the phone, flipping through the file of my latest case. "Detective Jones."

"You son of a bitch!" I hear shrieked across the line.

"Um…" I'm taken aback for a second.

"You got her pregnant!" the woman screams. And this time, she has my complete attention.

"I'm sorry. What?" I ask, confused and extremely fucking curious.

"Caleb, what the fuck? This is way worse than just trying to get back at me. Emma was innocent in all of this. And now…a baby."

Ah, yes. Sarah. I knew I recognized that shriek. I begin to be a smartass when her words suddenly hit me.

"Wait. Who's pregnant?" My stomach drops to my toes.

"Emma!" She confirms.

My mind is racing a million miles a minutes.

"I haven't seen Emma in two months." I'm so surprised that I somehow feel the need to explain things to *Sarah*.

"Well, she's ten weeks pregnant. You do the math."

Oh fuck.

I'm stunned into silence as I run over a hundred different scenarios that would make the baby Emma is—allegedly—carrying not mine. But those thoughts hurt even worse. I'm nowhere near ready to have a baby, but if she were to have a baby with someone else, I would never be able to recover.

I've been busting my ass to get myself to a better place the last few weeks. A place where I could let go of this vendetta I have against Sarah. A place where Emma and I can be together. I even started seeing some whack-job counselor Jesse hooked me up with. I'm really fucking trying to fix my shit, but now a baby?

"Damn it, Caleb! Say something!" Sarah yells, reminding me that the phone is still attached to my ear.

"I love her," is all I manage to choke out.

"Right. Of course you do," she says flippantly, and it makes my blood boil.

I've spent the better part of the last five years searching for ways to put this woman behind bars. Now, she's on the phone giving me shit. *Really?*

"Fuck you. You're really fucking lucky I love your sister, because she might be the only saving grace you have. You kill anyone recently?" I jab with the words from our past, and I can almost hear her face pale across the line.

"I'm trying to get better," she breathes.

"Stay out of my life. Forget I exist. God knows I've spent years trying to forget you." I slam down the phone and look around the room to see if the world really is upside down.

I lock up my computer and head for my car. I need to catch a plane to Savannah, but I have to make a phone call first.

Brett answers on the first ring. "Hello."

"I need Emma's address in Savannah," I say shortly.

"Well that took you long enough. I'll have Jesse text it to you. They exchange funny cards and shit. Why women do that I will never—"

"She's pregnant," I announce because I need someone to tell.

"Uhhhh…" He stutters across the line.

"My thoughts exactly."

"Is it yours?" he asks, sounding slightly awkward.

"I really fucking hope so, or Sarah is going to look like a real ass for calling me to drop this bomb."

"Oh shit!"

"Yep."

"You want to talk to Jesse? She's right here."

"Nah, I'm good. I just need to get to Savannah. Have her text me the address. I'm going to need you to cover for me for a few days."

"No problem, brother. Eli and I can fill whatever hours you need. Take your time."

"Thanks, man."

"Hey!" He catches my attention before I hang up. "She's pregnant. Leave the caveman in Chicago. Try some Romeo bullshit or something. If you act like a dick, I have zero qualms about beating your ass."

I bark out a laugh. "Qualms? Really, Brett?"

"I'm serious. She's my family. Don't go down there and show your ass. Just get your woman and bring her home."

"I gotcha."

"Keep me in the loop," he says before cutting the connection.

EIGHT EXCRUCIATING hours after I got the phone call from Sarah, I arrive at Savannah International Airport. I didn't even bother to swing by my house on the way to the airport. I'll buy whatever I need here. I'm reasonably sure Savannah has a mall or two.

It's nine p.m. when my cab pulls up in front of her house. There is not a light in the house on, and for a second, I worry that she's not home. But just as I walk up to the front door, the porch light flips on.

"Caleb Jones," he drawls, pulling open the door. The shadow of a giant I know to be Alex lingers behind him.

"Hunter Coy," I respond taking the final step to the door. "Where is she?"

"Sleeping," he answers shortly but pushes the door wide as an invitation for me to enter.

"I want to see her," I demand, stepping into the quaint townhouse.

"We won't stop you. But I want to know where your head's at first," he says, and for the first time since I met the asshole, I feel something similar to respect for him.

"I honestly have no idea. I'm guessing, by this little show of solidarity, it's true."

"Sarah called earlier. I know you talked to her. Emma does *not*." He moves to sit down.

"Where is she?" I ask again.

"Upstairs. In my bed," Hunter says with wicked grin that has me rushing toward him.

"Slow your roll." Alex throws a hand into my chest. "He sleeps on the couch. He's just giving you shit. First door on the left." He nods up the stairs.

I don't give Hunter a second thought as I fly up the stairs. I gently push open the door, and the light from the hall illuminates the room. I stand for a minute and watch her softly sleeping. Her long hair is cascaded behind her, and her body is completely absent of any blankets, exposing her long, creamy white legs. I can't take it a moment longer. I have to touch her.

I quickly toe off my boots and climb into bed behind her. Wrapping my arms around her waist and bending my knees into hers, I pull her tight against my body. She hasn't even opened her eyes, but for the first time in months, my body relaxes. I drag my hand under the camisole she's sleeping in and press gently against her belly.

"I'm not cuddling with you, Hunter. Take your ass to the couch," she says, scooting away from me. Her words make me smile and extinguish whatever smoldering jealousy I had about their relationship.

I follow her across the bed holding her tight, and just as she begins to huff and try to move my hand away, I whisper into her ear. "Hey, Emmy." Her entire body immediately goes stiff.

Very slowly, she rolls over to face me, nervously chewing on her bottom lip in the most unlike-Emmy way.

"What are you doing here?" she asks, but her bright eyes give her away.

"I'm here to take you home."

"Where's home exactly?"

"My house."

Her eyes go wide before suddenly narrowing. "Who told you?"

"Sarah," I say simply, and surprisingly, it doesn't even feel like venom on my tongue.

"Fantastic!" she says with enough sarcasm to shut down an entire clown college.

"Were you planning on telling me?" I ask gently.

The entire way here, I thought this was going to be a fight. I'm bitter that I just found out, and it's even worse that Sarah was the one who told me. But now, staring into Emma's face, whatever anger I was harboring is completely washed away.

"I just found out yesterday. I was headed back up to Chicago this weekend to visit Sarah, so I figured we'd talk then."

"I wish you had called."

"I wasn't sure what to say. This is all so surreal. I mean, I was on the pill. And let's be honest here—they make lifetime movies about shit less dramatic than our relationship. And on top of all that…I'm really scared."

"Oh, Emmy…" I let out a loud sigh and lean in to finally kiss her lips to show her some sort of reassurance. And while I'm at it, to selfishly take a little for myself too.

She quickly leans away. "What are you doing?"

"I'm about to make up for two months of separation." I follow her forward but never quite reach her mouth.

"I think you may have the wrong idea about things," she says uncomfortably, rolling away and sitting on the edge of the bed.

"We'll figure it out, Emmy." I desperately try to pull her back into…Hunter's bed. *Fuck that.* "Get dressed. We're going to a hotel." I need to get away from here. I don't care if they are just friends. I'm not taking her in another man's bed. And trust me—I will be burying myself inside Emma tonight.

"We're not going to a hotel. It's the middle of tourist season. A hotel in downtown Savannah will cost a small fortune."

"I don't care if I have to sell my left kidney to pay for it. We are *not* staying here tonight. Get dressed," I repeat, pulling on my boots and heading to the door to make sure it's shut and locked before she starts getting dressed.

"Caleb, we don't have to go anywhere."

"Get dressed, sweetheart." I watch as she crosses the room.

She's wearing nothing but a soft grey camisole and tiny pink shorts that I'm not sure are actual shorts or underwear.

"Stop staring," she says, pulling on jeans and a T-shirt.

"Please tell me you don't walk around the house in that."

"Oh Lord, no. Alex would die of an aneurism."

"Good. I knew I liked him." I grab her hand and head for the door.

"Hunter! I need your keys!" Emma shouts.

I prepare myself to exchange a few words with Hunter, but to my surprise, it's Alex who steps into my path.

"If she comes home crying, I will slaughter you. I've known Emma for over fifteen years, and I've seen her cry more in the last two months than I have in all those years combined. Man the fuck up, put your personal bullshit aside, and worry about her for once," he says, staring down at me. I want to say something dickish back to him, but he's fucking right.

"She'll be okay. I swear."

"She better be." He turns and walks back over to where Hunter is standing with Emma.

"Call me if you need anything." Hunter kisses her forehead, and it takes all I have not to rip his lips from his face.

"Come on, Emmy. Let's go."

Chapter
TWENTY-THREE

Emma

"JESUS, YOU really must have sold a kidney for this room." I walk into a huge suite in the new hotel right on River Street.

"Nah, it wasn't that bad. No worries. All my organs are securely intact." He smirks. God, I've missed him. "You hungry or thirsty? How do you feel?" he asks as concern slides over his face. His gaze flashes back and forth from my eyes to my stomach (with the occasional rake over my breasts).

"I'm fine. Can we sit and talk?"

"Yeah, of course." He motions for me to move to the couch.

No sooner than my butt hits the fabric, he slides in beside me—mouth aimed for mine. I barely have enough time to turn my head and dodge it. We have a lot of words that need to be said before we get to that point. I ache for Caleb's touch, but I know myself. If I kiss him now, I'll never want to stop and we will end up right back where we were months ago. I'm like an alcoholic when it comes to him. If I take even one taste, I'll be a goner.

"Please. We have a lot to figure out," I plead.

He groans into my hair but never moves away.

I can't think with him this close. I breathe in a deep whiff of all that is Caleb and quickly begin to lose my resolve. The image of Caleb pushing me down on to the couch while I drag my tongue up his neck has me letting out a soft moan.

"For fuck's sake, start talking, Emmy. I don't know how much longer

I'm going to be able to keep my hands off you."

"I don't blame you for the wreck," I start, but my voice is thick with desire.

"I know." He pulls away, but not before grazing his teeth across my shoulder. "We were both pissed and said some really shitty stuff. I didn't mean it—any of it. If I could go back, I would have handled that so much differently. I'm sorry, Emmy. "

I nod, knowing that, yesterday, this would be an extremely serious and more in-depth conversation, but now, we have much bigger issues to deal with.

"I'm pregnant," I say, chewing on my bottom lip.

"So I've heard. Sarah was all too happy to let me know this morning." He leans back and runs a hand over his face.

"I'm so sorry. She called me as I was leaving the doctor yesterday. I shouldn't have said anything, but she could tell I was upset. She just kept asking until I finally broke and told her. Yesterday was really rough for me."

"You should have called. I would have been here last night."

"I wanted to tell you in person. I was heading up on Saturday. I've been back and forth from Chicago for the last six weeks. I fly up for a few days once a week."

"What? Why?"

"Because I wanted to see Sarah, and I needed to keep my business going for when she gets out."

"Why the hell didn't you just stay up there? That must have cost you a fortune."

"Well I definitely accumulated some frequent-flyer miles," I offer a small grin, but judging by the look he is giving me, it's not enough of an answer. "I didn't trust myself to be near you," I whisper, and his eyes immediately go soft.

"Come here."

He doesn't have to say it twice. I move toward him and melt completely into his strong arms. He kisses the top of my head before dragging me across his lap. I nuzzle into his neck and ask him the real question.

"How do you feel about me being pregnant?"

"I have no fucking idea. I wish I could tell you I'm giddy with excitement, but that would be a lie. I just don't know. On one hand, I love you.

On the other, we're not exactly in the best place right now, and adding a baby to the mix just seems like a clusterfuck." He answers honestly, and even though he's right, it still hurts to hear him say it. This isn't how this was supposed to happen, but it's not like either one of us can change it now.

"You should know you can be as involved or uninvolved as you want. I don't want you to feel trapped, and Hunter said—"

"Fuck Hunter! If the next words out of your mouth have anything to do with him and my baby, I can't be held responsible for how I react."

"You're acting like a dick." I sit up with a full-blown smile spread wide across my face. "I've missed you. You're such an ass, but I've really fucking missed it."

"God, Emmy. You have no idea how hard the last two months have been."

I finally give in, and against my better judgment and all rational thinking, I lean forward and touch my mouth to his. I figured Caleb would devour me, but the slow, soft kiss he places on my lips is even better.

With his eyes wide open, his perfect lips move across my mouth. He slides a hand into my hair and the other around my back, forcing me against his chest. I go more than willingly. I move to straddle him, needing a connection. Even the one inch of space between us is too much. I need more.

"I need you, Caleb." I move to unbuckle his jeans, but he grabs my hands.

"Not yet, Emmy. I want this figured out. All of it. Because I want you to know that when I touch you this time, I will never *ever* let you go again."

"Okay." I drop my forehead against his, but as my one last show of rebellion, I roll my hips against his hard cock.

"Stop," he growls, taking my lips in another gentle kiss.

"All right, all right. Where should we start? The baby?" I peek at him through my lashes, not quite sure I want to have this conversation at all.

"I love you. And this is shitty timing, but I think as long as I have you, we can deal with the rest of it together." He lets out a sigh and rubs his thumb across my cheek.

I look around the room, trying to avoid his gorgeous blue eyes. I know I'm going to cry the minute I land on them.

I try to collect myself but continue to look down. "What about Sarah?

Avoiding her didn't exactly work out so well. I can't just sit by and watch you spend hours chasing dead ends that may or may not ruin her."

"Now this is where it gets tricky." He touches my chin, forcing my eyes to meet his. "Emma, I hate her. I will for the rest of my life for what she did—what she took from me. The blame game is a slippery slope, and I can't seem to find my way off it. You have always been amazing about my past—about Manda. You were even understanding to a point about the way I feel about Sarah. I think that's why I love you so much. You're so confident and strong, which is basically the exact opposite of me these days.

"So here it is. I want this with you, and I'll do whatever it takes to make that happen. You can't ask me to like Sarah, but you can ask me to stop obsessing about the hate. So ask." He stops talking, but my eyes go blurry. Of all the things I expected from Caleb, the words that just came out of his mouth were my absolute best-case scenario. Ones I never even dared to dream about. "Ask," he urges me as the tears escape my eyes.

"Stop with the box. Stop trying to break her. If you succeed, it would break me too."

"So. Ask," he repeats once again, waiting for me to find the right question.

"Love me more than you hate her. Please," I plead.

A small smile creeps across his face and he uses the pads of his thumbs to wipe under my eyes. "I can do that."

He suddenly stands with me in his arms and strides across the room to the bed. Gently laying me down, he positions himself on top of me, careful to avoid resting his weight on my stomach.

As he trails kisses up my neck, he stops at my ear and whispers, "I tossed the box the day you mailed back the ring."

"What?" I breathe in disbelief.

"I've been trying to get my shit together so that when I came for you, you couldn't say no. You had no idea, but I never planned to let you go despite your little 'move on' text."

"What text?" I scratch my nails down the back of his neck.

"The text you sent that night."

"Ah, that was Hunter. I didn't trust myself with my phone. I knew you would text when you got the package."

"Jesus fucking Christ, I really hate that guy."

"He did tell me you regretted trying."

"I'd apologize, but I think you know I'm a dick by now." He slides a hand teasingly under the edge of my shirt. "And apparently you missed it." He gives me a wink.

"You threw it away?" I ask again, running my fingers through his hair.

He doesn't say anything, just nods against my chest as he pulls down the neckline of my T-shirt to gain access to my cleavage.

"Come home with me in the morning. Move in with me, Emmy. I refuse to sleep another night away from you." He sits up to allow me more room to pull his shirt off.

"I can't. Sarah will need someone when she gets to come home. In a few months, they are going to start letting her do two weekends a month at home."

"Then stay at her place on those weekends, but you're living with me the rest of the time." It's not a question. It's a command. "You and that baby are mine. I want you under my roof permanently."

My chest warms at the idea of us as a family. I sit up and he drags my shirt over my head.

"If I say okay, will you stop talking and make love to me?"

"Absolutely."

He scoops a finger down into my bra to brush against my tender nipples. My back arches up off the bed when he makes contact. Fire spreads across my body and down to my core, drenching me.

"I'll do anything you want. Just don't stop touching me," I whisper as my hips begin to rock, searching for some type of friction.

Caleb drops his mouth to my nipple, sucking it and swirling his tongue in a relentless pattern. He settles on his side, pulls down the other side of my bra, and begins a different rhythm with his hand on my other breast. He's always been good with his hands, but this is unlike anything I've ever experienced.

"Oh God, Caleb," I moan as he continues. Every stroke sends a wave directly between my legs. "I want you inside me." I reach down, quickly trying to pull away my jeans.

"Not yet. Come for me, Emmy. Show me you missed me." He quickly switches his mouth to my other breast, sending me into a complete spiral.

"Fuck, Caleb!" I come, calling his name.

He slowly drags his tongue across my nipple one last time before releasing. He looks up at me with his signature smirk that almost has me coming all over again.

"That. Was." He stops and stands up to unbutton his pants. As soon as he pushes them to the ground, he crawls back up the bed. Wrapping an arm under my back, he drags me up the bed. "Unbelievable," he finishes just before crashing his mouth into mine.

Caleb

I CAN'T get close enough or deep enough. As my tongue rolls in Emma's mouth, the emotions threaten to overtake me. I need to be inside her, but I'm honestly not even sure that will be enough. I can't hold her tight enough to show her how I truly feel, and the words won't do this moment any justice.

I slide her jeans down her perfectly toned legs and sit in awe as I look over her body and into her eyes. I knew it months ago, but here and now, I am not only ready to admit that my life will never be the same again, but I'm willing to embrace it. I watch for a minute as she moves under my hand. Very slowly, I slide my fingers over her, teasing the way up.

I can't lose this woman again.

"You scare me," I admit. "I'm thirty-three years old, and I've never in my life felt like this before. *Never.* And it makes me doubt every single moment of my past. In some ways, you make me feel more lost than ever."

Her eyes flash to alarm, and she begins to sit up. I quickly silence her with a kiss. I don't need her to talk. I need her to listen.

Pulling away only an inch, I continue, "You see, every emotion I ever knew to be real just exploded around me. Love. Hate. Compassion. *Peace.*" I pause to give her a soft kiss. "I've described you as a whirlwind from the very start, but that's not true at all. Emmy, you are a natural disaster. You stormed in and stripped me bare. Say you're going to stay and help me rebuild. Swear to me, this is it for you. Because it sure as hell is for me."

She doesn't say a word. Instead, she leans forward, taking my mouth into an agonizing kiss. Showing me emotions with her mouth that her words would never be able to convey. Careful not to break the kiss, I slide inside her.

"Caleb," she breathes with the same contentment I feel in my chest. "You're it for me," she finally replies.

Five years after my life was stolen from me, in a hotel room in Savannah, Georgia, I finally reclaim it.

Chapter
TWENTY-FOUR

Emma

"I CAN'T believe you're pregnant!" Kara screams across the room. "That might possibly be the best-looking baby ever born. You should alert the Guinness Book of World Records now!"

I laugh, propping my feet up on Caleb's new coffee table. "I don't know. Channing Tatum's kid might have already secured that spot."

"Oh please. Mrs. Tatum has nothing on you." Kara's serious tone only serves to make me laugh more.

"I can't believe Caleb is going to be a dad," Jesse says, setting down a plate of cookies "When are you due?"

"February first. I'll be fourteen weeks tomorrow."

"How is Sarah taking this?" Jesse asks. She's not nosy like Kara. She's genuinely concerned. Brett is a really lucky bastard.

"Okay, I guess. She's not all that happy about me and Caleb. I think it's still weird for her. In her eyes, Caleb will always be Manda's fiancé and I'll always be her baby sister. As soon as we got back, I sat her down with her counselor and explained that this was my life and not hers. She said she understood but her attitude says otherwise. I just ignore it." I shrug and take a sip from the virgin daiquiri Jesse made me.

It's girls' night at Caleb's house. Brett and Eli came over to help Caleb with some stuff out in his workshop, so Jesse brought Kara and came over to keep me company.

"And how are you and Caleb?" Jesse questions, picking up a cookie.

"Now that is the million-dollar question." I sigh. "Caleb and I are great. Caleb and the baby are not so great."

"What do you mean?" Jesse asks, concerned.

They both lean in close, ready for some good gossip.

"I don't know. He doesn't talk about the baby at all. When I bring up decorating the room or names or even doctor's appointments, he basically shuts down."

"Well, you know guys don't get all excited about the planning the way women do. It's probably just such an abstract idea for him at this point. It's not like you have a big pregnant belly or anything yet."

"Hey, I've got a little bump." I rub my stomach.

"Oh please. I've eaten hamburgers that have made my stomach bigger than that," Kara says, causing us all to laugh.

"Just give him some time. You watch. He'll be passing out pink or blue cigars in no time." Jesse tries to reassure me, but I can't help that something just seems off.

Suddenly, Kara's phone rings and she excuses herself outside to talk. I instantly see this as my moment to ask Jesse something that I've been dying to know.

"What really happened the night that Sarah broke into your apartment? I mean, I know the gist of it, but I get the feeling from everyone involved that it became some sort huge, life-altering moment in y'all's lives, including Caleb's."

"It really was. It was horrible at the time, but that moment was a lot like the wreck except it changed everyone's life back to moving in a forward direction. Before that night, the whole group was living at a standstill."

"What did Brett say to her that night? I mean, he had to have said something because she had been struggling with this for years. And no offense, Jesse. Brett loves you unlike anything I've ever seen, but he had this misplaced guilt and responsibility to Sarah. How did he finally just walk away?"

"He finally let her go. He told Sarah that, wherever his wife may be in the heavens, he would always love her, but he accepted that it wasn't her anymore. He recognized that his wife died right alongside Manda."

"Oh wow," I gasp.

"It was the worst night of my life, but we are all better for it—that includes Sarah."

"Yeah, she definitely is. What about Caleb?"

"You want my personal opinion on what changed for him? Because really that is all I have to offer."

"Yeah. I'm just curious about his actions that night. Knowing him like I do now, I can't see him being in the same room with Sarah, much less rushing into a traumatic situation to carry her out. He said he did it for Manda, but the very next day, he went right back to hating her."

"That was Caleb's first experience with letting love triumph over hate. You should probably remind him of that sometimes." She gives me a gentle smile, and I have no idea what her last statement means, but before I can overanalyze it, Kara comes back.

"Well as very entertaining as you boring people are, Devon is coming to pick me up," she announces.

"Wait, what happened to the bartender?"

"No! Don't get her started on him!" Jesse yells just as Kara sits down to enlighten me.

"Okay, so we were finally getting down to business when, all of the sudden, his mom called. Okay, fine. Whatever. We've all got a mom. However, his mom was pissed, all screaming over the phone. Come to find out—"

"He bought her dinner using his mom's credit card while cruising around town in her Mustang," Brett finishes, interrupting her.

"Damn it, Hot Ass! You ruined the best part."

"Sorry, I have a seven-story limit, and that was number eight."

"Oh whatever. You suck," she says, heading to the front door. "Okay, ladies and sexy men, my chariot awaits. See you guys later." She smiles.

"Night, Kara!" we all yell in unison.

I turn to Caleb, who came in with Brett and parked beside me. "I freaking love her."

"Why does that not surprise me?" He gently kisses me.

"Okay, gorgeous. We need to get going," Brett announces, pulling Jesse to her feet.

"Why? It's still early." I whine.

"We'll hang out again soon," Jesse says over her shoulder as Brett pushes her out the door.

"Where's Eli?" I ask, turning to Caleb.

"He went out the back a while ago," he says, leaning in for another kiss.

"So what do you want to do tonight?" I move over on the couch and lie down with my head in his lap.

"It depends. How are you feeling?" he asks, sneaking a hand down the top of my shirt. Caleb may not talk about the baby, but he takes full advantage of my overly sensitive nipples and increased sex drive.

"Can we watch a movie or something then talk about that? It's still early." I pull his hand out of my shirt.

"Sure. What is the shortest movie ever made? I'll rent that."

I laugh, and he smiles down at me, licking his lips.

"I love you," I say, pulling his hand down to my stomach.

I really don't think too much about the implications until he snatches his hand away like my stomach burned him. I can't decide if I want to be pissed, hurt, or some wicked combination of the two. Regardless, I know I need a few minutes alone.

"I'll be right back." I try to keep myself from running to the bathroom.

I lean against the sink, hating myself for hiding away instead of asking him about it, but I don't want to hear his answer. I'm insecure right now, and it's an overwhelming and new feeling for me.

"Emmy, you okay?" Caleb knocks on the door. "You want some ginger ale or something?"

"Nah, I'm fine." I try to collect myself but give up and decide to confront him instead. I pull open the door and almost run into his chest.

"Hey, you all right?" He looks concerned.

"Why'd you pull your hand away?"

"What?" he asks, but he gives me a fake laugh that tells me that he knows exactly what I'm talking about.

"Start talking or I'm going to bed."

"It's weird," he says sheepishly.

"What's weird? My stomach? Because that's going to get a whole lot more weird over the next few months."

This time he doesn't even try to hide it—he openly laughs.

"Laugh it up. I'm going to bed." I push past him.

"Emmy, wait!" He follows behind me. "I just mean that it's weird that you're pregnant."

"Awesome!" I say sarcastically over my shoulder, but I don't get two steps before I'm plucked off my feet. He swings me up into his arms. I scream and try to fight his hold, but it's useless. "Put me down."

"Nope." He carries me into the bedroom and less-than-gracefully deposits me on the bed. His body quickly covers mine, and I turn my head, anticipating a kiss that I have plans to avoid. "Maybe I didn't say this the right way. It's weird that you're pregnant because I just got you back, and I'm a selfish prick who doesn't want to share you with anyone. Not even our baby. It's stupid and childish, but I worry that when he or she gets here it will change things. So right now, I'm embracing just being us, and I'll worry about the baby later."

"You don't have a whole lot of time before later becomes now." I give him some bitchy attitude.

"Look at you, all pissed off," he says, laughing.

"Of course I'm pissed off. I'm terrified, and I feel like I'm in this alone," I admit not only to Caleb but to myself as well.

"You're not alone, sweetheart."

"Well it sure feels like that. You don't talk about the baby—ever."

"It's been a month, Emmy. Give me some time to warm up."

"Where is my time to warm up? My whole life has already changed and it's just going to change more. What if you realize you can't handle this? I'm not sure I can do this on my own." I begin to work myself up into a frenzy.

"Babe, calm down. I'm not going anywhere. I'm going to love that baby more than any human has ever loved before. It's just going to take some getting used to the idea. This is why pregnancy is nine months long. Assholes like myself need time to adjust. I promise. It will be all right. I love you. You're it for me, remember?" He places a gentle kiss to my lips that immediately soothes me.

"This is just really hard. I don't even feel like myself. For the love of God, I can't stop crying all the time!" I yell, and I know he wants to laugh. I can see it on his face, but like a good man, he keeps it in.

"So what names do you like?" he asks.

I'm positive he doesn't want to have this conversation right now, but the fact that he is willing to ask for my sake makes me melt into his side.

"Collin for a boy. Laurel for a girl."

"Humm... Let's keep thinking on those." He smirks, and I pinch his chest.

"Thank you," I whisper.

"Of course." He places a deep kiss to my lips while dropping his hand to rest on my stomach. "It's me and you forever, Emmy. Anything else is just a bonus at this point. This is it." He gives a content sigh.

"This is it," I repeat back to him.

Chapter
TWENTY-FIVE

Caleb

"YOU NERVOUS?" she asks as we drive to the doctor. Immediately I feel like a dirt bag for not asking her the same question. *World's best father sitting right here.*

Emma has a doctor's appointment today and insisted I come. This whole baby thing is crazy town. I'm thirty-fucking-three years old. I should be able to handle a baby. Hell, I should have a whole house full of kids at this age, but for some reason, this baby scares the shit out of me. I'm not sure why I'm so nervous. I've *always* wanted kids, but I just feel like this is all wrong. Right woman, but the completely wrong time.

Little Collin or Laurel Jones will be entering the world in less than six months. At least those are the names as far as Emma is concerned. I have something a little edgier up my sleeve. Maybe something where my son won't have to wear a pocket protector, and my daughter…oh fuck that! I don't even want to think about having a daughter.

"Yeah. What about you?"

"I'm fine," she answers with a weak smile.

I want to shut down and pretend like none of this is happening, but based on our conversation a few days ago, I need to be there for her.

"Liar." I look over, flashing her a funny grin. I pray to the Lord it's not as forced as it feels, but based on her deflated reaction, I know it is. "So tell me what's going to happen. This is my first ever gynecology appointment, you know." I chuckle at my own joke, but Emma sits emotionless beside me. "Hey," I say to catch her attention. "Seriously, are you okay?"

"Sorry. I'm just really anxious and…worried. The nurse said they were going to do an ultrasound today. What if something's wrong?"

"Emmy, that is our baby you are talking about. It is way too stubborn for anything to be wrong. It's probably already cussing and telling dirty jokes."

"No, he isn't!" she yells.

"He?" I lift a questioning eyebrow.

"It needs to be a boy. You can't handle a daughter." She finally gives me a true Emma Jane smile, and just that one flash of her immediately calms my nerves.

"Thank God we agree." I pull into the parking spot and waste not a single second planting a kiss on her lips. I hold her against my mouth for longer than necessary, but I try to transfer some of my false confidence. I'm nervous as fuck but still manage to say, "Let's go meet our foul-mouthed son."

Emma

I HAVE a horrible feeling about this. I know it's just a simple routine checkup, but I feel like I'm going to puke. The butterflies in my stomach are threatening an all-out revolt. It's making me edgy, and even Caleb's being at my side isn't helping calm my nerves.

"Emma Erickson," the nurse calls, and I spring to my feet as I hear Caleb groan behind me. I can't even focus on him long enough to question it.

"That's me." I stop in front of her.

"Right this way. I'm going to need you to leave a urine sample then have a seat in the back waiting room. I'll let the ultrasound tech know you are here."

"Okay," I reply, hoping to God Caleb was listening to what she said because I'm so distracted I barely even registered her words at all.

"Emmy." He catches my attention. "Go pee in a cup," he finishes with a laugh.

"Right." I head into the bathroom.

When I come back out, I find Caleb standing in the hall staring at a huge board covered with pictures of happy, smiling families. I follow his gaze to a picture of a man sitting on the side of his wife's hospital bed. Their left hands are crossed, showing off their wedding rings as they hold a wrinkly newborn. It's a nice picture, but I could do better. I do envy them though.

They probably had time together, a life, a plan. I mean, it's not exactly like we are teens with an unexpected pregnancy, but the timing is all wrong.

Caleb was right the other night. I wish we had more time together, just the two of us. Part of me wonders if we would even be together if it weren't for the baby right now. Sure, Caleb said that he was trying to get his shit together before the baby bomb was dropped, but how much time would have passed before he just gave up completely? He's had to make a lot of changes to be with me. How long before he decides it wasn't worth it? Now, I have to worry that he's only here because of the baby. I know he loves me, but where were all of his heartfelt speeches before we fell apart?

While I love him for making it easy for us to get back together, I don't necessarily believe his motives. Caleb has sacrificed more than enough in his life. The last thing I want is for him to sacrifice his future just to do what he thinks is right by our baby. I saw his fake smile in the car today and heard his groan when we were called to the back. He can say whatever he wants to me, but I know that he feels obligated. He's a good guy. I don't doubt that for a second.

"Hey, I think we're supposed to wait back there," he says, wrapping his arm around my shoulders and kissing the top of my head. He leads me back to an empty waiting room, proving that he actually was listening to the nurse earlier.

No sooner than we sit down, a different nurse peeks her head around the corner.

"Ms. Erickson?" I immediately stand, but she continues to talk. "We are running a little bit behind this morning. It's going to be a few minutes, okay?" She kindly smiles, and I give her a quick nod before she's gone again.

I settle back down into my seat as Caleb picks up a parenting magazine and absently flips through it.

"We need to get married already," he says randomly with some emotion I can't pinpoint. Annoyance? Anger? Frustration? Whatever it is, it all leads to the exact same answer.

"Um, no we don't," I answer, quickly looking away.

"Excuse me?" he says entirely too loud.

"I said we don't need to get married. That is the very last thing we need right now."

"Are you fucking kidding me? You don't want to get married?"

"Wow, was that a proposal?" I ask sarcastically. We are in the middle of a doctor's office waiting room. This is definitely not the place to be having this conversation.

"Maybe," he responds with a blank stare aimed over my shoulder.

"You are such a romantic, Caleb Jones. Who knows? Maybe in few years, you can try that again." I've once again resorted to being a smartass.

"A few years?" He jumps to his feet and pushes a hand through his hair. "So let me get this straight. You don't want to get married?"

"No, not right now. Can you please calm the hell down?"

"What was all the 'you're it for me' bullshit then?

"You are it for me. What the hell is going on?"

"So let me get this straight. You love me, and I'm it for you, but you don't want to get married?" The anger—and if I'm not mistaken, fear—paints his face. "For Christ's sake, we're having a baby, Emma." The lack of my nickname suddenly makes me realize that this is really fucking serious, but he also just hit the nail on the head. *We're having a baby.*

"And?"

"Ms. Erickson, we're ready for you," the nurse calls from behind Caleb.

"Can we please talk about this later?" I whisper-yell, standing to head for the nurse.

"I've got to get out of here." He begins to walk away, but I grab his arm, stopping him.

"What is wrong with you? You can't just leave me here."

"I just got a really fucking bad case of déjà vu." He pulls his arm away and walks past the nurse and out of the room.

Stunned, I look around the room, trying to figure out what just happened. Did he really just walk out and leave me here alone? Yep. Completely alone.

"Ms. Erickson?" the nurse repeats, but I'm rooted to the ground.

I can't go in there alone. I needed Caleb to lean on, but he just walked out the door with no explanation. It was a fight. Not the end of the world. Yet here I stand, abandoned because Caleb needed to pout like a child. I don't think I have ever been so hurt in my life.

"Yeah, I'm ready." I walk forward to meet her. I'm so angry at him I can't even bring myself to cry.

Caleb

NO. NO fucking way am I doing this again. I will not, under any circumstances, beg another woman to marry me. Not even Emma, no matter if she is carrying my child. I will not be sucked into that black hole of heartache again. Once was way more than enough.

How is it even remotely possible for two people to talk as much as Emma and I do yet still be completely confused about where we are in our relationship? I may not have given her a proper proposal, but I sure as shit expected an overwhelming yes. I didn't really mean to propose at all, but if I have to listen to them call her Ms. *Erickson* one more time, I am going to lose my ever-loving mind. I told her a month ago that she was it for me, and I meant it. However, Emma obviously meant something completely different. I know we haven't been together long, but I know without a doubt, I want Emma to be my forever—just not enough to beg for it. I've been there and done that, and I'll never fucking go back.

Forty-five minutes later, Emma finally walks out of the doctor's office. The anger on her face matches my own.

"Take me to Sarah's," she says, climbing into the truck.

I try to respond calmly, but my voice is still raw from her rejection. "No. We are going home. We need—"

"I want you to listen to me very carefully, Caleb," she interrupts me while staring out the front window—not even bothering to look at me. "I will not argue with you. I will not debate this. I will not even pretend to entertain a conversation, explanation, or apology from you. I just experienced the scariest moment of my life alone because you 'needed to get out of there.' Did it ever occur to you to think about what I might need?

173

Because newsflash—I just needed *you*. You know what? Fuck it. Go home. I'll call a cab." She snatches open the door, and just as quickly as she got in, Emma gets out.

I don't have it in me to chase her anymore. For once in my fucking life, I don't want to have to fight for a future. Life's a struggle—I get that—but finding, loving, and marrying a woman should not be this damn difficult.

I watch as she paces the sidewalk in front of my truck for twenty minutes. I'm not about to leave her here, but I'm absolutely not willing to plead for her to come home. I'll make sure she's safe, but that's about all I have in me right now.

I instantly recognize the BMW that pulls up. Brett's tall body unfolds out then rounds the hood of my truck. He's got that fucking look in his eye. He's always pissed at me about something, but he can just take a number and get in line as far as I'm concerned today.

Brett leans in the passenger's side door. "You want to tell me why you are here sitting in your truck but Jesse just called me to come pick up your pregnant girlfriend?"

"Nope," I answer shortly, not taking my eyes off Emma as she heads for his car.

"Jones, I don't know what is going on with you two. This hot-and-cold bullshit has got to stop. You two are having a baby. This is bigger than Sarah. Whatever spat you two had—"

Just as Emma closes the door to his car, I swing my head over to face him. "I asked her to marry me, and she said no."

"Shit!" He begins cussing under his breath.

"I'm not doing this again. I'm not starting this cycle of hell all fucking over again."

"She's not Manda, Caleb," he whispers, looking back to make sure her door is really closed.

"No. She's carrying my child. It's worse," I say before putting the truck into reverse, forcing him to back away or get run over.

Emma

"SO YOU remember a few months ago when you two decided to get to-gether and I said I didn't want any part of it?" Brett says, climbing into the car.

"Not now. I called Jesse. I didn't expect her to send you."

"She had a class. But that's not what I was going to say. I'm glad she called me. I can actually fix this situation."

I bark out a laugh. It's going to take way more than anything Brett can provide to fix this.

"I'm pretty sure there is no magic fix for this one. He left me. That is more than enough to secure his spot on my shit list. I had a bad feeling about today. I was scared something was going to be wrong with the baby. I've been sick about it all morning, and he knew it too. Yet he still got his panties in a bunch over something stupid that could have been discussed at home and walked out, leaving me to deal with my fears completely on my own."

"Is everything okay? I mean, with the baby?" he asks, looking over with immediate concern.

It only intensifies the pain in my chest. Here is my ex-brother-in-law, worried about my baby, but Caleb didn't even care enough to ask in the two sentences we exchanged in his truck.

"Yeah, he or she is fine. Everything looked good and measured right on track. I was nervous for no reason, but he shouldn't have left me like that."

"No, he shouldn't have. That was a dick move. However, I heard he proposed."

I begin to laugh manically. "Is that what he told you? That he pro-posed? Now that's a fucking joke."

"He said he proposed and you said no." Brett looks over at me in confusion.

"Of course I said no. I'm not marrying him because he feels obligated because I'm pregnant. Oh, and let me tell you how he *proposed*." I put on my best deep asshole voice to mimic his. "'Emma, we really need to get married.' In the middle of a fucking doctor's office. It was so fucking ro-mantic my heart almost exploded out of my chest," I say sarcastically, rolling my eyes.

"Jesus Christ, Jones." Brett drops his head back against the headrest.

"So, yeah. Damn straight I said no."

"Would you have said yes if he'd done the whole one-knee-and-ring thing?"

"No! I'm sorry, but when I finally get married, I want the man to marry *me,* not because he feels like it's his duty. 'Oh, you knocked her up. Better put a ring on it.' This isn't 1950!" I scream, taking my frustration out on the completely wrong man.

"I hear you, Em. But I don't think you have the full picture. Caleb is my best friend, but Jesus Christ, he can be a pouty asshole when he wants to be. Just ignore that part until you hear his reasons. Has he ever told you about his relationship with Manda?"

I roll my eyes. Of course Brett is going to take Caleb's side. "I guess he's mentioned her a time or two," I say in a bitchy tone while looking anywhere but at Brett.

I wish he would just take me home already. *Home.* Do I even have one of those anymore? It used to be with Caleb, but I can't go back there tonight.

"Do you know about the part where he proposed to her almost daily and she always said no?"

My head immediately swings over to face him. "What?" I ask in disbelief. "I thought they were engaged?"

"Yeah. Manda agreed to marry him, but she would never set a date. She just wouldn't commit. It ate away at him. Then the night of the accident, she agreed to talk about it and possibly even set a date, but he lost her before they had the chance."

"Why wouldn't she commit?" I whisper.

"Oh, I have no idea, and neither does Caleb."

"Damn." I lean back, feeling a twinge of guilt, but only a twinge. That sucks, but what he had with Manda is very different than what we have.

"Yeah, it did a number on him. He always wanted a wife and a family, that whole white-picket-fence thing, but Manda just wouldn't settle down."

"That's not my fault though. I can't be expected to marry him just because she wouldn't. And I sure as hell am not going to accept him acting like a child at my expense either." The anger bubbles back up. And whatever guilt I did feel all but disappears.

"Shit, Emma. You are just as stubborn as he is. No, you don't deserve his bullshit, especially not right now." His eyes drop down to my stomach. "However, you do need to cut the man some slack. You struck a seriously painful nerve with him today."

I sit quietly, not responding. I don't know what to say. I'm sorry, but no matter what Brett says, I won't be made to feel guilty about this. I did nothing wrong. I love Caleb, but I refuse to let him take his issues with Manda out on me.

Brett finally starts the car and begins to pull out of the parking lot. "By the way, I think it's hilarious that you would think Caleb is noble enough to marry you just because you're pregnant. He's a good guy, but not that good. If he said anything to you about marriage, it's because he *wants* to marry you. That's a really big deal to him—as it should be."

"I'm not her," I say under my breath.

"Emma, no matter how much you try to avoid it, Caleb's past is going to affect you. He is who he is today because of his time with Manda. The same way I am who I am with Jesse because of my time spent with Sarah. Trust me. That was harder for me to accept than anyone else." This time, it's Brett who looks out the side window, seemingly lost in his past. A few seconds later, he continues. "He loves you, Em. Baby or not. Caleb wouldn't fight for you if he didn't."

"Yeah, he was really fighting for me today when he walked out on me."

"Sometimes you have to fight down the demons before you can help the angels," he says, causing the tears to spill over my eyes. "I wouldn't trade a single second of my life with Jesse, but that doesn't mean I don't still struggle with the way things went down with Sarah. Give him a break. I'm not telling you to forgive him. I'm just asking you not to give up on him."

"Are you happy?" I find myself asking.

"Extremely," he answers quickly and confidently.

"I know I've said it before, but I still stand by it—Jesse is amazing." I wipe away the tears from my face.

"You have no idea the depths of that woman's heart. And speaking of, I'm under direct orders to take you back to our place. She should be back by now. I think she's already got Kara and the entire chocolate section at Nell's on the way over too." Now this makes me smile.

"That sounds fantastic." I'm ready to change the topic. This is entirely too deep for us. Brett and I joke and laugh, not talk about the moments that will define our futures. "Hey, look! I've got ultrasound pictures." I drag them out of my purse.

He plucks them from my hand as he pulls up to a stoplight. "Aw, look! It has Caleb's black-and-white lines," he says with a laugh that has me joining him for a much-needed break from the heaviness.

"Thank you." I smile at him, and we both know that I mean it for more than just a ride home.

"Any time, Em. Any time."

Chapter
TWENTY-SIX

Emma

NOTHING HAS been the same since that day at the doctor's office. I stayed with Jesse and Brett for a night, then another night at my old apartment that I never even got to share with Sarah. But finally, I had to go back to Caleb's.

It's been three weeks, and with the exception of 'can you pass the salt' conversation, we don't even speak. It's awkward at best. I've cried myself to sleep more times than I can even count over the last few weeks, and if it weren't for Sarah, I would be gone. Hunter wants me to come home. Even Alex asked me to move back. I can't leave again though. He might have been able to leave me, but I won't take his child away from him. No matter how much he doesn't want it. Caleb may not be on my list of favorites right now, but I'll still love him eternally. I don't even have a choice about that.

I'm not used to these feelings of insecurity and vulnerability. I've never been like this about a man before. I've also never been pregnant before either. It's more than that though. Pregnancy might be expanding the seven hundred emotions, but they all have the same origin—a gorgeous man who's covered in tattoos and has the most brilliant blue eyes I've ever seen. The man who made me want to fight for forever. The same man who is too preoccupied to even realize that I'm still fighting for us.

Caleb stays gone almost every night until ten or eleven p.m. I was really worried at first, until one night when I was driving home from Kara's house and saw his truck sitting at the cemetery. And because insecurity is not a pretty color on me, I drove past and checked the following three nights in a row. He is always there. I don't want to be jealous. I said that I would always respect his past, but watching him run to her tears me open. I have given myself a million pep talks in the mirror about how strong I am and how every single moment of this self-imposed separation from Caleb shouldn't be complete agony. I don't need him…right? But no matter how hard I try, I can't lie to myself. *This is absolute hell.*

As my eight a.m. alarm begins buzzing in my ear, I silently beg for the clock to turn back an hour. I need to get up and meet with a Realtor. Jesse found a lead on a building near Nell's, the coffee shop where she used to work. I need a studio so I can really expand my business. But damn, I'm exhausted. I fell asleep fully dressed last night after a four-hour-long photo shoot for the local college. I hit the snooze button, but as soon as I doze back off, my phone begins to ring.

"May I please speak to Emma Erickson?"

"That's me," I say, desperately wanting to roll back over and go to sleep.

"Hi, Emma. This is Lynn, Dr. Parker's nurse. I was wondering if you would be able to come in this morning for an ultrasound?"

"Huh?" I ask, sitting up and rubbing the sleep from my eyes. "Why this morning? My next appointment isn't for another week."

"Yes, I'm aware. However, your blood work we took last week has a few unexpected markers. I'm sure it's nothing, but we would love if you could come in and let us take a look at your baby. You haven't had an ultrasound in several weeks. We would like to check on the baby's heart now instead of waiting until your twenty-week appointment."

"Oh, God. Is something wrong?" I question as fear consumes me.

"No, I'm not saying that at all. All I am saying is your blood work came back with a few abnormalities. We would like you to come in this morning so we can take a quick peek and make sure everything is okay." Her words do nothing to reassure me.

Numbness overtakes my body. This may not be the most expected pregnancy, but I unquestionably love my baby, and I know somewhere deep down Caleb does too. My heart begins to race as I rub my small bulge. My mind frantically tries to think of every possible outcome, but I feel like I'm in the dark. I don't even know what 'markers' are, but based on this phone call, I know they terrify me.

"I'll be there as soon as possible."

I ARRIVE home, walking on cloud freaking eleven (nine isn't even high enough today). I'm still mad at Caleb, and I hate that he wasn't there for me again today, but I didn't feel comfortable enough to ask him to come to the appointment with me. I was too scared that he would say no. I couldn't handle his rejecting me this morning, so I went alone instead. Apparently, those 'markers' the nurse mentioned on the phone were indicators of several possible birth defects. I can't thank God enough that they didn't tell me that until *after* they told me that our baby looked okay. However, the sense of relief I felt in that moment still has me reeling. So what did I do? I went out and spent a hundred bucks on groceries and cooked a huge-ass steak dinner to celebrate.

When Caleb walks in, I could care less that he is still a selfish prick. I just want some company at my party.

"Hey!" I shout across the loud music blasting from my iPad.

"What are you doing?" he asks, obviously bewildered.

"Dancing!" I spin in a circle that would have had him laughing his ass off weeks ago.

"Well, can you turn it down? I need to do some work and get some sleep," he replies, absolutely dumbfounding me.

"What happened to you?" I snap in his direction. "Where did the funny guy that I fell in love with go? You are always just a fucking dick now, Caleb."

"You want to know what happened, *Emma?*" The cold chill of my real name rolling off his tongue makes me flinch. I'm always Emmy or sweetheart, but for the last few weeks, I've just been Emma. "I asked you to marry me and you said no." He pauses for a beat before roaring, "I won't beg another woman to marry me!"

"You wouldn't have to beg if I thought it was really me you wanted to marry!" I scream right back at him. "I'm not Manda!"

"You don't get it." He begins to walk away.

"And here we are again. You get pissed and walk away. Am I responsible for your baggage with Manda? Jesus Christ. Look at us, Caleb! We live under the same roof, but that is all. Well guess what? Denial doesn't change the fact that there will be a baby here in few months. Damn it, Caleb. Grow up! At some point, you have to let go and start healing. I have no idea what the hell happened at the doctor's office, but is it worth all this?"

"Oh don't give me that, Emma. You ignore me just as much as I do you. This is the first time you have spoken to me in weeks, and it's only so you can bitch about what a dick I am."

"Can you blame me? I cry myself to sleep every night while you sit completely unreachable only fifteen feet away. Well, that is if you are even home."

"What the hell is that supposed to mean? I always come home. It's not like I'm out trolling the bars."

"I know you go to Manda's grave every night. Avoiding me and our life together in the here and now, all while engrossing yourself in the past. I swore I would never have an issue with your past, but up until now, you have never made me feel like the other woman. However, despite all of that, I'm still standing here because I fucking love you, and we have a child, even if you do avoid it at all costs."

"We don't have a child yet, so stop acting like it's toddling around in the den while I ignore it," he responds so fast it makes my head snap.

"Oh really? We don't have a child yet?" I stand up from the chair and pull my dress shirt tight against my stomach. "What the hell do you call this then?" I rub my rounding belly. I walk over to my purse, remove this morning's ultrasound picture, and slap it down on the table. He stares for a minute at the image but doesn't make a single move to pick it up. "Because I call that *your son.*"

I can't take it anymore. I turn and walk away, leaving Caleb and an "It's a boy!" ultrasound picture alone in the kitchen. *Fuck him for ruining this for me.*

Caleb

I CAN hear my pulse in my ears as Emma storms off, leaving me with the weird black-and-white image of our…son? I can't even begin to contain my rage as I stomp down the hall after her.

"You found out the sex of the baby today without even telling me you had a doctor's appointment?!" I stop at her—our—bedroom door.

"After the way you acted last time, I didn't exactly think you would care," she smarts back while slipping off her shoes and sliding on her favorite flip-flops.

"Wow, okay. So are you just doing this entire pregnancy on your own now?"

"That's the way if feels." She turns away from me and takes off her dress shirt before pulling on her favorite T-shirt.

"Well I sure as hell can't be involved if you don't tell me what the fuck is going on. I'm not a mind reader."

She lets out a loud sigh but finally turns to face me. "Look, I'm sorry. They called me this morning saying I needed to come in. My blood work had a few markers for birth defects so—"

"What?" I interrupt as my face goes pale. Things might be rocky with me and Emma right now, but that is my baby she is carrying. I must look pretty worried, because for the first time in weeks, she steps up to hug me.

"No, it's fine. He's fine. The ultrasound ruled out any defects. It was just precautionary."

"Are you sure?" I ask as I release the breath I didn't realize I was holding.

"Yeah, I'm positive. We got the all-clear. He's perfect." She holds me tight around the waist. With the relief still sliding through me, I put my arms around her shoulders and pull her flush against my body.

We stand in silence, just enjoying the moment of closeness.

"Why do you go to Manda's grave?" she asks into my chest, not stepping away but not looking up at me either.

I sigh and try to find the answer. I'm not completely sure why. All I know is that it grounds me.

"I don't know," I tell her, and she quickly steps away, wiping under her eyes.

"I know things are shit with us right now, but it still hurts knowing you spend almost every night there." Damn. I didn't even realize that she knew where I was, much less that it hurt her. "If I'm being honest, it worries me." This is by far the most we have spoken since the day at the doctor when I tucked my tail and ran. And the fact that we are talking now is shocking the shit out of me, but Emma continues. "I feel like you are sliding backwards in this relationship. When we first got together, you were so ready to move on and start a new life, but now…I think you are using your past as a way prevent yourself from dealing with us—the present."

She's not right, but she definitely isn't wrong.

"Emma, the past is safe. It already destroyed me once. It can't hurt me anymore. Unlike you, who has the ability tear me to shreds over and over again. I go numb when I sit at her grave. The feeling I so tried to avoid all those years is the only thing keeping me sane right now."

"Right," she whispers, and I know that wasn't the answer she wanted to hear, but it's the only explanation I have.

When I first started going there, I told myself that it was nothing unusual. I was just visiting Manda. However, as the days passed and I spent more and more time sitting on the ground blankly staring at her name, it began to shut me down. And God, that was a welcome change from the emotional upheaval I have been in recently.

"I think I'm going to head to bed. I'll clean up the kitchen in the morning." She moves to slide back off her flip-flops and crawls into her— *our*—bed.

"Can we talk for a minute?" I ask, feeling helpless. It was only a flash of my Emmy when I walked in tonight, and then again when she hugged me, but it was amazing how such a brief touch immediately soothed me.

"You're not the only one who needs to feel numb these days," she says, and I can hear the tears in her voice. She turns away from me and curls into the bed.

I stand, watching her, the sound of her soft sobs floating through the room. I could just reach out to touch her, comfort her, and tell her that I love her. But I can't, because every time I look into her eyes, my heart completely breaks. Different woman. Same scenario. I want a family and a forever with her, but once again, I'm left holding on to another woman who can't commit.

"Please leave me alone," she says to the wall.

Without another word, I turn and walk out of the room, very gently shutting the door with a soft click behind me. Suddenly, I realize that I don't need to go to Manda's grave for the pain to take over. The slight crack in Emma's voice tonight was more than enough to hold me captive for weeks. I slide down the wall just outside her door. I drop my head to my hands and listen to her cry. The bite from the pain in my chest over-whelms me.

Yeah. This will do. This is actually fifty times more painful that vis-iting Manda.

Four hours later, long after Emma has fallen asleep, I get up and head to my makeshift bed on the couch, feeling more lost than ever.

Chapter
TWENTY-SEVEN

Emma

I MUST have cried for hours before finally drifting off. I love him. He loves me. We are having a baby. That should be the end of the story, but life doesn't work like that. Caleb and I have this invisible barrier between us. First, it was Sarah. Then, for a brief moment, it was Manda. But now, it's just Caleb.

I wonder if this is how Brett felt for all those years fighting for Sarah. She was right in front of him, but he couldn't touch her. For a moment, my imagination gets the best of me and I wonder if it weren't for the baby if Caleb would already be gone. I miss him so damn much. If only we could get through this turmoil, I know we could be happy together. I wish I could help him leave Manda in the past and once and for all escape the ghost of their relationship that haunts him. Suddenly, Jesse's words from weeks ago float through my mind.

"He told Sarah that, wherever his wife may be in the heavens, he would always love her, but he accepted that it wasn't her anymore."

Suddenly, a ridiculous plan to help Caleb forms. Will it work? Who the fuck knows. But I'll try just about anything to get him back.

I throw on some clothes and rush out of my bedroom. It can't be earlier than nine a.m., but when I run through the den, Caleb is lying on his back with one hand propped behind his head, staring up at the ceiling.

"Don't leave, okay?" I say to him while rushing to the door.

"What the hell are you doing, Emmy?" he asks, and the use of my nickname almost brings a tear to my eye.

A broad smile crosses my face, and I shake my head. "I love you. Like a lot." I lift my fingers a good six inches apart and hold them up in his direction.

He nods, biting his lip, remembering exactly what that means. "I love you, too." He coughs, clearing the frog of emotion from his throat.

"I'll be right back. Promise you won't leave."

"I'll always be here. Always, Emmy."

I smile once again and head out to my car.

Caleb

"WHAT ARE those?" I ask thirty minutes later when Emma comes rushing back in the door.

"Balloons," she says matter-of-factly.

"And what exactly are they for?"

"Therapeutic healing."

"Excuse me?" I try to figure out what the hell she's up to.

"You'll see. I have a few things I need to say to someone."

"Um, okay," I answer as she grabs the permanent marker out of the kitchen drawer and sits down on the couch. She pulls one balloon from the bunch, drags it into her lap, and begins to write.

"Here." She hands me a bright pink balloon with black ink scrawled over the outside.

Thank you for Caleb. He's amazing, and I know you had a hand in that.

I look up at her, confused, just as she hands me the next balloon.

Thank you for Collin. Without you, he wouldn't be here. You gave me that. I'll never be able to thank you enough.

"Emma, what are you doing?"

She hands me yet another balloon.

Thank you for helping Sarah through this. She needs you and loves more than you will ever know.

And just when I begin to think Emma has completely lost it, she hands me her last balloon.

Manda, I didn't know you well, but I love you for all the things you have given me.

And that is when it hits me—she's talking to Manda via balloons.

"No," I whisper as my voice catches.

"Caleb, you can't stop me." She stands, snatching the balloon strings from my hand and heading out the front door.

It might seem ridiculous. I know she isn't really talking to my dead fiancée, but that doesn't mean I won't try to stop her from releasing those balloons.

"Emma!"

"Shut it, Caleb! I'm doing this and it's long overdue. She has given me more than I can ever thank her for, so damn it, I'm sending her four balloons." She wipes a tear from her eye and lets them go.

I watch helplessly as four pink balloons zigzag through the sky. It's more than I can take, and I find myself falling onto my ass in my front yard while they float out of sight. I'm not sure if it's the words written on them or the very idea of Manda actually receiving them that has me in a panic. I can almost see her face when she reads each one. The bright smile I know she would be wearing and the breathtaking laugh that would be sure to follow.

"Here." Emma appears at my side, holding out the black marker and six pink balloons and two white ones. "Get busy. You have a lot stuff to say. Let me know if you need more balloons." I begin to argue, but I can't get a word in. "Caleb, it needs to be said. You have people depending on you, and it's not Manda anymore. The pink ones are for her, and the white ones are for Sarah." My eyes grow wide, and she quickly amends her statement. "The old Sarah. The one who Manda and Brett loved. She's gone and you have things to say to her too."

"Emma…" I drift off because I've been an ass recently, and I know she deserves more. I stare at the swell of her belly, at my son, and know she's right. "I miss her," I finally admit, looking into her eyes.

"And that's okay, Caleb. I'm not asking you to forget her. But what isn't okay is you rolling around in your grief, pushing me away, and forcing me to do this pregnancy without you because of your issues with her. Sure, you might be present, but you aren't *here.*"

I lock my hands on top my head and let out a loud breath. "Sweetheart, no amount of balloons in the world is going to fix me."

"Maybe not, but a first step is better than no step at all." Her words make my heart ache.

"Emma, no matter how big of a dick I may act like, I love you and I love that baby. I just can't figure out how to let go of the past and embrace the future. I feel like I'm nailed down. The world keeps passing me by, but I am rooted without any way to let go."

"I know, so you better get to writing. I love you too, and that is the only reason I'm doing this. I need you, he needs you, and no matter what you think…you need us. Now, make sure this hurts like hell so you can truly let it fly away with those balloons." She turns and walks into the house, leaving me sitting alone in our front yard with a fistful of helium and a black marker.

I sit for a few minutes, trying to figure out how long I need to sit out here to make her believe I followed through with her elementary ploy, when suddenly a single bright red leaf blows across my foot. It's the middle of August in Chicago. There are nothing but green leaves on the trees this time of year, and while I know it's probably left over from last fall, blown from the yard of my neighbor who never rakes, I still take it as a sign from Manda. After uncapping the marker, I begin to write.

Four hours later and six pink balloons that are now more black than pink, I let them go and watch them float away, taking with them a huge weight off my chest. My words weren't all sweet and kind. Some of them were angry and even scathing. I've been pissed off for a long time, but you can't exactly take that out on the woman who lost her own life. However, you can't take it out on the woman you hope to spend the rest of your life with either.

I lie back on the rocky grass and stare into the midday sun, reminiscing over the days leading up to the accident and the ones immediately following it. It's been over five fucking years. I shouldn't still be gutted every time I think about the past. It may not have happened the way I wanted it to, but as I think about Emma sitting on my couch, probably drinking one of those nasty-ass smoothies she loves so much, I know I can finally move forward.

I reach over and pull away one of the white balloons I tied to the small bush in my flowerbed. As I look at the blank slate, I realize that this part is going to be harder than I ever could have imagined. I have hated Sarah for a long time. I can't muster anything to say to her. I think back on those last moments in the restaurant before Brett and I got called away. Sarah was always a little crazy…just like her sister…but she had a good heart before the accident. The four of us always had fun together, but remembering those happier times hurts like hell. Emma said to make it hurt. So sitting like a douche in the middle of my front yard, holding a single white balloon, I try to remember every silly moment of Sarah, Manda, and even Casey. It was always a blast when we were all together.

After a long day of strolling down memory lane, just as the sun sets, I pick up the marker and finish this whole stupid game. Using one of Sarah's white balloons, I send a final message up to Manda.

Manda, it took me long enough, but I think this will make you happy, and that might be the best reason of all.

I reach back, snagging the last balloon.

Sarah, I forgive you.

I rise to my feet, stretching my aching legs. Looking up, I whisper a final, "I love you," and let them go. I don't stand there to watch them fly into the sky. I have a woman and child inside who need me, and nothing will keep me from them ever again.

Fucking balloons.

Chapter
TWENTY-EIGHT

Caleb

I WALK back into my house hours after I walked out of it. I'm probably sunburned all to hell and back, I'm starving, and I need water something fierce, yet I only have one thing on my mind. I rush through the house, turning off the lights and locking the doors as I go. Finally, I reach *our* room and gently push the door open wide.

"Hey, you," she says when her eyes immediately jump to mine. She's sitting up watching TV, a million pillows propping her up

"I'm going to kiss you," I start, and her eyes go wide. "Then I'm going to make love to you." Her smile slides away as heat immediately fills her face. "And then we are going to make plans to spend the next one hundred years together."

Just as quickly as it fell, her soft smile returns.

"You always do make good plans."

"I'm sorry. I don't think I'll be able to say that enough. I pushed my own personal shit on you when you needed me. I'm so fucking sorry, Emmy."

Her lip begins to quiver, but she bites it to hold back the tears. "It's not all your fault. I might be a tad hormonal and have taken that out on you...a little bit."

"A tad?" I smirk and walk over to sit on the edge of the bed. I reach out and wipe away her tears before cupping my hand against her cheek. She sways into my touch. "I'm sorry." I repeat.

"You really are an ass, but I've missed you."

And that's it. I push my mouth against hers for an emotional kiss. One by one, I pull the pillows out from behind her until she's flat on the bed. I strip away the blankets and step back just to look at her for a minute.

Stunning—that's the only word I can use to describe the vision that lies before me. What I did to deserve her and the little boy growing in her belly, I will never understand. Emma was right. I need her. But right now, I really need to be inside her. The emotions buzzing around inside me are enough to make a man go crazy. I just need to show her—make her feel it too.

Grabbing the top of her yoga pants, I slide them down her legs. I take my time on the way down to appreciate her body—to appreciate her. She's quiet and still, which is a little unnerving. Emma is always playing for the upper hand in the bedroom—always trying to capture control.

"You're not going to argue with me? No smartass comments?"

"Not tonight." She lifts her hips off the bed as I hook my fingers in her panties and drag them down her legs.

"Nothing?" I ask again.

"No. I have a suspicion you need to do this one your way." She reaches out and rubs a hand up my arm.

Fuck. I love this woman. I look away long enough to man up when the emotion of her words overwhelm me. Life gave me a second chance, and regardless of how many times I almost screw it up, Emma is always there to help me pull it back together. I don't deserve her, but I'm going to selfishly keep her for the rest of my life.

Sliding my eyes back to hers, I'm met with a staggering combination of lust and love. I crawl onto the bed beside her and push her T-shirt up and over her head with one hand. Letting my eyes travel down her body, I stop at the small bump of her stomach. Over the last three weeks, Emma has really popped. Gone is her perfectly flat stomach, but in its place is something even more amazing. It's still so surreal to me that my son is growing in there. I run my hand tenderly over her bump, bending to place a small kiss near her belly button. I hear her whimper and my eyes immediately flash to hers, finding them full of unshed tears.

"What are you thinking right now?" I ask, sitting up to cup her cheek.

"I'm thinking I need you to be real this time. That I can't do this drama with you anymore. I want you to be my life, but I have to be yours. I'm sorry if you feel trapped because of the baby, but—"

"What?" My head snaps back as if she slapped me.

"I just love you and—"

"Emmy, I think you're confused about some things. I'm not trapped because of the baby. I want kids. I just wanted more time with you first. I'm not with you because I have to be. I'm with you because I will never in a million years be able to love someone the way I love you."

"I'm not afraid to commit. I'm not Manda. But when we do get married, I want it to be because were in love and want to spend forever together."

"Emmy, I love you and that has nothing to do with Manda or the baby or any other outside element you could possibly conjure up. I love you because you're smart and funny. You challenge me and call me on my bullshit. I'm sure that will one day get annoying, but for now, I fucking love it. You're quirky and artistic. Did I mention hilarious? Jesus, you make me laugh. I could sit here for hours and tell you why I want to marry you, and not a single one of them would have anything to do with that baby. People don't have to be married to have a baby."

Her cheeks flush to red as she lies naked before me. It's not from embarrassment at being exposed. No, this is Emma. She's excited.

I lean in and press my lips softly to hers. She tries to deepen it, but I pull away slightly and peck her lips a few more times. I climb off the bed and get rid of my clothes, never for a second tearing my eyes away from hers. I move back over her body and position myself between her thighs. I can feel the heat from her core, and it makes my mouth water. This is more for me though. This is a way to show her how deep I am in it with her. Even if she never wants to get married, this is it.

I slide inside her, bending down to capture her moan with my mouth. That's my girl. She's always ready for me, and tonight, even despite our issues, is no different. She's so wet and warm, and it feels like home. I slowly find my rhythm, letting all the emotions take over.

Grabbing my ass, she tries to encourage me to go faster—begging and pleading with me to fuck her.

"Stop," I breathe into her mouth.

"Please, faster. Fuck me harder, Caleb," she demands, showing me a quick flash of the woman I'm used to. But it's so much more than fucking for me this time. She was right, I need to do this one my way.

I lift her arms up over her head and pin her wrists together between my hand, holding her in place while I work her body with my cock. She wiggles and squirms beneath me. She may want it fast and hard, but tonight, she's getting it slow.

"Tell me you're mine." I lean down and suck her nipple into my mouth. I graze it with my teeth as she arches her back up off the bed. I said slow—I didn't say I wouldn't be rough. I can at least give her that. I work my hips around in a circle but never pick up speed.

"I'm yours," she says, thrusting her hips off the bed as quickly as she can. I still completely, and she drops her head back against the bed, releasing a frustrated growl.

"Tell me you'll marry me," I boldly ask. I'm hopeful that she'll say yes, but it won't destroy me this time if she doesn't.

"Are you asking me to marry you in the middle of having sex?" she asks sarcastically.

"It's my favorite place in the world. It just seemed right." I toss her a smirk, and she laughs, rolling her hips to resume her earlier movements.

"Tell me you would have still proposed today, right now, even if there was no baby."

"I can't do that."

Her hips still against the bed. "Then the answer is still no."

"If there was no baby, you wouldn't have said no at the doctor's office, but if it wasn't for the baby, we wouldn't have been at the doctor's office, so let's go back a little further. If there wasn't a baby, I wouldn't have flown down to Savannah when I did and we might still not be back together." She rolls her eyes at my logic, but I begin my slow rhythm inside her once again. "You can't play the what-if game, sweetheart. You can only look at the now. And right now, I'm telling you that I love you and want to spend the rest of my life with you."

"Caleb."

But that's all she says, because I suddenly quicken my pace inside her, giving her exactly what she wants—and needs.

Bringing my lips back to her mouth, I claim what's mine. I don't care if she marries me anymore. She is absolutely mine.

Emma moans my name as she gets close to the edge. Her legs squeeze me tighter, and I gently bite the lobe of her ear.

"Let go, Emmy. Just let go... I've got you."

And with this promise whispered in her ear, she falls apart around me. One last thrust and I make good on my word and follow her off the edge. Going still and holding her tight against me, we both come down from bliss. I raise myself up and look in her eyes. The tears I saw before are still slowly trailing down her face.

"Hey, what's wrong?" I ask softly, slightly alarmed.

"It's just that you are really bad at proposals."

"It would appear that I am," I respond, causing her to laugh.

"Happy tears," she explains, pointing to her eyes.

I smile and kiss the tears on each cheek before lightly pressing my mouth to hers. I bring my hand to her face and tuck a stray hair behind her ear.

"I love you. You have put up with all my shit, but swear to you that I will do everything in my power to always be the man you deserve. We don't have to get married. This is enough."

"Well, that's a shame, because I was just about to say yes."

"Emmy," I warn before I get my hopes up.

"Let's get married, Caleb."

"Stop," I whisper, dropping my forehead to hers.

"I'm serious. You're hot, and I'm about to get really fat. I figured I should snag you while I've still got it."

"Swear to me you're serious about this," I beg as my heart pounds in my chest.

"This is it, remember?"

"I fucked up the proposals, but I swear I'll get everything else right. I swear, Emmy."

"No you won't, but that's okay too," she whispers, pulling me down for a passionate kiss that ensures I will be back inside her in three...two..."Fuck, Caleb."

One.

Chapter
TWENTY-NINE

Emma

"ARE YOU ready?" I shout across the house.

"I've been ready for three hours!" Caleb shouts back.

"It's not my fault that maternity clothes are hideous!"

"Hurry up, Emmy."

I sigh, staring in the mirror, pulling down my fitted dress over my large belly. I look like a sleepy cow on my wedding day. *Fantastic!*

It's been two months since Caleb and I got 'engaged.' He went out and bought a ring the next morning while I was still sound asleep. I woke up to him sliding it on my finger. He never exactly asked me to marry him, but I still said yes.

Today is the day we agreed to get married. I figured Caleb would have rushed me to the courthouse as soon as I accepted, but I was actually the one who had to pin him down to pick a date. I thought for a brief second that he was having cold feet, but he just smirked and picked a random date off the top of his head. It ended up being in the middle of the week, but we decided just to stick with it.

Today, in front of court-appointed witnesses while six months pregnant, I will become Mrs. Caleb Jones. Not even a year ago, I would have laughed my ass off if someone had told me I was going to be in this situation today. It's been quite the ride, but I've never been more ready for anything in my life.

"Let's do it!" I say, walking into the den, only to come to a screeching halt when my eyes find Caleb. He's wearing dark washed-out jeans, a white button-down with the sleeves rolled up to show off his amazing tattoos, and a simple black tie.

I will not have sex with him. I will not have sex with him. I will not have sex with him.

"Take your clothes off."

"You first," he says with a wicked smile.

"Jesus, you look hot." I walk over and straighten his perfectly straight tie.

"I look like a hobbit standing next to you." He kisses my lips with the gentle brush, refusing me the full connection he knows I'm longing for.

"I love when you lie to me like that," I mumble against his lips.

"Let's get out of here, Ms. Erickson."

Caleb has been calling me this for weeks now. It used to kill him to hear my last name, but ever since we set a date and he knows it's going to change, he can't seem to say it enough.

The courthouse isn't exactly a long drive from our house, and I'm thankful for that when nerves take root in my stomach. I have no idea why I'm nervous, because I've never been more sure about anything. Caleb and I agreed that today would just be us. We made plans to have Jesse and Brett, Kara and whatever random guy she is dating, and even Eli and Casey join us for a cookout at our house to celebrate this weekend.

We don't talk a whole lot about Sarah anymore. He knows when I go visit her, but he never has a single word, negative or positive, to say about her. It's almost like she is a person he has never even met. To say the least, it's really fucking weird for Caleb not to have an opinion.

"I got us a room at a bed and breakfast for the night," Caleb announces as we park in front of the Steel House. "Those are kind of Southern, right?" he asks with a huge glowing smile.

"Why? We live like two miles away?"

"Because I'm marrying the love of my life and she insisted on not having a wedding, so I felt the need to waste some money on a hotel room." He leans over to kiss me. I try to dodge him just for fun, but he grabs the back of my neck, sealing his mouth over mine.

After Caleb is done with his mini make-out session in his truck, he hands me a key.

"I love you. More than anything. You know that, right?" he says, holding my face. He uses one hand to stroke across my cheek and his other hand to rub my rounded stomach.

"Yeah, I know that." I suck his bottom lip into my mouth, roughly dragging my teeth across it before releasing.

"Mmm, sweetheart, you better get your ass into that room before I change my mind."

"About what?" I move even closer into his body, causing him to growl.

Suddenly, he opens his truck door and scoops me up, placing my feet on the curb.

"Go!" He points to the door then turns to adjust his pants. I have to laugh, but it only causes him to flash me a smirk that drenches me.

My dress is a long, fitted white maxi dress with a black sweater over it. It's simple—just like our non-wedding. I didn't bring a pair of spare clothes for tonight, and if I don't want to have to change my panties, I should probably go inside.

I blow a kiss over my shoulder and head into the ritzy house. The kind lady at the desk points me toward our suite, and I head straight inside, dropping the old-school metal key in the bowl in the entryway. I look around the lavish room Caleb has had decorated with dozens of orange roses. I pull my phone out to text him when I hear a familiar voice from the other room.

"About time you showed up!"

My heart stops and those fucking hormonal tears immediately spring to my eyes.

"Sarah?" I round the corner to find my sister sitting with her feet kicked up on the coffee table, drinking a glass of faux champagne, and eating chocolate-covered strawberries while watching Judge Judy.

"Hey, preggo," she says, standing to greet me.

"What the hell are you doing here? I mean…how are you here? Wait, are you even allowed to leave that place? Did you escape?" My concern only serves to make her burst out laughing. She falls down sideways on the couch next to her and laughs it out for a full minute before sitting back up.

"Jesus, that reaction alone was worth the deal I made with the devil just to be here." She smiles, wiping under her eyes.

"What are you doing here?" I repeat.

"It's your wedding day."

"I didn't think you were allowed to leave Building Foundations for another six weeks?"

"I'm not, but your little fiancé pulled some of his cop strings and got me a day pass. No worries. There is a uniform planted at the front desk in case I get squirrely." Her voice is filled with sarcasm.

"Sarah!"

"I'm kidding. Stop." She walks over to stand in front of me. "I'm not going to lie. I'm not sure how I feel about you marrying him, but given this basketball you are smuggling, I don't think I have many options."

"I'd marry him even without the baby," I declare just so she knows that this isn't a union based on our reproductive progress. I'm marrying Caleb because I'm pretty sure the world would crumble under my feet before it ever let me walk away from him again.

"I hate him," she states boldly.

This isn't the first time we have had this conversation, but it is the first time she has been so blunt about her feelings. This is definitely my older sister Sarah and not at all this new woman she claims to be.

"I also believe he's a really good and honest man." My head snaps up to meet her eyes. "If he wants to marry you… Well, you could definitely do worse than Caleb Jones." She shrugs, and I tackle her.

We are both careful with my belly, but we laugh hysterically while rolling around and wrestling on the hotel floor. A few minutes later, she helps drag my pregnant butt back up off the floor.

"There's a note for you over by the door. I swear I haven't read it…more than twice." She winks, pulling a pillow over her lap on the couch.

Emmy,
I know I didn't do the proposal right, but I wanted to at least make today special for you. Everyone deserves to be surrounded by family, no matter what. We aren't getting married until four, so enjoy the time with your sister. I'm just down the hall if you need anything.
I love you,
Caleb

I stare at the note, reading it over and over again until Sarah finally interrupts my thoughts.

"He bought you a dress too. It's in the bathroom."

I jerk my head up. "You know he wasn't talking about just me needing family, right?" I ask, because to me, it's painfully obviously why Sarah is here. I love her, and I love that she's here, but even Caleb knew that she would want to be here to watch me say I do. "He did this for both of us," I choke out.

"And that is why I've labeled him a good man today."

She tries to play it cool, but her eyes still gloss over with unshed tears. We both try to restrain the emotions. Erickson women don't cry. Oh, who the hell am I kidding? Between the two of us, we have cried the likes of Lake Michigan over the last five years.

I try to change the subject. "What's the dress look like?"

"It's hideous. Some summery orange and white number."

"What the hell is wrong with you? That sounds gorgeous." I rush toward the bathroom as she rolls her eyes.

I pull the garment bag off the hanger to find a floor-length white cotton sleeveless dress with a plunging V-neck. *Yep. Caleb definitely picked this.* Sure, it's going to show off a fair amount of cleavage, but the real drama is at the bottom. Just below my knees, the white fades into bright orange. I can't even put into words how much I love it. It's different, but stunning. Just like my man.

I whip out my phone and immediately text him.

Me: Thank you. Thank you. Thank you.
Caleb: I love you and you are very welcome. Now, stop texting me and hang out with Sarah.
Me: What room are you in? I want to come say thank you.
Caleb: I'm with Brett and Eli smoking cigars on the roof deck. You should probably thank me tonight.
Me: Oh God, does Brett know Sarah's here?
Caleb: Yes, now stop with the million questions and have fun. Lunch will be up in an hour.
Me: I love you.
Caleb: I love you too, Emmy. Always.

Caleb

"WAS THAT Emma?" Eli asks, pulling a puff off one of the cigars he brought.

"You ever see Caleb wear a shit-eating grin that big and it isn't because of Emma?" Brett says sarcastically.

"Shut the hell up, asshole." I play with my phone while trying to get rid of the big-ass smile I can't seem to wipe away today.

"What'd the ole' wife have to say?" Eli asks.

"None of your damn business. However, she was worried about whether you knew Sarah was here or not," I say to Brett, who is quietly puffing on his cigar.

"As long as I don't have to deal with Sarah's bullshit and Jesse isn't within a twelve-mile radius of her, I told you, I'm cool with it."

"Yeah, I know."

"How are *you* doing with Sarah being here?" Brett asks, turning the tables on me.

"It's weird. But I knew how happy it would make Emma, so it's worth it. I can promise you one thing. There will be no alcohol or car keys anywhere near those two today. I'm not risking anything with her."

I'm trying to let it all go with Sarah—really fucking trying. And to a point, I've been successful. Her memory doesn't eat away at me like it used to, but forgiveness isn't a cure-all either. I'm more than willing to admit that it does ease the burn though. Hate is a painful emotion to keep alive for any period of time.

I turn my attention to Eli. "So what's up with you and Casey?"

"She's Casey," he answers with a shrug.

"You two doing it for real now that she moved back to town."

"I am, but I don't think she is," he says shortly.

"Well don't puss out and let her go this time."

"Yeah, sure. Just like you didn't let Emma go?" His tone is sharp, and it's obvious I've struck a nerve.

"Hey, I'm getting married today. Obviously we figured it out."

"Well I'd appreciate if you keep your mouth shut about shit you don't know anything about. Not everything can be figured out." He stands up and heads to the rooftop bar, leaving Brett and me staring at each other with wide eyes.

"Damn. She's really fucking him up," Brett whispers.

"Nothing new there, my man. She's been screwing with him for years now."

A few minutes later, Eli walks back over with three beers, handing one to each of us.

We sit in comfortable silence just watching the world around us.

"Did you ever think we would be here?" I find myself saying out loud. "I mean, in those dark days after the wreck, could you have even imagined being in a place this good again? I'm about to get married and have a baby on the way, Brett's about to propose, and Eli has another chance with Casey. That wreck fucked us all over, but somehow we have all pieced together the crap we were handed and made something better."

I look up to catch Eli and Brett looking down at their beers, seemingly lost in the past. However, for the first time in years, I'm not there with them. I'm getting married to Emma Jane Erickson today. You couldn't drag me out of the present if you tried.

Chapter
THIRTY

Emma

IN A white-and-orange dress and with my sister at my side, I officially became Emma Jones. Caleb and I agreed to wait until the real wedding after the baby was born in order to write our own vows, but he still surprised me with a few sentences about how much he loved me. It was really sweet, and of-freaking-course I cried.

Sarah and Caleb didn't even acknowledge each other at the courthouse. They didn't speak, but it wasn't really all that awkward either. Just having them in the same place at the same time meant the world to me.

"You really have to go?" I ask Sarah as we stand outside the courthouse. Caleb walked away to make a few phone calls. I'm sure he was calling his sister and the rest of our gang to announce that we have officially tied the knot.

"Yeah, I need to get back before six," she says, pulling me into a hug. "I'm really glad I got to be here today."

"Me too." I squeeze her tight. "Hey, and only a few more weeks before they start letting you come home on the weekends."

"Oh goodie. Just in time to listen to you complain about your swollen ankles and heartburn," she teases while rubbing my belly.

"See you on Wednesday?" I yell as she walks over to the unmarked police car that escorted her here.

"You know where to find me!" she shouts back.

God, it is so good to see her finding herself again. She actually seems happy these days. A feeling I know all too well.

"Hey, beautiful," Caleb whispers behind me, wrapping his arms around my stomach.

I turn in his arms, which is not exactly the easiest feat these days. "Let's go back to the hotel and make this whole thing official." I nibble at his neck.

"I'm starved. Can we stop and grab some dinner first? And then go back and really grab dinner?" He rolls his hips into mine.

"Mmm, I could eat too." I wink up at him as we stroll down the sidewalk. "How come your sister didn't come to the ceremony too? You know I wouldn't have minded."

"I wanted it to be just us today, but I knew you would want Sarah there. So that, my love, is what you call a compromise."

"Compromise? What the hell happened to my asshole boy—I mean, husband?"

"He took the day off," Caleb says, stopping in front of a little Italian restaurant. "Come on. We should probably carb load for the bedroom marathon I have planned for tonight."

He gives me a half smile that sends flutters down to my core.

"Mr. and Mrs. Jones," he tells the hostess with pride.

"Right this way." She grabs two menus and leads us past a ton of empty tables to a back room that has a curtain separating it from the rest of the restaurant.

"Go ahead." Caleb pulls back the curtain and guides me inside.

Sitting at a long rectangular table is every person I think I know in this world. My eyes slide down as they take in the smiling faces looking back at us.

Brett, Jesse, Kara, Eli, Caleb's sister Lindsey and her wife Deena, Alex, and—

"Hunter!" I squeal as he rises to his feet and heads in my direction.

"Emma Jane Jones. Holy shit! You really did it." He pulls me in for a hard hug.

"You are such a liar! You said you couldn't make it up here this month."

"Well it wouldn't have been a very big surprise if I'd told you I was going to be here." He leans forward and kisses my forehead like he always does.

I swing my head around to face Caleb, who is watching us. His arms are crossed over his chest with his left hand on top. He's mindlessly spinning his new tungsten ring with this thumb, and instead of the glare I was expecting him to be shooting at us, his face is painted with a warm look of contentment.

"How long have you been planning this?" I ask Caleb, stepping away from Hunter.

"Since about ten seconds after you told me you wanted to get married at the courthouse," he answers, reaching a hand out to catch me.

"I love you," I say quietly as he tugs me against his side.

"Good, because you're stuck now." He lifts my hand and plants a kiss on my wedding ring.

As my eyes drift around the eloquently decorated room, I catch sight of a small three-tiered cake in the corner. "You got us a wedding cake!"

"My baby loves cake. Of course I got one." He rubs a hand over my stomach and around to my back, pausing just before it drifts down to my ass.

"Which baby?" I ask teasingly.

"Both. Now heads-up—here comes Brett and he looks happy as hell."

I turn around just in time to crash into Brett's arms.

"Congrats, Em. You finally made an honest man out of him."

"I know. I'm really excited to finally lose my virginity."

At first, he curls his lip. Then he bursts out laughing. "I can tell." He glances down at my swollen belly.

After that, each person heads our way. Caleb's sister claims him and Kara grabs my hand, pulling me aside.

"You are a bitch!" she whisper-yells at me while standing on her toes and peeking over my shoulder.

"Excuse me?"

"I thought we were friends? But it's obvious you don't like me at all!" She flashes her wild eyes back to mine.

"What the hell are you talking about?" Kara is off-the-charts crazy, but even this behavior is strange for her.

"Your two best friends are gorgeous guys and you didn't think to introduce them to me once. What is wrong with you?" she asks with the most serious look I have ever seen on a face outside of Caleb's.

I immediately try to stifle my laughter, look up, and try to match her tone. "You're right. That was very rude of me."

Aly Martinez

"How do you know them?" she breathes.

"Well, I grew up with Alex, and Hunter and I used to date."

Her head snaps over to me. "You lucky whore," she says before looking down and telling my stomach, "No disrespect intended, li'l man."

I can't help it. I have to laugh. Caleb's eyes fly to mine from across the room, and I wave him off.

"They are both single, so which one are you interested in?"

"Both. At the same time," she says with a dreamy gaze.

"That would be a maybe with Hunter and a hell no with Alex. Sorry, lady, but you're going to have to pick one."

"Hunter." She all but drools after saying his name.

"Excellent choice." I smile. "Hey, Hunt, can you look here for a second?" I call across the room.

"What's up, sugar?" he drawls, and I swear Kara moans.

"I've been rude. You may have already met, but I want to officially introduce you to my very, very good friend, Kara Reed."

Hunter tips his beer to his lips while sliding his eyes over her petite body. I glance down at my wedding ring and thank the Lord that I will never have to do the dating game again.

He tosses her a wink before saying, "Nice to meet you, again, Kara Reed. I'm Hunter Coy." He extends a hand with a very obvious twinkle in his dark brown eyes.

"Okay, well I need to get back to my husband. I'll catch up with y'all in a bit."

I leave as they continue to shake hands for entirely too long. But before I go, I have a little additional information for Kara. I lean in close to her ear and whisper one single word.

"Eggplant."

Oh yeah. She definitely moans this time.

I brush off my hands from a job well done and head back to my man.

"Hey, you." I cozy in close to Caleb's side.

"Hey, Emmy."

"This is perfect." I lean up for an all-too-brief kiss.

"Well, I told you I screwed up the proposal. I wasn't going to screw this up too. Besides, it's still small and intimate like we planned. I pretty much consider everyone in this room family."

"Thank you." I lean my head against his chest and loop my arm tight

206

around his hips. As I trace the tattoos on his forearms, with a dozen people chatting around us, the whole crazy world all ceases to exist.

Caleb

AFTER AN incredible night of lovemaking with my wife, I dragged Emma home at the crack of dawn. She groaned and whined, begging for me to just let her sleep. But I was almost as excited as a kid on Christmas.

See, I've lied to Emma a lot recently. And while I normally wouldn't be very proud of that trait, today I am damn near ecstatic.

"Jeez, Caleb! What the hell lit a fire under your ass this morning?"

"It's October first," I announce, pulling her out of the truck and into the backyard.

"And?" she asks, thoroughly confused.

"Your due date is in exactly four months. In less than one hundred and twenty days, I will meet my temporarily named son, Collin. By the way, I'm still holding out hope for something not so preppy." She playfully slaps my chest, and I smile huge, knowing what's to come. "So I realize we are not even twenty-four hours into our marriage yet, but I already have a confession to make."

"Is it that you have been secretly hiding a bed in the backyard? Because I could really use a pillow and, like, eight more hours of sleep right now."

"Jesus, Emmy. Talk about stealing my thunder. That is eerily correct."

"Which part? About the bed or the fact that I need more sleep?" she asks, looking up through tired eyes.

"Just give me a minute. I need to tell you a story." I dramatically clear my throat. "So back in February, I met this amazing woman, and even though I had no idea what to do with it, I fell in love with her damn near the minute I laid eyes on her. She was beautiful, but what really surprised me was the fact that she was smart and funny as hell."

"Caleb, are you cheating on me with this other woman? Because I'm not sure I could blame you—she sounds fabulous," she says teasingly.

I ignore her jokes but pull her against my chest, tracing my hands down her back and over her ass. "A few days after I met her, I realized I couldn't stop thinking about her. I tried so fucking hard because I had absolutely zero business being with her. So I began building a table that I had been plotting in my head for years. I used the finest Bubinga wood I could find on short notice. I spent every waking hour trying to forget her, all while building my dream table.

"Emma, this table killed me. Even the simplest of tasks turned out like crap. It had a million flaws, and no matter how hard I tried, I just made it worse every time I tried to go back and fix them.

"Then one night, just as I was finishing this annoying table, I got a phone call from that spellbinding woman, and when I picked up the phone, she was crying. It scared the ever-loving shit out of me. With that fear, I realized that there was no point fighting it. It wasn't the smartest decision to pursue her, but it was definitely the best one I've ever made.

"The next day, as I looked around my workshop, I realized that stubborn, flawed table that I finished, the night I decided that you were mine, really was us. I moved it into my house the minute the polish dried."

"What happened to it? I haven't seen it since I've been back." She blinks up at me while fighting back tears.

"I tore it apart it the night you sent back Manda's ring."

"Oh," she breathes in disappointment.

"See, Emmy, that wood was never meant to be a table. Our relationship is not simple or straightforward. It's not perfect the way young couples dream about. It's rough and flawed, but it's ours. And sometimes, if you get really lucky, something truly beautiful can come from the imperfections."

I release her and swing open the door to my workshop, revealing the crib I have spent hours upon hours working on over the last two months.

"Oh my God," she breathes, and tears immediately flood her eyes. She walks over to it, dragging her hands over the smooth curves and rounded edges. "Is this the table?" she manages to squeak out.

"Most of it. I had to add to it, but I used as much of the table as possible. And look." I walk across the room to my workbench. "I made shelves to hang on his wall from the extra pieces." I smile, and she covers her mouth and continues to cry.

"This is... I just... This is perfect. I love it. I don't even know what to say. I'm probably going to cry every time I look at this now. It's beautiful."

"Don't cry. I'm sure little Gavin will be doing enough of that for you pretty soon."

"You mean Collin, and he and I can cry together then." She wipes away the tears and heads over to wrap her arms around my shoulders. "When did you have time to do this?"

"You know all those bookshelves that I told you my buddy asked me to build?"

"You lied to me!" she shouts, but her smile never falters.

"It wasn't a total lie. He did ask me to build a bookshelf, but it was only one, and I told him I couldn't do it until I finished this project first." I smirk, and as usual, she immediately softens.

"Thank you for this, and for yesterday, and for including Sarah. Seriously, Caleb, it was better than any wedding we ever could have planned."

"You're welcome, sweetheart. You ready to go inside now and take a nap?"

"Suddenly, I'm very awake. See, I met this guy back in February. He is so freaking hot. And when he isn't acting like an ass, he does the sweetest, most romantic things for me. I kind of love him."

"Kind of?" I question with a raised eyebrow. "Because he sounds like a definite keeper."

"Yeah, you're right. I think I'll keep him," she says just before pressing her lips to mine in a sensual kiss.

Chapter
THIRTY-ONE

Emma

THE DAYS have been flying by since Caleb and I got married. It's been calm and peaceful and completely unnerving. Last weekend, Sarah came home for the very first time. True to his word, Caleb gave me a kiss on Friday and didn't give me one bit of grief about spending the weekend with her. He didn't exactly pack my bag or anything, but he didn't pout and complain either.

Between doctor appointments, decorating the nursery, continuing to build my photography business, the holidays, and just enjoying being married, I've been running at a full sprint for the last few months. With Christmas a few days behind us and just over five weeks before my due date, I need to slow down. I'm getting bigger and more uncomfortable, but there is too much stuff to be done. February is just around the corner.

I can't even believe Collin will be here soon. I still panic a lot about being a mom, but Caleb is cool as a freaking cucumber. I kind of hate him for it, but he spends his nights trying to keep me relaxed. He usually uses his body to do it. He's a giver like that. It has absolutely nothing to do with sex. At least that is what he claims.

In other news, Brett finally proposed to Jesse. A few weeks ago, he surprised her after her college graduation by renting out an entire bowling alley. It was adorable. Not as sweet as my surprise wedding and crib, but hey, not everyone can land their very own Caleb Jones. However, I think Jesse is still extremely lucky. Brett is a great guy, and no one in the world can miss how much he loves her.

Everyone was there when Brett finally got down on one knee—her family, his family, all of Jesse's friends, and surprisingly enough, Hunter Coy. It seems he has taken quite a liking to our resident vegetarian. He's been up here almost every other weekend for the last two months. He claims that it's just to visit me, but Kara is never far from his side.

Eli was even there too, but not surprisingly, Casey was absent. She and Eli are still dating—or something like that—but she never hangs out with us. I guess I can understand why. This group is a constant reminder of what she lost. It can't be comfortable to hang out with the men who used to love your best friends and the new women who have filled their lives while you're two best friends are gone completely. Hopefully Eli is understanding and doesn't give her crap about it. I've only heard from Casey twice since I ran into her at the coffee shop all those months ago. Once she called, but when I picked up, she said that she had the wrong number. We talked for a few minutes and she asked about Sarah. Call me Dionne Warwick, but I have a feeling it wasn't such an accident at all. A few weeks after that, Eli stopped by with his truck to pick up some barstools Caleb had made for a mutual friend. Casey waved but never even got out. Manda used to live here with Caleb, so again, I can't even blame her.

"You going to be away this weekend?" Caleb asks while we sit at the dinner table on Thursday night.

"Yes and no. Sarah asked if she could just be alone on Saturday night. So I was thinking maybe we could do like an old-school date night. I'll have to sleep at her place, but maybe you could pick me up, take me to dinner, make out in the truck for a little while, and then you can drop me back off afterward. Kiss me on the front steps then go home with blue balls. It will be just like high school again."

He barks out a laugh. "Wow. You even planned my blue balls. You've thought of everything. How could I possibly turn down an offer like that?"

"Okay, okay. Fine. If you take me to a fancy restaurant, I'll give you a hand job in the truck. But only because I love you and not because I can be bought with food right now."

"Oh God, please tell me you didn't give hand jobs after dates in high school."

"Caleb! Don't be ridiculous. You know I was a complete virgin when we met! I have never even laid eyes on another man's naked form other than yours," I lie innocently, batting my eyelashes. .

"I love you, Emmy, but I don't believe that for even one second. I'm getting hard just thinking about the way you expertly rode me that first night." He walks around the table and kisses my mouth before carrying my plate to the kitchen. "All that matters is that I'm the last naked man you ever see."

"I can't wait to not be pregnant anymore," I announce as he walks away. I want to have sex with my husband. The kind where it's rough and deep and you can't walk the next day. But the watermelon I'm carrying is not exactly conducive to sexy time.

"You're beautiful, so stop. There is plenty of time for dirty sex in the million years to come."

"Oh all right, I'll stop complaining. Does that mean we have a PG-13 date planned for this weekend?"

"PG-13?" He asks in horror. "You just offered me a hand job. Thank God we aren't having a girl, because I'm starting to worry about the cred-ibility of your rating system." I start giggling and stand to slide under his arm. "Yeah, babe. A date sounds great."

"SARAH, WHERE is your curling iron?"

"I don't have one. Why?

I walk out of the bathroom and into the den, where she is sitting watching some trashy reality TV.

"You don't have a curling iron?"

"Just use the straightener to curl the ends under."

"That won't work! I was going for sexy wind-tousled curls." I shake my head like a shampoo model.

"Oh good Lord. You are pregnant and going out on a date with your husband. Just don't wear yoga pants and I think he will be impressed."

"This is probably true, but I at least want to try and look nice. I'm going to run back to our place and grab mine. You need anything while I'm out?"

"Nope." She looks up with a smile.

"Hey, I'm really glad you're feeling better. I love having you home again." I pause at the door and look at her just casually sitting on the couch.

She looks so peaceful, not at all like the woman I saw in the counselor's office a few months ago. It's a shame that it took her this long, but I feel like she is finally finding herself again.

"Yeah, me too," she softly answers.

I race down the stairs, plotting how I can get in and out of the house without running into Caleb. I bought a cute long grey skirt and form-fitting pink shirt that fits over my big pregnant belly just for tonight. I don't look great but I feel better than I have in a long time. I want to surprise him, not run into him half dressed in our hallway.

Thankfully, when I pull up to the house, his truck isn't there. I'm digging through the bathroom cabinet, tying to be as sneaky as possible in case Caleb comes home, when my phone rings. I swear I must jump about ten feet in the air, because it scares me to death. I don't even have a second to glance at the caller ID before I'm pulling it to my ear.

"Hello."

"I want to see her," I hear Casey's broken voice say on the other end of the line.

"Who? Are you okay?"

"Sarah," she answers shortly.

"Well she's home this weekend. Maybe I can talk to her and get back to you to set up a time—"

She interrupts. "No, I mean today."

"Shit, Casey. I don't know. I need to talk it over with her first. She's doing really well, but I don't want to set her off—"

"Call her. Tell her I miss her and I want to see her."

"Casey—" I start, only to be interrupted yet again.

"Please, Emma. I'm begging you." Her voice breaks.

"Yeah, okay. Let me talk it over with Sarah. I'll call you back."

"Make sure you tell her I miss her. And call her Danika. Promise you'll do that," she says urgently.

"Yeah, of course. I promise." I quickly say goodbye and hang up.

I make my way to the den and flop down on the couch, wondering if this is a smart move at all. Sarah is doing so well, and Casey sounds desperate to rekindle something. This could definitely send Sarah into an 'I'm not the same person' tailspin. This has emotional breakdown written all over it.

But on the other hand, it would do Sarah some good to have some friends. She needs to be surrounded by people who love her, and that isn't just limited to me. I sigh to myself and pick up my phone. This should be her decision, not mine. I said from the beginning that I wasn't going to try to fix her. She is a grown woman who can make her own choices.

"Are you having another curling iron emergency?" she says jokingly when she answers the phone.

"No, Casey Black just called and she wants to see you…today," I blurt out. I mean, really. What's the point in sugarcoating it?

"Why?" she asks with an icy chill to her voice.

"Because, Danika, she says she misses you."

After I relay Casey's message, I fully expect Sarah to burst into tears from hearing whatever inside joke I just reminded her of. Instead, she starts quietly laughing.

"What do you think?"

I have to admit that this is the most shocking moment of the last five minutes. She asked for my advice.

"Are you asking what I think? Seriously?" I say in shock and disbelief.

"Ha. Ha. Seriously. You knew me before, and you know me now. Do you think Casey would be receptive to the changes?"

"Sarah, I love you. But I have to say it. Your tastes have changed, you don't drink anymore, and you have different hobbies. I'm not trying to minimize your *changes*, but deep down, you are the same Sarah Kate Erickson you have always been. Only now, you aren't stricken with grief and self-loathing. So dare I say this is the best Sarah Kate you have been in years?" I pause to allow her time to yell at me or argue with me, but it never comes.

"Bring her over."

"Are you sure?" I ask, once again stunned.

"Yeah. I could use a little Anastasia Beaverhausen in my life again," she answers.

I'm clueless about what the hell that means, but the lift in her voice lets me know she's excited.

"We'll be there soon."

Thirty minutes later, I'm sitting inside my car in front of Sarah's apartment. I decided to wait outside for Casey so I could have a little chat with her about Sarah before their reunion. Her Mercedes SUV finally rolls into the parking lot.

I walk over to where she parked. "Hey, lady."

"Hey, Emma," she says softly, climbing out of the car.

"So listen, I wanted to tell you a few things before we go in." I go straight to the point. It's freaking freezing outside, and snow is steady falling from the sky.

"Okay." She motions me to the breezeway to escape the weather.

"I'm sure you heard that Sarah suffered a head injury after the accident, but she's dealing with it. It's changed her a good bit. So if she acts a little different than you're used to, just don't mention it, okay? She's pretty sensitive about it." I try to rush out the abridged version of Sarah's medical issues before the wind and chill freeze us both into icicles.

"Yeah, of course," she answers, and we head upstairs.

I briefly remember my date with Caleb and know that I need to push him off a little while. He isn't going to be happy about it, but this is a really big deal for both Sarah and Casey.

Me: Something came up. Long story. Can we push dinner off an hour? I'll call in a few and fill you in. Love you.

I press send and walk into the apartment with Casey in tow.

Chapter
THIRTY-TWO

Emma

"YOU STILL watching that shit?" I ask Sarah as I walk through the front door.

"You still knocked up?" she responds with a huge smile as her eyes drift to Casey. It slowly fades as I turn to find Casey barely standing—her face suddenly pale.

"Hey, you okay?" I grab her arm and try to pull her down into the chair next to the couch. She bats my hand away, insisting to stand on her own two feet.

"I thought you were dead." The tears work their way through her entire body before finally falling from her eyes. "You weren't breathing, and you were so cold and still," she whispers.

"Casey, what are you talking about?" Sarah says, walking forward, but Casey throws a hand up, blocking her progress, knocking over the lamp on the end table in the process.

"She loved you," she chokes out, and we all know who the *she* is that she is referring to.

"She loved you, too," Sarah says back, drying her own tears.

The room is silent and more than a little awkward for a few minutes while the two old friends stand uncomfortably.

"I killed her," Casey blurts out, and for a minute, the world has been spun completely off its axis.

Sarah slings her eyes to me as I sling mine to Casey.

"You what?" I ask.

"I killed her," she repeats. "The wreck was my fault. I was driving. Oh God, I'm so sorry." And with that, Casey folds to the floor.

Sarah rushes toward her, and I immediately jump in the middle, more stunned than ever.

"No, you weren't. Shut your mouth! Shut your fucking mouth!" Sarah explodes over my shoulder just before sobs catch in her throat.

"I did it. And I thought you were dead too. I left you both on the side of the highway, cold and alone." Casey curls her legs into her chest and begins to rock.

"No, you didn't. You weren't even there that night," Sarah tries to state matter-of-factly, but it comes out as more of a plea.

"I killed Manda!" Casey finally screams, and it forces Sarah to her knees.

"No, you didn't. *You weren't there,*" Sarah cries, crumbling in my arms.

Casey never once raises her tone as she begins to explain. "I was out with Jason McAdams searching for more pills. You called and said you had too much to drink. You thought you could drive home, but then you weren't so sure. You pulled over at that gas station down the road from Westies. I was too ashamed to tell you I was high. And above and beyond that, I was too high to think logically. I had Jason drop me off with you. Then I got behind the wheel and drove Manda to her grave."

"No! No, no, no! *You weren't there!*" Sarah once again screams at an eerily calm Casey, who is still crying but staring at the floor.

"I was. None of this was your fault." The hopeless tone in her voice is alarming. It's painful to listen to, and it's even worse to know that she has been living this lie for all these years. My heart breaks for her and the whole damn group of innocent people this affected.

I can see the exact moment Sarah shifts from denial and rage and begins to rationalize her way out of this.

"Where'd you go? Where the fuck did you go, Casey? If you were there, someone would have seen you. It's not like you could walk home. I've been to that tree a million fucking times. You couldn't just walk away. Where did you go, God damn it?!"

"Eli was the first on the scene."

Sarah and I both suck in a huge breath at the implications of that statement.

"Eli wasn't there that night," I say softly. I asked Caleb this very question a while back. Eli was on duty, but he was off at a domestic disturbance call. According to Caleb's 'box,' Stephens was the first on the scene.

"No, he wasn't as far as anyone else is concerned, because he was driving me home. Sarah, I swear, we both thought you were dead. When Eli pulled up, I was wandering around high and desperate. It was obvious Manda was gone. Even in my haze, I could recognize that. But you—I tried to bring you back. I tried to help but you just wouldn't wake up." Casey's words are heart wrenching as she gets lost in her memories.

Tears openly fall from all of our faces as I distantly hear my phone ringing in the corner. Sarah and Casey might both be sitting on the floor, but I'm the only thing standing between them. I'm not about to move.

Caleb

"WHERE THE Fuck is she?" I begin to pace around the house Brett just bought without Jesse knowing.

"Chill out. She's fine."

"She's fine? Remind me to tell you that when Jesse is eight months pregnant and disappears."

"Jesus Christ, she didn't disappear. She texted you, like, thirty minutes ago that something came up."

"She also said she would call in a few minutes to update me, and now she isn't answering her phone. What if—"

"She's fine! If you're so worried about it, get the fuck out of here and go check on her."

"I'll look like a dick for checking up on her," I say, pacing the floor, but my mind is already made up.

"You *are* a dick. I think she's used to it by now. Go barge in on her drinking coffee with her sister, but let me know when you find her," he answers, dragging a tape measure up the wall.

"I'll just give her fifteen minutes. Maybe call her another dozen times," I say, absent of all humor. Realistically, I'll probably call her thirty times over the next fifteen minutes.

I peek out the window and look at the heavy snow falling on the fro-zen roads. *What if she's hurt or stranded?*

Fuck it. She can be pissed.

"I'm out of here." I yank open the door and head for my truck.

Emma

"I WAS all over the place when Eli got there. He put me in the back of his car to keep me from wandering away. He immediately went to work on you and Manda. Finally, he came running up to the car and sped away. I tried to stop him, but he said there was another car and ambulance a minute out and they would take care of you."

"Why the fuck would he have left us there? He could have saved her!"

"She was gone. The minute I hit that tree, Manda was gone. Her green eyes were wide open, looking at me when I found her." All three of us flinch at her painful memory, and Sarah throws a hand to her mouth as her stomach threatens to revolt. "Please don't blame this on Eli. He loved me. He knew I was high, and we both thought you two were gone. The plan was that I would go and turn myself in as soon as I sobered up, but when you didn't remember anything, I sat back and allowed you to self-destruct because I was too afraid to face the consequences." She sucks in a stran-gled cry.

"No. Please stop. Just stop," Sarah begs, remembering the night she has no memory of through Casey's words.

"I'm so fucking sorry, Sarah. I should never have agreed to drive you guys home that night. I sure as hell shouldn't have waited five years to tell you this. I was just…"

"Shut up," Sarah snaps at her. "Shut up, and never mention this again. This begins and ends here." Sarah wipes her tears on the backs of her sleeves and rises to her feet. I stand beside her, looking puzzled by her response but not willing to drop my guard. "As far as everyone is con-cerned, I was driving the car that night. It's over. Let it go."

"I can't do that. I honestly can't live like this for even a minute longer. I'm done. Being buried beside Manda would have to feel better than this."

"Casey. Don't say that." I try to stop where her mind is headed, yet once again, Sarah is the one who makes the real impression.

"I've lived with that guilt for years. I've tried to kill myself more times than anyone even knows. I've been burdened with the blame of this entire incident for entirely too long. I've lived it, owned it, and most recently moved on from it. I will be damned if I will sit by and watch you be publicly stoned for this. I've been there and done that. It fucking sucks. Just let it go. Please. You don't want to open this back up."

"I'm sorry." Casey again chokes on a sob.

"You still taking pills?" Sarah asks rationally, and I might even say levelheadedly.

"No! I swear. I had a problem for years before that night, and exactly one week after the accident, I checked myself into rehab in Ohio. It's been a long road of bouncing back and forth between sobriety, but I've been sober for three years and four months now. I'm done with that shit."

"Good. Then you've done your time. I've already been crucified. I won't let the same thing happen to you."

"Stop being nice!" Casey shrieks. "I kept this shit from you for almost six years. Hit me. Hate me. Berate me. Do something. But don't fucking be nice! I killed her. I fucking killed Manda! *Hate. Me!*"

I feel him long before I see him. An arctic breeze flows through the air just before his voice slides across the room.

"You did what?" Caleb asks, suddenly standing in the door way with a fire brewing in his eyes.

Chapter
THIRTY-THREE

Caleb

WHAT THE fuck is going on? I came up to the door and heard a woman screaming. Luckily it was unlocked or I would have torn the damn thing off the hinges to get to Emma. When I walk in, before I can fully assess the situation, Casey says words that cause my heart to still.

"I fucking killed Manda. *Hate. Me!*"

My eyes fly around the room trying to put the pieces together to somehow form a coherent thought. I can't see Casey's face, but I have no doubt it probably matches the tear-stained cheeks of Sarah and Emma.

"You did what?" I ask, and it's like a kindergartner with a globe gave the world one big spin. The room morphs into chaos. Sarah rushes over and stands in front of Casey, blocking her from me as if I were a madman who just broke into the house.

"No!" she shouts, pushing Casey completely behind her—shielding her with her body.

Emma comes running up and starts talking quietly into my face, but I swear I can't focus on her. My mind is reeling, but I can't quite connect the dots.

"Make him leave!" Sarah screams at Emma.

For just a split second, all the women go silent. Or maybe my ears just seek out the words I've longed to hear among the voices.

Casey whispers, "I was driving. It's all my fault."

"What the fuck is she talking about?" I ask Emma, not dragging my eyes from Sarah, who is still protecting Casey. "What *the fuck* are you talking about?" I finally roar into the room.

"We need to talk, babe," Emma says, pushing me toward the door, but I hold my ground.

"Someone start talking, and for fuck's sake, make some God damn sense."

"I remember the accident," Sarah rushes out frantically. "You were right. I was drunk. It was all my fault. Casey was just trying to protect me."

"Sarah!" the girls shout at the same time.

"I did it. Now please leave," Sarah says nervously.

"You're lying."

"Come on, Caleb. Let's get out of here." Emma once again tries to drag me away.

But I only take a step closer. I want to get a look at Casey and see if I can get a read on the situation. Why the hell would she say that she killed her? Casey wasn't even there the night of the wreck.

I push down my anger, knowing that it will get me nowhere. I ignore Emma's pleading and Sarah's demands and begin talking to the only woman in the room who can give me the answers right now.

"What's going on, Case?" I ask quietly.

"No, don't talk to her. Get out!" Sarah acts like a mama bear herding her cub, but finally Casey turns and looks me right in the eye.

The pain on her face knocks me back a step. I haven't seen something this bad since the night I carried Sarah out of Jesse's apartment. It's the look people get when they know there is no going back.

"Just talk. Tell me what's really going on," I say gently, but the inferno is burning inside me.

"I was driving that night. I was high and I killed Manda." I can barely make out her words over her chokes.

"No, you didn't," I breathe, rejecting her confession.

My eyes slide to Emma, who is crying and nervously sliding her hair into a ponytail. I figured she would be all in my face, but I think even she knows that I need the space.

"Don't take it out on her, please. Let me pay for this. Hate me," Sarah begs as her lip begins to quiver.

"You were *not* fucking there!" I scream, suddenly losing it completely.

I begin to pace around the room, trying to wrap my mind around this.

I have a million questions, but I'm so enraged that I can't even force out the words. I finally land a punch through the drywall, which seems to level me. *This isn't happening.*

"Start at the beginning," I snap.

"She was—" Sarah starts, but it's obvious she's trying to protect Casey. I won't get the truth from her.

"Not you. *Her.*" I menacingly point my finger at Casey. The anger in my voice has Emma jumping into action.

"Nope. Not here. You are not doing this right now. If you want to talk, great. But if you want to intimidate her like that, you can do it another day when she is emotionally able to defend herself."

"Back it up, Emma," I say coldly.

"Shut it up, Caleb," she responds, challenging me and blocking my view.

Casey pulls in a deep breath and bares it all. "Sarah thought she could drive but pulled over at a gas station when she realized she couldn't. I had a friend drop me off, but I was all fucked up."

"What the fuck?" I say as adrenaline rushes through my system. *How the fuck did I miss this all these years?* "Where did you go? Stephens would have seen you."

"I wasn't there when Stephens showed up."

"Well where the fuck did you go? You couldn't just disappear!" I roar, stepping close, but Emma stops me with a hand to the chest.

"Please calm down," she says, but there is damn near nothing that can ease the rush of my emotions right now. Not even Emma.

"Where?" I demand again in a lower voice.

No one speaks up. They all just stand frozen, and I suddenly realize, judging by their faces, that this is about to get a hell of a lot worse.

"Eli was first on the scene," Emma answers when it's obvious Casey isn't going to.

My ears begin to ring as that night starts to unfold in my mind. All of the missing pieces finally click together to form one perfectly devastating puzzle.

Eli Tanner, one of my best friends, has held the answers to what really happened that night all along. He sat by and watched me running myself ragged while investigating it for years. He watched Sarah fall apart from the grief and the hatred eat me alive. He stood quietly while Brett watched his wife repeatedly try to kill herself over something she'd had nothing to do with. Casey may have been driving, but Eli could have saved us all years ago.

"I'm going to kill him," I growl through clenched teeth.

And in this moment, I mean those words with my entire being.

Emma

"WAIT! PLEASE!" I yell as Caleb turns to stalk out of the apartment.

He doesn't even acknowledge that I'm following him as he strides down the sidewalk to his truck.

"Damn it, Caleb! Stop!" I slip on the ice while trying to keep up with him. I'm not even sure he can hear me as rage controls his body.

He jerks open his door and climbs in his truck. I rush around to the passenger's side and climb in too. I absolutely refuse to let him do this alone.

"Get out," he says calmly, starting his truck.

"No, I'm going with you. You are not confronting Eli about this alone."

"Get. Out. I don't want you anywhere near this. You're not fuckin' going with me."

"Then you will have to physically remove me from this truck, because hell will freeze over before I get out. Cuss, scream, say hateful words—whatever you need to do. But I am not budging."

He looks over at me with wild eyes. He's looking right at me, but his eyes never actually connect with mine. They're glazed over as if he were drunk, flashing around the truck, probably at the same speed his mind is racing.

"Whatever." He finally relents and peels out of the parking lot.

My only saving grace in all of this is that Eli lives a good thirty minutes away. I have a little bit of time to try to talk Caleb down.

"He was trying to protect her."

"Fuck him," he snaps back at me.

"She was all fucked up, and he was trying to protect her. You would have done the same for me. Or Manda."

His eyes swing to me. "I never would have left two dying women on the side of the road. I'm sorry, Emma. Not. Even. For. You."

I cringe at the truth in his words, and he goes back to silently driving.

I'm not defending Eli. What he did was vile. He silently watched his friends crumble just to cover his own ass. That's not a man, even if what he was doing was out of love for Casey. This whole situation is fucked up, but something or someone has to defuse Caleb before he explodes on Eli.

"He thought they were both dead," I whisper, but it only serves to fuel his fire.

"Well he's a fucking idiot then. It doesn't take a genius to check for a pulse. You're not talking me out of this, so please be quiet. He watched all of us fall apart for years without saying a God damn word. Casey at least had the decency to take off and disappear from our lives. Eli has sat in my fucking house pretending to be my friend while keeping this secret. I'm going to kill him!" He bangs his hand on the steering wheel, pushing his truck even faster.

"Please slow—"

Before I can even get another word out, he hits an invisible patch of ice, causing the truck to swerve.

"Caleb!" I scream before the silence takes over.

Chapter
THIRTY-FOUR

Caleb

"EMMA," I croak out as the ringing in my ears rouses me back to consciousness.

I open my eyes to find my truck lying on the driver's side. I'm resting against the crushed glass from my window. I painfully turn my head to the side to find Emma hanging lifelessly, suspended by her seatbelt.

"Emma!" I scream, reaching for her, but I can't quite touch her. I fight against my seatbelt, desperate to get to her. Oh God. "Emma, please. Hang on, sweetheart. I'm coming. I'm coming," I chant as I struggle to get the damn restraint off.

It's fucking stuck, and I'm pinned to my seat while Emma might as well be dying inches away from me. She hasn't moved, and her head is hanging at an unnatural angle. Bile threatens to rise into my throat as I look down at her pregnant stomach being pulled snug by the seatbelt. I'm going to lose them both. I can feel it. The cycle of my life is about repeat itself.

My body finally kicks into gear and a jolt of adrenaline hits me hard, sending strength through my veins.

"Emma!" I yell while frantically pushing and pulling on the buckle of my seatbelt until, with the most magical click I have ever heard, it becomes unstuck.

I kneel up and immediately check for a pulse, ready to start CPR even before I can free her from the truck. I won't lose them. I'm reclaiming my life here and now. The rhythm of her heart against my fingers rejuvenates me.

The relief is short-lived. She's still alive, but even as I stroke her face, she doesn't wake up.

"Are you okay in there?" I hear the voice of a Good Samaritan from outside.

"Call 911!" I scream, continuing to work to get Emma free. "Come on, Emmy. Stay with me," I plead. "I need help! I need to get her out of here."

"Can you lift her? I'll grab her if you can get her up to the door," The man says.

I can hear him climbing onto the side of the truck and trying to pry open the stuck door. I reach up, pull the lock, and push into his pulls. Together, we manage to get it open.

"I'm getting you out of here," I say, unclipping her seatbelt before I press her up and out the door, into the arms of a stranger. "Be careful with her. She's pregnant." I call out as she disappears.

I reach up and pull myself out of the truck, jumping down to the road and racing to her side.

Someone has covered her with a blanket to keep her warm. I pause just steps away, paralyzed by my memories. I've seen a woman I love lying on the side of the road before. It's only the realization that this one is still breathing that propels me the last few steps to her side.

"Emmy, wake up, sweetheart." I drop to my knees beside her. My heart is racing as she lies motionless.

In the distance, I hear the sirens screaming. The lights bounce around the darkness as emergency crews surround us. Paramedics nudge me out of the way as they begin to work on her.

"Sir. I need you to step over here." My body follows the command, but my eyes are unable to stray from Emma. "What's your name, sir?"

"Caleb Jones."

"Okay, great. And who is the woman?"

"My wife, Emma Jones." Her name lodges in my throat as my voice gives out.

Shock has rendered me unable to form coherent thoughts, but all I know is that I need to get back to her. Even four feet away is too far right now.

I turn and head back towards her, only to get pulled away again. "Sir, please. I need you to answer a few questions."

"Later," I snap and shake off his touch. "Don't fucking touch me again." I resume my stance over Emma, and just as they begin to load her onto the stretcher, her hand clumsily lifts to pull away the oxygen mask. "Emmy!" I shout, and she immediately reaches out to the side, searching for me. "I've got you, babe. I'm right here." Relief at just this small sign of life consumes me.

"Okay, load her up!" The paramedic yells quickly, moving us both into the back of the ambulance.

Chapter
THIRTY-FIVE

Caleb

"WHAT'S WRONG with her? Why is she so out of it?" I ask, pacing the hall of the emergency room. Two doctors and a nurse are inside, checking her over.

"Sir, I'm not sure. Let us look at her and the baby. We can't give you any answers until we get a better idea of what's going on," a nurse says, passing me by and heading into Emma's room.

The entire way here, Emma mumbled incoherently and drifted in and out of consciousness. I can't take this anymore. I need some answers. My imagination is running rampant, and I don't know how much longer I'm going to be able to keep it together.

"Mr. Jones." The doctor steps into the hallway.

"How is she?" I stop in front of him pushing a shaking hand through my hair.

"Her vitals are stable for now. We are going to focus on the baby for a minute and then take her back for a few more in-depth tests."

I rush out a breath, willing my pulse to slow.

"As you know, Emma still has five weeks until her due date. The baby is not quite ready to be born yet, but after a trauma like this, sometimes it's safer for us to go ahead and take the baby."

"Wait, will he be okay? I mean, if he's born now? Isn't it too early?" The fear that just faded immediately climbs again.

"Most babies his age do just fine with some extra care. Besides, as long as everything looks good, we will leave him safely where he is now.

Why don't you go in and sit with her while I run down and grab an ultrasound machine." He tries to give me a reassuring smile, but none of this feels right.

I walk into the room, and the air is filled with the soft and steady whooshing of our baby's heartbeat. Emma is hooked up to a bunch of monitors, a white blanket covering her.

I drag the chair from the corner of the small room over next to her and lean down with my head next to hers. "Hey, sweetheart. I could really use a glimpse of those blue eyes right now."

She immediately turns her head towards me but barely cracks an eye. However, the minute the corner of her mouth lifts an inch, I completely lose it.

Tears fill my eyes. "Oh God, Emmy." I've been holding it together for years, but this—this is just too much.

Suddenly, her fist begins to beat on the bed between us as a scream tears from her throat.

"No. No," she whimpers, and before I can even process what's going on, the sounds filling the air slide from quick and steady to slow and sluggish.

I frantically press the nurse call button, terrified to leave her, but as I look toward the door, I catch sight of the massive amount of blood pooling between her legs, soaking completely through the blanket. I jump to my feet and sprint into the hallway.

"Help! I need a doctor! I need a doctor, *now*!"

A startled nurse comes running down the otherwise empty hall.

Not a second later, doctors and nurses fill the room.

"Get her to the OR. Call anesthesia and have them meet us there. She's abrupting, people. Let's move," I hear the doctor yell as they unlock the wheels on her bed and push her out of the room. I don't even get a second glance as she is rushed past me.

"Caleb!" I faintly hear shouted from behind me, but the agonizing pain in my chest won't release me long enough to focus on it.

I stand immobile in the middle of the hallway as the images of Emma bleeding out hold me hostage.

"Jones!" I finally recognize Brett's voice and his fingers snapping in front of me.

I manage to get out only one sentence before the potential devastation levels me. "I can't lose her."

My legs give way as I crash to my knees. I bargain with every possible god in the universe to let her live or, at the very least, take me with her.

"It's okay. She's going to be okay," He begins to frantically repeat.

"Come on, Caleb." I hear Jesse's Tinker Bell voice in my ear as I'm practically dragged into a waiting room.

"This isn't happening. Please, someone wake me up," I beg as this all-too-familiar feeling strangles me.

Everything moves in fast forward around me as I sit rooted to a chair in the middle of a hospital. I've been here before, only this time, I'm responsible. Why the fuck was I driving so fast?

I look over to Brett and say words that only an hour ago sent fire through my system. Now they seem inconsequential. Who cares who was driving? The result will always be the same.

"Casey was driving the night of the wreck. Eli helped her leave unnoticed."

"What?" He looks at me like I've obviously lost it.

"We'll talk about it later. I don't even care anymore. I just need this entire nightmare to stop. It's like a chain of events that were set into motion just to destroy me. And if anything happens to Emma, I have no doubt it will."

Brett squeezes my shoulder reassuringly but says nothing else.

Time passes, but that's all I know for sure. I don't have a clue how long it's been or if that's a good sign or a bad one. I know that Jesse never leaves my side. She's been holding my hand since I sat down. At some point, I remember Sarah and Casey showing up and Brett storming over to them. I just block it all out. Occasionally I catch sight of Brett pacing around us. And regardless how much I will it to stop, the world still spins beneath me.

"Emma Jones?" a nurse announces, and it has me springing to my feet.

"Yes!" I quickly rush over to her, Sarah hot on my heels.

"Are you immediate family?" she asks, and much to my surprise, it's Sarah who answers first.

"I'm her sister, and he's her husband."

I turn with silent gratitude. She offers me only a small nod.

"Follow me."

"Please. You have to give me something here. Is she okay?" I beg.

"She will be," she says with a warm smile.

Tears finally flood my eyes as I fight to keep some semblance of composure. I stumble backwards, but Brett grabs my arm to stop me from planting my ass in the middle of the floor. *She's alive.* Emma's heart is still beating. That's all that matters—

"What about Collin? I mean…the baby. What about the baby?" I ask as fear creeps back into my throat.

"He's great. Little small, but he'll be okay too. Come on. We'll stop at the nursery to see him first while they finish up with Mom."

"Oh God. They're okay. They're both okay?" I ask again because I need to hear it one more time before I can trust it.

"Everyone's okay," Brett says, gripping the back of my neck and trying to catch my eyes. "Get it together. You have a son. Don't make his first memory you crying like a puss. They're *both* okay," he reiterates.

"Yeah, I'm okay." I try to shake it off, but I know that, until I lay eyes on Emma and Collin, I won't be able to relax.

"Let's go meet your son, Mr. Jones." She leads the way down the maze of halls. After stopping at a nurse's desk, she wraps a plastic hospital bracelet on my arm. "That is the key to your son. Don't take it off, don't lose it, and you will be just fine." She smiles over at us both.

"Will I be able to see him too?" Sarah asks from behind me.

"Well, now that is up to Mr. Jones. All visitors must be accompanied by a parent. So as long as he gives the A-Okay, we can go back now."

Forgiveness is a very abstract term. It doesn't erase the past. It's not a magical switch you can flip or a stained rug you can just turn over. It's merely a scar that covers the deep, dark gash that hate carved in your soul. I forgave Sarah months ago for something, it turns out, she never did, but it didn't delete the years of hate and loathing I once felt. I'm not sure Sarah and I will ever be close. And even though the rational side of my mind says that I should be begging for forgiveness from her, my stubborn heart isn't there yet. However, the most amazing woman I have ever met once told me that a first step is better than no step at all.

"Yeah, of course she can see him," I answer, catching Sarah's eyes with a tender nod.

The nurse leads us back to a large room with babies in small beds lined against the wall. I look at each one as I pass, searching for one who looks like Emma. *Damn it!* I'd give anything for her to be here with me right now.

"Here he is." The nurse stops in front of a little bed with the tiniest baby I have ever seen in my life.

"Oh my God," Sarah breathes from behind me.

"Oh, shit… I mean… Oh God," I stutter in awe.

He's lying naked except for a diaper. There's a tube in his mouth and wires and monitors covering his tiny chest. Warm tears slide down my face before I even realized they were falling. I've seen him for less than thirty seconds and I know unquestionably that I would give my own life to protect him. I didn't think I would ever be able to love another person as much as I love Emma, but looking at this tiny baby we somehow created together proves me wrong completely.

"He's so small. Is he going to be okay?" I ask, moving even closer.

The nurse giggles for a second before answering. "Yeah, he's actually a pretty good size for his age. He weighed in at five pounds two ounces. I first want to congratulate you on your new baby. He is a very handsome little man. How about I go over what we have done with him so far and tell you how he's doing?"

"Yeah, um… Sure," I say absently as my eyes stay glued to his tiny chest rising and falling.

"I know it's overwhelming and a lot to take in. You will probably forget half the stuff I tell you as soon as you walk out the door, but don't stress. We are here twenty-four hours a day, and there is no such thing as a 'dumb question.' First, let me give you his footprints so I don't forget."

She hands me a piece of paper with impossibly small footprints. I stare at it for a minute, trying to figure out what the hell I'm supposed to do with them, when she keeps going.

"Those are yours to keep, a small memento for the baby book. I sure bet your wife would love to see it." She pauses to smile. I absently nod. "So like I said, he's doing very well for being five weeks early. He's breathing on his own, which is wonderful, and he has a very strong heart rate. He is breathing a little fast, but that's very normal for babies that are born by C-section. That typically resolves itself in a few days. The tube we placed in his mouth will be used to feed him until his respiratory rate slows down. Eventually we will remove it and he will take all of his feeds by bottle or by breast. The tube goes right into his stomach so he does not have to put forth the *work* to suck and swallow the milk…"

I pray to God that this is not the only time she is going to tell me this information because this sounds important and I can't for the life of me process her words as fast as she's saying them.

"The wires you see on his chest and foot are hooked to this monitor. They allow us to watch his heart rate, respiratory rate, and how well his body is oxygenating. Because he is small, we placed him in an isolette to help keep his body temperature normal. As he grows, we can slowly drop the temperature and then place him in an open crib. When he is in an open crib and eating all of his feedings by bottle or the breast, then he will be ready to go home.

"Now I know you want to know how long he is going to be here, and I will tell you what I tell all my parents. He is running the show." Yeah, that's definitely Emma's baby. I laugh to myself. "If he does everything as he is supposed to, then he could leave as early as a week. As a rule of thumb, we tell people to expect them home by their due date. Your son, Mr. Jones, is doing very well, and we will do our best to get him home to you and your wife as soon as we can."

Oh, I definitely understand those words and enthusiastically nod my head.

"Now, would you like to hold your son?"

"What? No." I put my hands up and instantly back away like she's holding a weapon. I know it's my child, but I can't hold him. He's too frail. What if I hurt him or pull out that little tube that's in his stomach? No way. I can't do that.

"I'll hold him," Sarah says with a grin before turning to look at me. "I mean, if that's okay with you." She immediately glances down at the floor.

I look over at the little guy all alone. He needs someone to hold him—someone who loves him—even if I'm not man enough to do it.

"Yeah, go ahead." I wave to the nurse my approval.

They wrap all his wires into a blanket, and before I know it, they pass my entire life into the arms of a woman who, just hours ago, I would have told you stole everything from me. I watch as she cradles him with such tenderness that it make me jealous. Besides the doctors and nurses, Sarah Kate Erickson is the first person to ever hold *my child*. Who would have thought?

She looks down, runs her hand over his blond peach fuzz, and pulls his arm from the blanket. When he curls his tiny hand around her finger, I completely change my mind.

"I'm ready. I want to hold him."

Her eyes flash to mine. With the same knowing smirk Emma gives me, she stands and hands him off to the nurse.

"Okay, Dad." The nurse steps back over. "His temperature is getting a little low, so how about we try some skin-to-skin?"

"What the fu—I mean, what's that?"

"If you don't mind, we'll need you to take off your shirt—"

I immediately peel it over my head without another thought.

"Well, okay then," she responds, laughing. "I'll unwrap him and put him against your chest then cover you both in a blanket. It's great bonding time for the little guy, and it also helps to keep his temperature up."

Sarah moves to switch positions with me, and I know the exact moment she sees my back because she releases a loud gasp. Not many people expect me to have so many tattoos. I don't show them off or advertise them. I got them for myself. No one would understand the real emotion and meaning behind them anyway—well, except for Sarah.

"No wonder Emma fell for you so quickly," she says under her breath, but it makes me crack a much-needed smile.

Only minutes later, the nurse lays Collin on my chest. The feeling of fulfillment washes over me with a rush, immediately calming my nerves. This is my baby boy. *God, I wish Emma were here.*

"Hey." I catch the nurse while she is covering us with blankets. "Is there any way for you to check on my wife? They told me she was fine, but I need an update."

"Sure. Not a problem." She once again smiles warmly at me. I seriously need to have Jesse make this woman a muffin basket.

"Can you ask them when I'll be able to see her? Wait, can I take him with me to see her?" I ask, desperate to see her but unwilling to leave him.

"No, he has to stay here, unfortunately. She'll be able to come down and see him soon enough. Just take lots of pictures of him with your phone in the meantime. She'll want to see them as soon as she wakes up." Yep, this woman is totally getting chocolate chip muffins from Jesse.

I lost my phone during the accident, but Sarah quickly pulls out hers and starts snapping pictures.

As if instinctually, Collin's little head flops to the side. He looks up at me and opens his eyes. It completely steals my breath and sends my emotions spinning.

"Hey, buddy." I gently kiss him on the head as my eyes begin to water.

I've been through a lot in my life, but I am not emotionally equipped for this moment. I wrap my arms tight around him, holding and protecting him as best I can. This is overwhelming, and the very idea that I get to spend a lifetime with this little boy *and* his mom has me turning my own head to hide the tears.

"Manda didn't want kids," I hear Sarah say from the corner.

"What?" I ask, completely dumbfounded.

"The reason she wouldn't marry you is because she didn't want kids. She knew you did, and she couldn't live with the idea of you sacrificing that for her. She was terrified you would eventually resent her for it."

"No, that's not true. She and I talked about having kids a million times."

"No, *you* talked about it a million times. Manda just never corrected you. She was planning to tell you the night of the accident." Sarah closes her eyes when the memories become too much.

I lovingly kiss the baby and wait eagerly for her to continue.

"One of the last things I remember from that night is standing with her in the bathroom at Westies. She was panicking that you were going to leave her when she told you." Sarah chews her bottom lip as the painful memories spread like wildfire through the room.

"Not possible." I curl him even closer into my chest.

"She was a mess. She loved you so much, but she never wanted to be a mom. She was too scared to tell you but more afraid to lose you."

"I wouldn't have left," I whisper to keep my voice from cracking while looking down at Collin asleep in my arms.

I'm not lying. I wouldn't have left, but I also wouldn't give up this moment of holding my child for anything. Despite my earlier fears and reservations, I've always wanted kids and a family. It happened sooner than I was prepared for with Emma, but sitting here now, I know I wouldn't change it for the world. Sarah is the last person I want to have a chat with, but ironically enough, she is also the only person who will ever understand.

"I loved her, and if you had told me this years ago, it would have devastated me. I would have done anything to hold on to Manda. Absolutely anything—except give up this." I pause to allow my racing mind to catch up. "Manda was water, but Emma—she's air. I couldn't have survived without either one of them, but this right here—this is life."

"This is full circle, Caleb. That night…the wreck—it was only a single moment, but it destroyed us *all*. Maybe this is where we're all reborn. We're all involved in this one miracle tonight. Think about it. Me, you, Brett's out there with Jesse, Casey has probably already left to be with Eli, Emma's recovering, and right now, your son is cuddled against Manda's name over your heart. Maybe *this* is the reason and culmination of all of the hurt. It all happened just to get here—just to get to him." Her words sink into my heart, and I can't say that I disagree with her.

Originally hate, pain, remorse, and grief ruled my life. But now, love, acceptance, and forgiveness have led me to this minute. Somewhere deep inside, for the first time in almost six years, it finally gives Manda's death a purpose. One that doesn't fill me with hate or resentment. Instead, it's filled my arms with a blond-haired and sure-to-be blue-eyed baby.

"Jesus Christ, how much therapy have you been through?" I joke through the emotions.

"You have no freaking idea." She smiles back. "I have no doubt that Manda gave this to you. All of it. She loved you, and she was just twisted enough to enjoy watching this whole thing play out. I think she sent Collin just to make sure you wouldn't screw things up with Emma."

"Yeah that sounds about right for Manda." I sigh, closing the conversation and the blast from the past.

I've said it a thousand times before, but while sitting here holding all five pounds of my son's tiny body, I realize that it's officially time to move forward.

Chapter
THIRTY-SIX

Emma

"EMMA. WAKE up. You with us, Emma?" I hear through the fog.

Bright lights shine down on my face, but I'm still trapped in the truck with Caleb.

"Caleb!" I scream, but it only comes out as a gurgle.

My throat is killing me.

Where is he? Why isn't he here? Oh God. What happened to him?

"Welcome back, Mrs. Jones," I hear a woman's voice say from beside me.

I turn my head, but I'm barely able to pry my eyes open to see her. Jesus, how did I get so drunk?

"I... Where... Caleb..." I try to form a sentence, but the words all float away.

"Don't worry. Your throat is going to be sore," she answers, reading my mind. "It's from the intubation. We had to do an emergency C-section, but don't worry. That baby of yours is strong and doing well."

Oh God, Collin. How the hell could I forget about him? Wait, it's too soon.

"Now, before you get all excited, take a deep breath and relax. He is absolutely fine and his daddy is in there holding him right now as we speak."

Yep. I'm going to cry. Oh shit. Caleb is with him. I...I...

"I want to see them." I finally squeeze out a string of words.

"Hey, you really are there." She stops tinkering with the computer and turns to face me.

"Is he okay?" I grumble against the sandpaper in my throat.

"He's going to need a little extra care, but he looks great. Does he have a name?"

"Collin," I rasp.

"That's a good name. Strong, masculine, and easy to spell." She turns back to her computer. This woman is crazy, but if I could just get my thoughts together, I would probably love her. "I'm going to call down to the nursery and let them know you're awake." Yep, totally love her.

I nod and drift back to sleep.

"Emmy. Wake up, sweetheart," I hear whispered from beside me.

I turn my head and open my eyes to see the most amazing thing in my life. Caleb—alive, healthy, and uninjured—is sitting beside my bed, hunched over, holding my hand.

"Hey, you."

His eyes fly to mine, and the fear on his face transforms to relief. "Oh God, Emmy," he breathes, moving up the bed to kiss me.

"How's Collin?" I immediately ask when my senses return.

"He's absolutely perfect. He's so small, but apparently that's okay since he was early. He's got some tubes and wires, but *apparently* that's also okay. Oh wait, I have pictures." He pulls a phone from his pocket and begins scrolling through the images until he finds the perfect one. "Here." He thrusts a pink iPhone into my face.

"He's beautiful," I gasp as all of the oxygen is most definitely sucked from the room. "When can I see him?" I move to sit up before pain hits me and pins me to the bed. "Oh God! Shit!" I screech and throw a hand over my stomach.

Before I have a chance to catch my breath again, I hear Caleb shouting in the hallway. A nurse comes rushing in, and I glance over to find worry covering every inch of my husband's gorgeous face.

"What's going on, Emma?" The nurse immediately begins to check my blood pressure and moves the blanket to look at my stomach.

"Nothing. I'm fine. I just tried to move and forgot about my stomach. He just overreacted…a little," I say and begin to laugh, but it only makes it hurt worse.

"Real funny, Emmy. I've had a hell of a day. You'll have to forgive my *overreaction*," he says sarcastically and half pissed off.

"There's my man! I recognize that asshole." I smile, and he just shakes his head but finally chuckles too. He walks over to resume his spot next to my head, grabbing my hand and pulling it to his mouth.

"Okay, well, let's see what we can do about getting you some more pain medication and, after that, maybe get you in a wheelchair and down to see that handsome fella of yours."

"That would be great," I respond, and Caleb mumbles something about Jesse's muffins. "Let me see the rest of those pictures." I turn to Caleb as the nurse walks out of the room.

He pulls out…Sarah's phone?

"Hey, how'd you end up with that?" I ask.

"Sarah went back with me to see Collin."

My eye brows lift in shock. "Wow, that's a big step for you."

"She was actually the first one to hold him." He floors me once again.

"Oh God. I died, didn't I?"

"Ha. Ha. Smartass." He kisses my hand again.

"Thank you," I say genuinely.

"I think everyone's going to be okay, sweetheart. It's always going to be strained, but it's all going to be okay."

"I want to cuddle with you," I whisper, desperate to get close to him.

"Well there is no way I'm crawling in that bed with you after I saw what's going on under that blanket. You need to relax and try not to move. That has got to hurt like hell."

"Well, it's not fun." I smile, and he brushes the hair away from my face.

"Here." He leans over the bed and buries his face into the side of my neck, rubbing his stubble over my cheek. I nuzzle in close for the brief and much-needed moment of closeness. "I love you. I'm so fucking sorry about today. I lost it and that almost cost me everything."

"We're all okay, remember?" I try to soothe him the way the he always does me. I reach up and run my hand through his hair and down his neck. "Tell me about Collin," I ask to try to get his mind off the internal what-if game I know he's playing right now.

He immediately sits up and scrubs his hands over his face. "He's perfect. I swear I've never loved anyone so much. He's so tiny, but I think he looks like me."

I laugh as his eyes light while talking about his son. *Our son.* And it doesn't even matter that I haven't seen him. We're a family.

Chapter
THIRTY-SEVEN

Emma

THREE DAYS after the accident, I was released from the hospital. It broke my heart to have to leave Collin there, but it really tore up Caleb too. For a man who was originally so hesitant about the pregnancy, he sure as hell has embraced fatherhood. Caleb spent every single night sitting by my side or holding his son—sometimes the magical combination of both.

The minute we got home from the hospital, he deposited me on the couch and went to work finishing off Collin's room. This included cleaning every nook and cranny with a toothbrush because he was terrified of germs getting anywhere near his baby. Let me just say that, there is something insanely sexy about watching your big, buff, tattooed husband on his hands and knees scrubbing the floor.

Caleb took two weeks off work and drove me back and forth to the hospital every three hours to feed our little man. Once, I had a doctor's appointment during a scheduled feeding, so he dropped me off, went up to the hospital, and fed him a bottle on his own. It melts my heart to watch them together. My gruff prick becomes a big ole' softie when his baby's involved.

Exactly ten days after he was born, Collin Mitchell Jones came home. Since Caleb gave in and let me pick the first name, I couldn't argue when he chose his father's name for the middle. The day we picked him up from the hospital, I felt like I was walking on the clouds. Caleb, however, was a nervous wreck. He asked the nurses a million questions while I stood behind him silently laughing and shaking my head. He even took the car seat to three different police officers' houses to have it checked to make sure it was installed properly. They weren't even on duty, but Caleb still forced them out to his new SUV to check it. Normally I would have been offended that he wouldn't take my word on something, but I have to admit that, after both of the car accidents that changed our lives, I was relieved to know we had done everything possible to keep him safe.

Today, Collin is one month old. It's been an extremely long month. We are both exhausted. Collin isn't fond of sleeping, I still cry at the drop of a hat, and Caleb still obsesses about germs and hand sanitizer. (Thank you, NICU Nurse Autumn, for that.) Hunter and Alex are finally coming up to meet Collin for the first time. We held them off for as long as possible so I could really recover and enjoy their visit. We decided to do a little get-together, and as much as it pains me, I can't have everyone I love together in one place. Caleb and Sarah have marginally made up, but there are some bridges that can never be rebuilt. There will never be a future where Sarah and Brett can ever be in the same room. While I hate it, I can't say that I blame him.

I don't know the full details about what happened with Caleb, Brett, and Eli, but everyone is still alive and no one—that I know of—ended up bloody. I do know that they decided amongst themselves not to pursue an internal investigation against Eli's actions that night. After hearing the whole story from Casey and Eli, they decided that they didn't want them to pay for it criminally. Casey got the help she needed, and they all agreed that she had paid the price. What I can say is…having a baby changed Caleb's outlook on life. He never would have given Sarah that leeway. While it burns, it also makes me happy that no one else will be weighted down with the responsibility of that night.

I don't completely understand their decisions about this, but I don't have to. I'm Sarah's sister and Caleb's wife, but on a very surface level, that accident didn't involve me. I'm more than happy to voice my opinion in most situations, but in this one, I just have to sit back and let them figure it out.

Ultimately they asked Eli to quit the force. They both agreed that they didn't want a man like that serving beside them. I think deep down Caleb understands that he was trying to protect Casey, but their friendship is permanently severed. I asked him the other night in bed if he hated them now. I was worried that he was going to fall back into his dark space with a new vendetta against Eli and Casey, but he quickly put my fears to rest. He told me, "There is no way I can look at you and that baby and have any room left in my chest for hate." It was a really fucking good answer.

"Look at this little man!" Hunter says, pulling the baby from my arms. "Does he look like me?" He holds him up against his face.

Caleb lets out a growl and rolls his eyes. He has surprisingly warmed up to Hunter since we got married. He still pretends to be annoyed with him. I mean, let's be honest. Hunter is a little over the top.

"You want a beer, man?" Caleb asks.

"You know it." He kisses Collin and hands him over to Kara, who is eagerly awaiting her turn.

"So what's up with you two? Y'all getting serious?" I ask as she coos, running her finger over his little nose.

"Something like that. We met up in Georgia last weekend at his best friend's wedding. He introduced me to his mom and everything."

"Wait, Mason and Lacey got married?"

"Yep. Apparently she got knocked up too. I'm making Hunter wear two condoms from now on. This shit is contagious."

"Wow. I can't believe he went to the wedding. I'm going to have to get a full update on how that little reunion went down."

Jesse shows up with Brett behind her. "Can I hold him?"

"Sure thing." Kara passes him over.

Tonight, we're moving the party over to Sarah's place after Brett and Jesse head home. I know right now she is with Casey preparing dinner. Casey won't stick around though. She might be close with Sarah and friendly with me, but she avoids Caleb at all costs. Trust me. That's probably for the best.

Sarah and Casey have become close again since the truth came out. It's great to see them together again. Casey helps Sarah learn to live again and Sarah helps Casey let go of her grief. They need each other more than anyone ever knew.

I look around the room for a moment. Jesse and Kara are huddled together, talking about how adorable Collin is and debating who he looks like. Caleb, Brett, Hunter, and Alex are all in the kitchen sipping beers, talking sports, and laughing like old friends. It's not everyone, but this moment, right here is as close to perfect as it can get.

Caleb catches my eye from across the room, and we stare for a second before he tosses me his signature smirk and a wink. I smile back as he mouths, "I love you." I don't say anything in return. I just hold up my fingers about an inch apart. His face warms at the memory and we both laugh at our unspoken joke. The truth is that no amount of space in the world could adequately portray how much I love Caleb or our life together. *This really is it.*

Oh God. I'm going to cry again.

Damn.

Epilogue

Caleb

Six Months Later...

"CALEB, YOU are not taking a baby into a tattoo parlor."

"Parlor? You really are from the South. And apparently the 1800s. And why not? It's not run by a biker gang," I tease, unbuckling Collin from his car seat.

"Don't they like smoke and stuff inside?"

"What?" I laugh at her comment. "No, they don't smoke! Emmy, have you ever even been to a tattoo *parlor*?"

"Well, no," she says hesitantly, and I shake my head.

"Well I'd let Collin crawl on the floor at this place. They have done all of my ink over the years. Seriously, this place is the best. It's clean, and sterile, *and* smoke-free. I swear." I pull her into my side and kiss her forehead. I hold Collin on my hip and push my sunglasses up to sit on my head so I can nuzzle his chubby cheek before going inside. "You ready to get your first tattoo, li'l man?" I ask, and as expected, Emma rolls her eyes.

"What are you getting done anyway? Do you even have any space left?" she asks, pulling away Collin, who's squirming from my arms.

"Oh, I've got plenty of room for you, Emmy." I slide my hand down her back and squeeze her ass.

"What do you mean, for me? Caleb, what are you getting done?" she demands, but I just laugh and head inside.

"Come on, sweetheart."

I pull open the door and walk into the familiar shop. I've spent many painful days in this place. It's so fucking nice to be here for something I want instead of a feeling I need.

"Jones!" I hear Paul shout. "What's up, man? Long time!" He walks over and stops in front of Emma and Collin. "What's up, little Jones?" He gently pokes his stomach with a finger. "Jesus, if that isn't your kid, I would suggest hitting Maury Povich up for a paternity test. He looks just like you!"

"Paul, this is my wife, Emma, and son, Collin. Emma, this is Paul. He's done one hundred percent of my tattoos. I won't let anyone else touch me."

"Wow. Well I have to say you did a fantastic job on his back. I'll have to send you some of the pictures I took a few weeks ago," Emma says with a huge smile.

"Yeah, send 'em over. I never thought he'd finish, but it turned out pretty badass." He turns his attention back to me. "Give me a minute. I'm transferring your stuff now."

"I thought this was an impromptu stop?" She spins to face me.

"Yeah, I totally lied." I shrug but can't wipe the smile from my face. "Oh and Brett and Jesse should be here in about five minutes to pick up Collin."

"What!" she screams.

"Oh and we're going out to dinner afterward."

"What!" she screams again.

"And I packed him his pajamas and enough bottles to get us through ten o'clock. So after dinner, I'm taking you home and fucking you against the wall, maybe on the stairs, and definitely in the kitchen. "

"What." This time she breathes the word as heat floods her eyes.

"Come on, Emmy. I knew if I'd asked you about this, you'd have said no. I haven't been alone with you since he was born. I packed his bags and dropped them off with Brett this morning after the gym. It works out for everyone. I get to have loud sex with my wife without fear of waking the baby, and Jesse gets her baby fix for the week."

"I don't know…" she starts, but the door opens and Jesse comes skipping into the shop.

She addresses Collin first. "Hey, cutie!"

"Jesse, I don't know about this," Emma says as Jesse plucks him from her arms.

"Em, it will be fine," Brett says as he joins the group.

"Oh and the best part. I was worried about the whole car seat switch, so Brett's just going to take the SUV and leave us the BMW." I smile eagerly.

"Be careful with my baby, asshole," he snaps as he hands over the keys.

"I could say the same." I look down at Collin, who's giggling while Jesse blows raspberries on his cheek.

"Come on, sweetheart. It will be fine," I urge.

She finally relents. "Yeah, okay."

"I'll text lots of pictures," Jesse promises, using Collin's hand to wave over her shoulder as they walk away.

Emma's eyes look a little teary as the door closes behind them, so I pull her into a hug. After pushing her hair off her shoulder, I place a wet kiss on her neck. She immediately relaxes into my arms.

"He'll be fine. He loves Jesse."

She nods, biting back the tears as Paul comes out from the back.

"You ready, man?"

I turn to Emma and ask, "We ready?"

"Did you draw it?" she asks, referring to my soon-to-be new tattoo.

"Yeah. I did."

"Then I'm ready." She stands on her toes and pecks my lips.

Two hours later, I finally stand up and look in the mirror.

"Holy shit. That is gorgeous!" Emma gasps when she sees my newest additions.

I had the word *Stolen* filled in with green ink—the same color as the bird's eye. I didn't need that word anymore, but I wanted to keep it as a reminder of how I got here. In a grey section at the tail of the bird, I had the word *Reborn* added in sky-blue ink—almost the exact shade of Emma's and Collin's eyes. But my absolute favorite part is the addition of their names. On the left side of the bird's body, I had *Emmy* added vertically in black script, and on the right is *Collin*.

"What the hell are you going to do if we have more kids?" she asks from behind me as she inspects every inch of my new markings.

"Are we having more kids?" I ask with a laugh.

"Well yeah, eventually." She steps around in front of me.

"Okay, two more, but that's it. I like to keep things symmetrical," I say, and she stands on her toes to kiss me.

"I love it. Like a lot. Maybe even more than I love you," she teases, kissing me again a little deeper.

"You hungry? Because I really want to skip dinner right now. That wall at home is calling my name." I pull her tight against my body. Then I slide my hand down the back of her pants, cupping her ass like no one can see us.

"Yeah, that's definitely a better idea."

We finish up and I all but throw my credit card at Paul in a rush to get out of there and get home. No sooner than I sign my name on the receipt, I grab Emma's hand and drag her to the parking lot. Just before we get inside the car, I suddenly swing her around and push her up against the door, kissing her with a deep and promising kiss.

"You know that's permanent, right? No getting rid of me now," she explains against my mouth.

"That's the plan, Emmy. That's the plan."

The End

Read more about Hunter Coy in

Savor Me: A Novella

Available Now!

AND

Brett Sharp's Story in

Changing Course

Available Now!

Coming Summer 2014

Among the Echoes

"I don't know who you truly are, Riley. But tiny flashes of that woman whisper around the room between us. I will find the real you among the echoes—and I will make her mine." —Slate Andrews

Acknowledgements

Not too long ago, I decided to start writing. It was a huge decision for me and quite possibly one of the best ones I've ever made. Along the way, I have met some truly amazing people who have selflessly given their time and support to me. I have also seen the true colors of the friends I have had for years as they have blindly taken my back during this new endeavor. I can't thank everyone who has helped me, but here is where I try.

To my family: I love you. I don't think I will ever be able to say that enough.

Mike, you have listened to me talk books for more hours than I care to admit. Thank you for keeping the wild animals that we call kids while I go away to signings, and all the nights where I lock myself away to meet deadlines. I kinda love you….a lot.

Lunny, Toots, Grey, and Hoppy, mommy will one day cook vegetables again. Enjoy the pizza and chicken nuggets while you can.

Mom, Dad, Lori, Jennifer, Jay, Matt, Yeah, I wrote another book. No, none of you are allowed to read this one either. Let's just pretend this never happened. M'kay.

Juan, Wilma, Anthony, Ashley, and Telisse, What can I say? Seriously, don't even try to read this one either. (Except for Ash, she is allowed. After all, she did practically write one of the best lines in here.)

To Bianca J, Adriana, Bianca S, Tracey, and Krissy I have absolutely zero idea what I would do without you ladies. You read every single rough sentence of Stolen Course. Then you helped me make it in to something better. I love you all for not sugar coating it. Yes, even you Mean B.

To Ashley Baumann: I can't thank you enough for Caleb's amazing tattoo. I gave you my idea, and you took it to a whole new level. You are truly talented and above all that, you are just plain awesome.

To Ash T: I don't even know how many hours you spent listening to me ramble about this book. Thank you for helping me plot and plan. And also for not being afraid to say, "Yeah, that's dumb." You are a rock star.

To Fall: Wow…you pulled out all the stops for Caleb and Emma. Thank you for spending so much time pumping up the sexy factor in this book. Caleb deserved some heat, and you more than brought it. You are the cheese in my macaroni. (I hope you remember this convo or that is a really stupid joke.)

To Danielle: I WANNA COME HOME!!! Wahhhhhh!!!!!

To Jessica VW: Your pimping hand has got to be tired. Thank you so so so much for forcing everyone you meet to read my books!

To Stacey and Tessa: You ladies make me want to be a better writter (← yes I spelled it that way on purpose.) I love you both so hard.

To the IRAC Ladies: I know this technically doesn't exist anymore, but each and every one of you have had a huge impact of my writing life. I'm sad it's over, but it was one hell of a ride. I have never laughed harder, learned more, or seen more dirty pictures than when I hang out with you ladies. I hope I get to meet each and every one of you in person eventually.

To the Bloggers: Oh God! This is so stressful. I'm going to leave someone off, I can feel it. I'm sorry. There are so many of you who have reached out to me since I started writing. I wish I could list you all.

K & T Book Reviews, Short and Sassy Book Blurbs, The Rock Stars of Romance, Crystal's Many Reviewers, A is for Alpha B is for Books, For the Love of Books, Schmexy Girl Book Blog, Love Between the Sheets, Three Girls and a Book Obsession, Biblio Belles Book Blog, White Zin Bookends….and to each and every blogger who took a chance on Changing Course. I love love love love all of you!!!

To Mickey Reed: You rocked my freaking socks off! You are amazing and I laughed so freaking hard at your gifs. Thank you so so so so much!

About the Author

Born and raised in Savannah, Georgia, Aly Martinez is a stay-at-home mom to four crazy kids under the age of five, including a set of twins. Currently living in Chicago, she passes what little free time she has reading anything and everything she can get her hands on, preferably with a glass of wine at her side.

After some encouragement from her friends, Aly decided to add "Author" to her ever-growing list of job titles. So grab a glass of Chardonnay, or a bottle if you're hanging out with Aly, and join her aboard the crazy train she calls life.

Facebook: https://www.facebook.com/AuthorAlyMartinez
Twitter: https://twitter.com/AlyMartinezAuth
Goodreads: https://www.goodreads.com/AlyMartinez

Made in the USA
Las Vegas, NV
28 October 2024

10600856R00152